Dead in the Loft

Susan Williamson

ENJOY!
Susan Williamson

Cactus Mystery Press
An imprint of Blue Fortune Enterprises, LLC

DEAD IN THE LOFT
Copyright © 2020 by Susan Williamson.

This book is a work of fiction. Names, characters, businesses, organizations, places, events and incidents either are the product of the author's imagination or are used fictitiously. Any resemblance to actual persons, living or dead, events, or locales is entirely coincidental.

For information contact :
Blue Fortune Enterprises, LLC
Cactus Mystery Press
P.O. Box 554
Yorktown, VA 23690
http://blue-fortune.com

Book and Cover design by Wesley Miller, WAMCreate, wamcreate.co

ISBN: 978-1-948979-42-9
First Edition: September 2020

Reviews for Dead in the Loft

Dead bodies seem to follow Molly Lewis around. This insider's view of the Saddlebred world of gaited horses, wealthy owners, and weekend-long horse shows is balanced against shady horse sales, a drug deal gone nasty, a copperhead snake used as an assassin, and animal rights advocates playing for keeps. A good read awaits... Enjoy.

Dave Pistorese, author of *Skeads, An Honorable Man*.

Murder and mayhem abound in this cozy mystery. As the horses are put through their paces, bodies drop, frauds are perpetuated, animal rights activists create chaos, and Molly finds her life in danger. She must solve the crimes before whoever is out to get her is successful!

Patti Procopi, author of *Please... Tell Me More*

When Molly and John begin working at Mills Stable things quickly take a bad turn. The reader is quickly immersed in the world of horse shows, horse farms and nefarious animal rights activists. A body is found in the hay loft and other unsettling events begin to happen. For a suspenseful murder mystery set against the backdrop of horse farms, you couldn't find a better book.

Peter Stipe, author of *The Art of Love* and *The Fairy Garden*

Dead in the Loft is a titillating murder mystery that will delight those who love the genre. However, it is also a book about horses and those who train, care for and show them in competition. The book is entertaining, informative, and full of realistic detail. The characters ring-true and the reader will be drawn to finding the solution to more than one mystery in the book. Susan's character development allows to reader to identify with the main character and follow with baited breath as she discovers the truth.

Christian Pascale, author of *Memories Are The Stories We Tell Ourselves*

Dedication

This book is dedicated to all of the riding instructors who put their heart into their work, rain or shine, heat or cold, because they truly believe in the power of a horse-human connection.

Chapter One

"MISS MOLLY, COME QUICK. THE sink fell off the wall and water's going everywhere."

"What do you mean the sink fell off the wall? Can you turn the water off?" Molly had visited the ladies' room several times that day, and as far as she knew, the sink remained firmly attached.

"It's spraying all over."

"I'll be right there." Molly looked at the six riders she was instructing in the indoor arena. "Halt your horses and dismount. I have something I have to take care of. That's right, stop and jump down and hold your horses."

Judy Franklin, one of her favorite parents, walked over to Molly. "Can I help?" Judy was a horse person and comfortable around the kids.

"Just keep an eye on these guys while I see about our latest plumbing emergency."

Sure enough, the bathroom sink was off the wall and water sprayed everywhere. There was a cutoff, but Molly couldn't turn it without a wrench. Everyone else who worked at Mills Stables was gone to the horse show and they probably had all the tools, as well. Molly ran for the main cutoff at the back at the barn and managed to turn it off before searching for tools. There were none to be found, so she went to the office and called her boss's brother, Jim, who lived down the road. He promised to come see what he could do about it.

Judy stood chatting with the girls and keeping an eye on all the horses. "Not too close, Sarah," she told her tall, slender daughter. "Keep your horses out of kicking range of each other." She tucked her neat blonde crop behind her ear and stepped between her daughter and another rider.

"Thanks, Judy," Molly said. "Okay, let's get you all back on your horses and to work." Molly gave each of her six riders a leg up while Judy held the horses. Molly told her students to go to the rail and pick up a sitting trot.

Jim walked into the arena, armed with a tool box.

Molly pointed back toward the bathrooms. "It's the Ladies' room—you'll see the water."

Jim headed that way and walked back to the arena a few minutes later, taking off his cap and running a hand through his full head of snow-white hair. "No way this sink could have just fallen off, unless somebody sat on it."

Molly suspected that's exactly what happened, but so far, the girls involved weren't fessing up. She called for the class to line up and dismount. Her students untacked their horses and hosed them down before turning them out for the night. Jim grumbled from the bathroom while she finished cleaning out the holding area.

Forty-five minutes later, she had everything in order, and Jim had the water in the bathroom turned off, but he was unable to reattach the sink.

"I'm not sure where the stud is and the cheap plumbing broke, so I can't fix this until I get the parts. But I've got it cut off, I think. Turn the main back on and we'll see."

Molly opened the main valve behind the barn, and the sink cut-off dripped only slightly. She found a mop and cleaned up the water before putting an out-of-order sign on the bathroom door. At least now the horses would have water. These things always happened when everyone was gone.

It had been her dream to work in a big show barn, but the reality was much different than her dreams. Who would have thought the home of several world champions would be so shoddily managed? Molly called Bingo, her Jack Russell, who had been busy searching for rats. Jack Russells were good for that, at least. She walked slowly to the house, wondering what she could eat.

Molly kicked off her stinky boots at the door and walked in. She fed Bingo and found cheese and bread for dinner. She was too tired to prepare anything else. Her husband, John, had gone to the show in Lexington, Kentucky with everyone else. He called when she got out of the shower. "How goes it?"

"Someone sat on the bathroom sink and pulled it off the wall, but Jim finally got the water cut off. How about at your end?"

John sighed. "We thought we had everything done for tomorrow, then Carter came back from playing cards with his buddies and decided to work two horses. We had just washed their tails and then of course they got dirty working so we had to wash them again. I'm beat. A little communication would help so much."

"Yeah, tell me about it. But I guess we'll make it. We'd better get sleep. Love you."

"Me too. Take care, Molly."

Molly had pushed for the move from Marsa Farm to Carter Mills Stables in central North Carolina thinking it would be their best chance to really get to work talented horses and show at the top shows. But she hadn't counted on being treated like slave labor. Everyone had to prove themselves in life, things would surely get better with time. But six months in, she didn't see that happening. She hoped she hadn't talked John into a new work situation that was much worse for him.

~ * ~

Molly yawned as she walked to the barn. How could it already be morning? She wheeled the grain cart down one side of the wide barn aisle and up the other before taking it out back to feed the horses in the outside stalls. Lofts above each side of the barn held hay. She climbed into the right loft to throw hay down into the stalls and the extra bales for the horses on the other side and in the outside back stalls. She stomped her feet to scare away rats and looked carefully before touching any hay bales.

Her boss hadn't gotten around to asking anyone to help her clean stalls, so she grabbed a pitchfork and headed out to get the tractor and spreader where they sat behind the barn.

She turned the scissors, which substituted for an ignition key, and the tractor reluctantly coughed and sputtered to life. She eased it into gear and drove into the barn. The tractor wouldn't start again if she shut it off. The battery was iffy in the best of times, so she rushed through the stalls, trying to ignore the diesel fumes. By the time she got to the outside shed row, the gears were getting a little balky. After the first stop, the gearshift lever refused to go anywhere that would result in forward motion. Disgusted, she pulled the choke and shut down the engine. Could Jim fix this, too?

Her boss, Carter Mills, called as she walked back in the barn. She told him about the sink and the tractor. "You're just not driving it right," he said. "You say Jim's going to fix the sink?"

"He said he'd try to find the parts and fix it this afternoon. But he needs the credit card to get the parts. Is that okay?"

"He can't pay for them? Oh, all right, but be sure to get it back. Everything else okay?"

"I guess."

Carter's wife, Ellen, her other boss, called next. "How is everything?"

"A few mechanical and plumbing problems, but I just talked to Carter about those."

"I hope you're not working too hard. I just remembered I scheduled an introductory lesson for a very nice family this afternoon at two o'clock. Did I tell you about that?"

"No, and I have a make-up lesson scheduled then."

"Who is it?"

"Sarah Franklin."

"Well, call Judy and reschedule, she'll understand. These

are really nice people."

Molly knew better than to argue. "Okay," she said, knowing that "really nice" was code for "really rich." No doubt, Ellen had already driven by their home and checked out where the child attended school.

Stephanie, one of her advanced students, came to help about noon, and Molly started working horses or turning them loose in the round pen. She tried not to get a show horse out if no one else was around. The "very nice people" were late, throwing the rest of her lesson schedule behind, but at least Stephanie was there to help her.

~ * ~

Stephanie fed grain but Molly didn't like to ask students to go up in the lofts. That area was too dangerous and too creepy. At six-thirty, Molly had a break and took time to climb into the left loft since there was little decent hay remaining on the right side. She sniffed as she climbed the ladder. *Must be a dead rat up here*. She gagged as she moved a bale of hay to open it, and the smell grew stronger. She moved the next bale out from the wall and gasped. It was a dead rat all right, but the human kind.

She froze for a moment, telling herself this wasn't real. But the odor told her it was all too real, and nothing could be done for the victim.

Chapter Two

MOLLY RECOGNIZED THE DEAD BODY as one of the less than desirable local characters who periodically appeared at the barn to ask her boss for money. She had no doubt they helped themselves to anything not locked up. She didn't know his name, but she knew she had seen him before.

She hurried down the ladder and ran to the phone. She was shaking despite the heat.

"911. What is your emergency?"

"I just found a dead body in the loft. I'm at 3636 Brant Road."

"Ma'am, is that in the city or the county?"

"I don't know for sure. I recently moved here."

"I can't decide who to call for you if I don't know if you are in the city or the county."

"Don't you have maps that tell you that?"

"Well, part of Brant Road is in the city, but there's a small area that's still in the county—which are you?"

"I'm telling you, I don't know. But I'm on a horse farm. Does that help?"

"I'll notify the sheriff's department. Please stay on the line."

Several children and their parents had arrived for the next scheduled group lesson. Molly pondered what to say. Trying to compose herself, she stuttered, "There… there's been an accident. I need to cancel this lesson. I'll call you tomorrow to reschedule. I'm very sorry."

She stuck the phone in her pocket and turned away. Parents followed her, peppering her with questions. How could she politely ask them to leave? She went into the men's room, splashed cold water on her face, and washed her hands.

Sirens squealed in the distance. Some parents gathered their charges and left, but others talked quietly among themselves. At the end of the barn, she met the first arrival—an emergency response team. She directed them to the ladder and explained what they would find. Radios squawked as she went to the office to call her boss. Both husband and wife's phones went to voice mail. *They are probably down at the show ring now*. She tried Carter again and left a message.

Farling County deputies were moving the bystanders back. They told everyone to go into the lounge and stay there. A uniformed man approached and introduced himself as Deputy Horne. "How did you come to find the body, ma'am?"

"I was in the loft, feeding hay, and I smelled something dead. I… I thought it was a rat." Molly realized she hadn't finished feeding the horses "I need to go back up there and hay the rest of the horses."

"Not just yet. Did you recognize the man you found?"

"I've seen him around here, but I don't know his name. He often came to talk to my boss, Carter Mills."

"And where is your boss?"

"He's in Lexington, Kentucky, at a horse show."

Molly gave him all the information she had, and he finally excused her to see about the lesson horses. She quickly unsaddled the horses in the holding area and began to lead them out to their pasture. A deputy went in to talk with the remaining parents and students. Stephanie met her as she headed toward the pasture. "Miss Molly, what's going on?"

Molly said, "I found someone in the loft. There was an accident. You should probably call your mom to pick you up."

"Is it someone you know? Are they hurt bad?"

"Stephanie, the deputy asked everyone to go in the lounge. You can join them until your mom gets here."

"But I…"

"Please, Stephanie, just go." Stephanie was a good kid, smart and hard working. But Molly couldn't explain this situation now.

~ * ~

Molly was pushing a wheelbarrow full of grain from stall to stall when the ambulance crew lowered the gurney with the body to the barn floor. The deputy introduced Molly to Detective Stearns, a tall, well-built man with seriously blue eyes which focused intently on her. He asked her to repeat what she had told the deputy.

She asked him, "What about the parents and kids? They were just arriving when I found the body. Can they go home?"

"Yes. We're getting contact information, but I guess you have that as well, right?"

"The students and their parents? Yes."

"Do you have an office where we can sit down?"

Molly led him to the office, and he agreed that it might be good to start a pot of coffee. Again, she repeated what she knew, which wasn't very much. She gave the detective her boss's phone number, and he called and left a message on Carter's phone.

She tried to think about a timeline. The horses had left for the show early the morning before. She had fed that morning, last night, and this morning, and she hadn't smelled anything—or had she? She tried to think about this morning's feeding. Then she remembered. Most of the hay on that side of the barn had molded after a roof leak. She hadn't even gone up there the last two feedings, just threw hay down from the other side of the barn. But she had used most of that hay and went to see if she could salvage one bale for the two remaining horses on that side of the barn. It had been really hot that afternoon, no wonder the body had begun to smell. She wondered how long it had been there.

The detective's phone rang. "I have to take this. Excuse me." While he spoke to whomever, Molly went out to finish her chores. Crime scene tape blocked the ladder, and she climbed the opposite ladder to look for more hay.

The police were still working when Carter called her cell phone. "Who was it, Molly?"

"I don't know his name. He's that guy with the straggly beard and gray ponytail who comes around in a golf cart to talk to you."

"Oh, hell, Freddy? He probably got drunk and went up there to sleep it off. Maybe got too hot and died. Why'd you call the police?"

"He's dead, Carter. I couldn't just leave him up there."

"Jim coulda taken care of it. Does anybody know?"

"I had six students and parents waiting for their lessons. It's kind of hard to hide an ambulance and a string of deputies. They finally let everyone go home."

"Horses all right?"

"Yeah. I'll check them all before I leave." She called Detective Stearns to the phone to talk to Carter.

Molly checked every stall and thankfully found nothing amiss. Stearns handed her back the phone and told her she was free to go home. She called to her dog and walked to the house. Too tired to eat, she dragged herself up the stairs and into the shower. She wanted to call John but knew he might only get a few hours of rest and hated to wake him. She checked to see if the alarm was set on her phone, then in a fit of rebellion, turned it off, along with the lamp.

Would the police be back in the morning? At least there weren't any lessons scheduled until afternoon. Carter thought Freddy had just passed out and died from the heat. But if he was really drunk, why would he climb the ladder to the loft and go up where it was so hot? Molly had been through one murder investigation. She wasn't looking forward to another. But she had no reason to think Freddy's death was suspicious.

Chapter Three

BINGO WHINED ENOUGH TO WAKE her a little before eight o'clock. Molly didn't feel like she'd slept at all. She forced herself to roll out of bed and find clean jeans and a t-shirt. Her back ached. She fed Bingo and grabbed a banana before walking to the barn.

The heat and humidity hung heavy, making every breath a chore. The banging of metal pierced the air. Jim stood behind the barn, hitting the tractor with a hammer—whether for a particular purpose or pure frustration, she didn't know. He alternated his hammering with removing his cap and wiping the sweat off his forehead. She grabbed the grain cart and began feeding the noisy horses who were kicking, pawing, and whinnying to let her know she was late. The loft ladder on the dead body side was still blocked with yellow tape. Finding a few decent bales in the other loft, she fed hay and pitched down the last of the hay on her side for feeding.

With the tractor out of commission, the wheelbarrow would have to do. She grabbed a pitchfork and began cleaning stalls. After turning out the horse most likely to kick her, she was able to do a thorough job on his stall. She hadn't been able to clean it yesterday.

With that done, she checked for calls. The answering machine held a message from Carter, but her return call went to voice mail. Outside the window, police radios chattered. Uniforms and what looked like evidence techs swarmed into the barn. So much for the natural causes theory. She ran to alert Jim.

"Carter told me about Freddy last night. You think he didn't just pass out and die up there?" Jim asked.

"Don't know, but the police are back. Does he have family around or anything? Do you even know his last name?"

"He had a brother used to live around here, but I don't know where he is now. Has a sister, too. She keeps an eye on him. Freddy's name is Pedigo. We played poker when he was straight enough to know what card was what," Jim said.

Detective Stearns walked behind the barn. "Ms. Lewis, can I have a word?"

Molly introduced Jim and followed Stearns to the barn office. He called back to Jim as an afterthought. "I'll need to talk to you, too."

Detective Stearns settled heavily in the spare chair, stretching his boot-clad feet out in front of him. "Ms. Lewis, who would have had access to the barn loft in the last forty-eight hours?"

Molly sat down on the other side of the desk, brushing her

short hair away from her eyes. "Anyone who wanted, I guess. I mean, there's no gate at the road and no lock on anything except the office and the lounge. I'm here until about eight or nine most nights, and then I check the horses around ten. I can see one side of the barn from our house, but I can't see the driveway and parking area. The grooms live in trailers by the drive, but they're all at the horse show."

"Aren't you afraid here, a little thing like you, all by yourself?" Condescension dripped from his words.

Molly wanted to ask if he had missed his harassment training, but she said instead, "Why would I be afraid? Are you thinking Freddy didn't die a natural death?"

"I thought you didn't know his name."

"I didn't until I described him to Carter and Jim Mills— they knew him."

"Someone bashed his head in. Are you sure you didn't have an argument with him? He might have tried to get friendly with you. Or maybe you encouraged him…"

Molly shuddered at the thought. "Ugh, no. I am happily married, detective. My husband is at the horse show with the rest of the crew."

"We'll need to search the barn and premises. We can start now or I can come back with a search warrant."

"I'm not the owner, so I guess you'll need to ask Carter. Can we teach lessons tonight? I have students scheduled from four o'clock on. If I can't teach, I'll need to let everyone know."

"How many people are we talking about?"

Molly looked at the lesson roster. "Two private lessons and then three groups of five."

"I'll get back to you on that."

As usual, Carter wasn't available, but the detective left a message and said he would keep trying to call him. In the meantime, Stearns asked Molly to send Jim back to the office. She was excused to finish her stall cleaning.

The sweet mare in the first stall muzzled her arm and looked at Molly with her large brown eyes, ears pricked forward. "No treats right now, Annie, but you'll get out to play in a bit," Molly said as she scratched the mare's neck.

Annie jumped as heavy boots walked across the barn loft above. The detective must have gotten permission for a search. Would they search all the stalls as well? The shavings pile? And what about the manure pile? She giggled. That would take time. The barn phone had been ringing nonstop, but Molly let the answering machine pick up since she didn't know what to tell people. She had left her own phone in the office as well for the same reason.

When she wheeled the next wheelbarrow load of manure out, Jim was back at the tractor and cranked it to life. He managed to get it in a forward gear and pulled it into the barn. Molly's heart lifted, and she and her aching back thanked Jim. He grabbed a pitchfork, and together they finished the stalls.

When Jim pulled the tractor and manure spreader out of the barn, he had to stop. A State Police car blocked his path. The trooper and a plain clothes officer approached Molly. "Are you in charge here, ma'am?"

"For the moment. The owner's gone to a show. Do you need Detective Stearns? He's inside."

"Stearns? What's he doing here?   Wait, is this the

homicide site? We're actually here on another matter. You have a Bobcat on the farm?"

"Yes, it's in that shed." Molly pointed to a large shed behind the barn which held round bales, shavings, and the Bobcat.

"I'm Trooper Thompson and this is SBI Detective Long from major crimes. We need to look at the serial number on that machine."

"Ah… ah, okay."

She watched as they consulted a clipboard and walked into the shavings shed. When they wrote something on a clipboard, she guessed that wasn't good. The detective made a phone call before striding back to her.

"Ma'am, we're going to have to take possession of this Bobcat. It's stolen merchandise. Do you have a bill of sale or receipt for it?"

"I have no idea. But I can ask my boss." Wonderful. How would they get round bales out to the lesson horses? And it would be the wheelbarrow for shavings. Bummer. "When are you picking it up?" she asked, hoping they could use it one last day to put fresh shavings in front of each stall.

"We have a wrecker on the way."

Time to call her bosses. Molly shut herself in the office and first listened to messages. Both Carter and Ellen had left messages for her to call. Several parents had called to cancel lessons. Molly hadn't watched the news, but guessed the discovery of a body was on the air. Perhaps the news even mentioned the fact that it was a homicide.

As a riding instructor, Molly answered to Ellen, but taking care of the barn and the show horses was Carter's bailiwick. Working for a couple who often gave conflicting orders was not easy. She decided to call Ellen first.

Given the number of cancelations, Molly told Ellen she thought they should cancel the rest of the lessons for the day at least. Ellen agreed and thought Molly should call all the adult students and parents of the young riders to tell them the murder had nothing to do with Carter Mills Stables and Riding Academy and that no one even knew the poor man who had crawled up in the loft, obviously high on drugs.

To Molly this sounded like he who doth protest too much, but she replied, "I'll cancel the students we haven't heard from already and then start returning calls. But I still have to get all the horses out, and I need to tell you about the Bobcat. The State Police are repossessing it, said it's stolen."

"You'll need to talk to Carter about that. Did you tell them you needed it?" Ellen asked.

"I don't think that matters to them. They're picking it up right away." After going over a few more items of business, she hung up and called Carter.

Carter's response was, "Oh, hell. That damn Ronnie didn't tell me it was hot."

"They wanted to know if you had a bill of sale for it."

Carter snorted. "Hell, no. I bought it from Ronnie—you know Ronnie?"

"I don't. What do you want me to say to any show horse customers who call?"

"Why would they call? You mean about Freddy? Was it on TV?"

"I'm sure it was. I haven't exactly had time to watch. You gave them permission to search the barn?"

"Sure. We didn't have anything to do with this. My buddy

in the DA's office said they'd get a warrant and it would look better if I said okay."

"Makes sense. Jim got the tractor going. But we won't have a Bobcat for shavings and round bales. I'll try to get the horses out today."

"Yeah, that'd be good. Got to go."

Molly had planned to jog a few of the more seasoned horses while Jim was around to help hitch them to the two-wheeled training cart, but the tire was flat on the remaining jog cart, and the grooms hadn't left her a complete set of harnesses. She put ankle guards and bell boots on Annie and turned her out in the outdoor round pen. Then she long lined a Hackney pony, Butch, in the arena. High and fast trotting Hackneys were energetic riding and driving ponies that originated in England. Butch was cranked, snorting and leaping, and her spirits lifted with his exuberance. Working a horse always made her feel better.

She untacked Butch and left him to cool in cross ties while she retrieved Annie. The mare had a fine time playing and rolling and was now covered in sand and sweat. Molly hosed her off outside and took her back to her stall. Then she put another horse out in the round pen and prepared to work a young, gaited filly in a bitting rig, a harness and bridle designed to help her head set, in the indoor round pen. By the time she had groomed her, wrapped her legs, and added bell boots and ankle guards, the roll-back had pulled in behind the barn. She realized she hadn't given the state police the Bobcat key and went to find it.

Detective Long handed her a stack of paperwork. "I need this signed," he said. He followed her into the barn as she signed it, handed it back to him, and went to bridle the filly. The young horse danced beside Molly as she led her to the round pen. The filly looked out the door, snorted, and took off trotting around the enclosure. The detective watched, amazed. "How do you get her to pick up her feet like that?"

"She's bred to perform. She's showing off for you because she wants to."

A sweating and disheveled Stearns emerged from the tack room and walked up to Long. They shook hands and spoke in subdued voices.

Molly put another horse out to play and went to the office to begin returning calls about that day's lessons. Stearns had told her that they could resume lessons on Saturday, so she listened to the rest of the phone messages and returned calls accordingly. A birthday party was scheduled for Saturday afternoon, actually two parties, and she realized she hadn't heard from either one. She'd better call.

The first mother was clueless about the incident so Molly didn't enlighten her. As Molly went over the party details, the woman asked about the cowboy. *What?* Ellen had told her they would have a cowboy doing lasso tricks. News to Molly, who told her the cowboy couldn't make it but that they had lots of fun in store for the birthday boy and his guests. That reminded Molly to check the birthday supplies and be sure there were enough craft items and prizes. The second mother had heard about the murder and decided to cancel her party.

The phone rang incessantly. Before she knew it, feeding time had arrived and so had a much- needed load of alfalfa. Molly had called Jim and Jose, a Mexican who sometimes helped at the barn, to come help unload it. Molly climbed into the loft to help stack, but she didn't think she could throw the sixty-pound bales up to the loft. John had asked Carter if he ever considered getting a hay elevator, since a used one wasn't too expensive. Carter had just laughed. And while he pretended to work alongside his employees, he never threw bales up. Covered in dust and sweat, and coughing, she grabbed a cup of water and an allergy pill from the office before paying the hay supplier.

When she checked on the lesson horses in pasture, she realized they needed a round bale. Jim and Jose managed to push one round bale down from where it was stacked on another. With a lot of grunting, they maneuvered it out of the shed and pushed it into the pasture with the tractor while she held the gate and shooed away the hungry horses.

Jim left for home, and Molly collapsed in the office chair. She dug fifty cents out of her pocket and bought a Diet Coke from the machine. She realized she hadn't had lunch and was suddenly starving. She found a candy bar in the office and sat down to try to organize her thoughts. Stearns and the deputies were gone, and she wondered if they had found anything during their search.

Freddy had evidently been bashed in the head up in the loft. Why was he up there in the summer heat? How had he gotten there? There was no sign of his golf cart. The detective hadn't asked her any more questions, and she didn't know what Jim had told him. Jim probably knew where Freddy lived.

Time to go home. When she walked out into the barn aisle, she realized she hadn't emptied the payment box for two days due to all the commotion. She grabbed the key from the desk and opened the box to find several checks. She recorded them on the computer and fixed a deposit slip, but she needed to check the mail at Carter and Ellen's house as well. After calling Bingo, she walked to her house and her car and drove the short distance to the Mills' home. She was supposed to open anything that looked like it might be a customer payment and deposit it.

There was an envelope from a long-time customer who didn't have any horses in training at the moment, Jean Montrose, but knowing it might be a past due payment she opened it. *Whoa.* The check for $50,000 said "new horse" in the comment line. No one had told her to expect that. She wondered if she would be in trouble for opening it. She tried calling Carter and Ellen and heard only voice mails. She checked her messages and found one from Carter telling her a new horse would arrive that evening and that she would have to pay the hauler. She left the large check locked in her bosses' home and drove to the bank to make the deposit of the other checks.

Bingo stood with his paws on the dash as she waited in line at the drive-in window of the bank. He knew a treat would be coming and sure enough Molly received a dog biscuit with her deposit slip.

Because a new horse was scheduled to arrive, she returned to the barn and shoveled shavings into the wheelbarrow. Selecting an empty stall, she bedded it, checked the waterer, and threw in a flake of hay.

Chapter Four

MOLLY TOOK BINGO HOME BEFORE making a quick run to the grocery. Milk, cereal, tuna, bread, and salad mix went into her cart before a juicy-looking steak jumped in as well and then cookies. She knew she had potatoes and was fantasizing about her first real meal in two days.

She unloaded the groceries and fed a whining Bingo before opening a bottle of wine and putting a potato in the oven to bake. She made a salad, poured Italian dressing on the steak to marinate, and opened her own mail. Then she took a quick shower. The potato was done, so she heated the broiler and cooked the steak. She didn't often buy steak, for health as well as budget reasons, but she thought she had earned this one. *I wonder how John is. He's probably eating well, at least because the guys insisted on their meals.* She kept looking out toward the barn driveway. There were no windows on that side of the house, but she could see the driveway from her back door. Bingo would probably alert her if a big rig pulled in. The meal was as good as she had anticipated, and she sighed with pleasure.

Her phone rang and she hoped it was John, but Carter was calling to see if the horse had arrived yet. "Damn, I gave the hauler your number."

"I haven't heard from anyone yet." She hesitated, then decided to mention the check.

"Good, good," he said. "You can leave it at the house. Ellen will let you know if she wants you to deposit it."

"Okay. The hay came, too. Oh, and I haven't heard anything else from the sheriff's department."

She hung up and her phone rang again. This time she was glad to hear John's voice. She asked, "Did Carter tell you about finding Freddy?"

"Yeah. Sorry you had to go through that. Are you okay?"

"I thought it was a dead rat. When I moved the hay—I saw him. I knew he had to be dead. It was awful." Tears began welling in her eyes.

"What do the police think?"

"They think he was killed in the loft, but I don't know with what. And I don't know why or even when. And I don't really want to talk about it. I'm waiting for a new horse to arrive. How are things there?"

"We worked all the horses today. Carter was here early to supervise. Of course, the show doesn't start until Monday, so we have time to clip the ones who show tomorrow. I'm guessing we'll work the horses who show later in the week again tomorrow, but probably not the ones who go early. Carter likes them fresh, you know."

Molly told him about the Bobcat and the broken tractor. "Oh dear, you have had your hands full. You need to get to bed."

"Tell that to the man bringing a new horse. But I will. You be careful and get some rest yourself. Love you, bye."

She decided to do her nightly barn check and hope that the horse would arrive while she was there. Bingo sniffed for rats as she peered in each occupied stall. She had checked all the inside stalls when Bingo began barking, and she heard the roar of a diesel pulling in the drive. The dually truck pulling a six horse goose-neck stopped at the open barn doors. The driver got out and began dropping a ramp on the side of the trailer.

Molly walked out to meet him. "Hi, got a horse for us?"

He turned and looked at her with a smile. "I might. Have a check for me?"

"I will, as soon as we get this horse off and settled."

"Let's get 'er done." He walked up the ramp, a lead shank in his hand.

When he flipped on the interior trailer lights, she could see three horses, all of which began to whinny and paw. He went to the middle horse on the right side, clipped on the lead, and took off her cross ties and front bar. The horse walked quickly down the ramp, and they followed Molly to the freshly bedded stall.

The mare—Molly had looked to see which sex—was a dark liver chestnut. Her only marking was a small star on her forehead. She walked right to the automatic waterer and began to drink, always a good sign. She was about sixteen hands, the equivalent of five feet, four inches tall, and wore only keg shoes. She finished drinking, dropped and rolled in the clean shavings, then jumped up and shook before looking for hay.

"What's her name, do you know?" Molly asked.

"I'll get her paperwork," he said as he walked back to the truck.

He handed her Coggins, proof of a negative test for equine infectious anemia, required for all horse sales, shows and transport, and a health certificate along with a copy of the mare's papers.

"Come on back to the office and I'll write you a check."

She laid the papers on the desk and paid him. He still had two horses to deliver and was eager to hit the road. He thanked her and walked back to the idling truck.

Molly locked the office and called Bingo, because morning would come soon.

~ * ~

Feeding was a chore, but Molly always enjoyed the horses' eager nickers for hay and grain. The new mare looked alert and ready to eat. She realized she hadn't even glanced at her papers and didn't know what to call her. And then, one of the trainers might change her barn name. Carter never kept up with the horse's names, registered or barn names. He would just tell someone to get that bay colt out, when there were three bay colts in the barn, which made for confusion on everyone's part.

Molly finished feeding the horses in the barn and then wheeled the grain cart out to the fence of the lesson horses' pastures. Of course, all the feed pans were turned over. She climbed over the fence and shooed horses back while she righted the rubber pans. Dumping grain, she watched the horses struggle through their pecking order. Buttons, the beginner pony she and John had brought with them, had quickly aligned himself to Johnny, the biggest and baddest head of the pasture. Johnny allowed Buttons to sneak bites of grain, which the fat pony did not need.

She put up the lesson list on the clipboard in the aisle and assigned horses and saddles beside each rider's name. Hopefully, Sarah and another student would come help today and receive an extra lesson. She had given up trying to teach on Saturday mornings when everyone was working at the barn. There was too much commotion with customers riding their show horses and Ed teaching the show riders afterward, but at no certain time. She once had to move a horse and rider three times during a thirty-minute lesson—from the indoor arena to outside, then back inside. It was embarrassing, and she had lost the student because obviously the rider didn't feel cherished. But she had scheduled several make-up lessons for that morning since she had the barn and the arena to herself.

Jose had come to help her clean stalls, and she heard him start the tractor. After they finished, he would let the horses out in the round pens while she taught. Sarah and Katie arrived and began catching lesson horses from their pastures. They noticed the new horse and asked what her name was.

"That's a good question," Molly answered. "We'll go see right now."

She picked up the paperwork. The mare had been shipped from CC College in Kentucky. Her registered name was listed as "Pendiana Poppy" with "Poppy" being her barn name. She was ten years old, and her Coggins had been pulled in

Pennsylvania, so the mare hadn't been at the Kentucky college for long. Keeping a horse in training or even boarding could be expensive, and owners often donated horses to colleges with a riding program because the tax write-off was more beneficial to them than the money they could get from a quick sale. The schools could use the horses in their riding programs, but if they had more than they needed, they often leased or sold the donated horses. Molly had no idea what Poppy's job would be or what her background was.

With Sarah and Katie's help, the lessons went smoothly. Her last lesson was scheduled for eleven and the girls would ride in the group. They worked on equitation patterns—working off the rail individually in circles and figure eights—since the arena was quiet and all theirs. Sarah rode Johnny who disliked being asked to move away from the herd.

"Sarah, use your leg, don't let him turn around. No. Shorten your right rein and make him go down the rail like you asked him—use your left leg to straighten his body. Now tap him."

With coaching, Sarah legged the recalcitrant gelding to the end of the arena and managed to execute a canter circle before reversing and trotting back to the line-up. The other riders offered encouragement.

Molly smiled. She loved teaching. "Good job. See, you really can do it if you use your legs."

Sarah was smiling, sweat running down her face and tendrils of auburn curls escaping from her helmet. "Thanks."

Katie was aboard Zoom, a five-gaited horse who preferred doing his fast four beat rack to trotting. And as Molly expected, he took off racking down the rail. Katie tried to pull him back which only increased his desire to rack, the fast and impressive four-beat gait taught to five-gaited horses.

"Katie, bring him back here. Make a circle and then turn him loose. Say, 'whop trot'—no pressure on your reins."

"But he'll take off," she whined, continuing to pull on the horse as they came back toward Molly.

Molly understood, but she knew the horse and the rider. "Loosen up, now," she said as Katie came to a stop beside her. Katie loosened her reins and Molly grabbed the rein from the side and began running toward the rail. "Whop trot," she said to the horse. "Drop your hands and touch him on the neck, but don't tighten up," she said to the rider.

Katie was too startled to argue, and Molly turned Zoom loose as he trotted boldly down the rail. "Keep trotting," Molly said. "Just trot your circle and come back, one thing at a time."

Katie was grinning when she came back. "It worked."

"Imagine that. Now do it again, and stop and ask for a canter when you get to the end. He canters better from a stop. So, stop him, tip him to the rail, use your outside leg and say canter."

The canter was a little fast, and the circle was a little large, but Katie handled it and remembered to release him as soon as she pulled him down out of the canter. He trotted back to the line-up, as mannerly as could be.

Molly sent all the riders back to the rail, and they finished up with a canter. She reminded the girls to wash their hot horses and get ready for the birthday party while she checked messages. Carter called on the barn phone and wanted to know about the new horse. "Have you worked her yet?" he asked.

"Didn't know I was supposed to," she said, checking her watch.

"Sure. Get on her. See what she does. She's supposed to be a kid's horse."

"Is she going to be a lesson horse?"

"I didn't say that. Just try her out."

"Okay. I think I have time before the birthday party."

Molly asked Katie to tack up Poppy. "Let's try a snaffle and two reins with a running martingale—I have no idea how her mouth is."

Experience had taught Molly to be leery in mounting a strange horse, but a horse coming from the college and before that a training barn was less risky than someone's backyard outlaw, and she had seen her share of those. She put on her helmet, just in case. The mare stood quietly while she mounted, and walked off willingly, ears forward. Poppy began to jig, and Molly urged her on into a trot rather than fight with her. The mare's neck came up and back, and Molly shortened her now flopping reins.

"Wow," Sarah said. "She's really cute."

Molly could feel the mare pounding the ground and could tell from the bounce that she had plenty of hock action. Horses who stepped high behind were bouncy. But Poppy was out of shape. Two trips around and she was breathing heavy. Molly pulled her down. "Whoa, walk."

Poppy was willing to flat walk after trotting, and Molly took her twice around so that the mare could catch her breath. Then she asked for a canter and was rewarded with a slow, easy gait. She brought her down again and reversed, enjoying the mare's ground-covering trot. The second canter was equally good although it took Molly two tries to get it. The mare was tired.

She rode her to the middle and petted her neck. "Good girl." Molly slipped off and handed the mare to Sarah, saying, "Be sure to wash between her legs, she's really hot."

The birthday parents were unloading food and presents into the lounge, and Molly went to greet them. Twenty-five children were expected, so she had planned for two ponies for pony rides and a table for crafts and another for face-painting. Her helpers were set up and ready. The children were well behaved, thank goodness, and appeared to enjoy the rides.

The barn phone rang as she was putting away the party supplies. Carter wanted to know how the new horse was.

"Really cute and easy to ride, but out of shape."

"Good, good. Got another horse coming tomorrow," Carter said.

"Do you know what time?" Molly could see her day off—between feedings, at least—spiraling down the drain.

"Actually, I told them you'd meet them at Monty Blair's barn in Wytheville. You know where that is, right? You can use your truck and trailer."

The day off had now vanished. "Who's bringing the horse?"

"Oh, what's his name, from Bluefield. I gave him your number."

"What time?"

"I think about eight in the morning."

Molly didn't groan although she certainly wanted to. She suggested several names as to who might be bringing the horse. Carter finally agreed that it was someone from Dreamwood Farm and said he didn't have a phone number. Molly had been looking forward to a day off, but it was not to be.

She and Sarah fed grain to the horses.

Sarah saw her dad drive up outside the barn. "My dad's here, I'd better go. Bye, Miss Molly."

"Bye, Sarah, and thanks for all of your help."

She decided to fuel up the truck and hitch to the trailer before she ate dinner. Fortunately, the trailer tires all looked okay. One never knew around here, but she didn't want a flat tire while hauling a horse.

~ * ~

Molly groaned when the alarm rang at five. She rushed through feeding and managed to be on the road by 6:45, Bingo happily sitting in the passenger seat. There was no traffic going up the mountain, and she made good time to pulling north to Wytheville. She never minded driving up a mountain, but coming down with a loaded trailer made her nervous. She pulled up outside the barn and left the truck idling to cool the engine. When Molly walked into Monty's barn, she saw a groom feeding the horses. He didn't know about the horse that was coming or he didn't understand much English, Molly couldn't decide which. She went back outside and shut off the truck. Monty himself showed up about nine and offered her a Diet Coke, which she gladly accepted. He didn't know anything about her meeting someone with a horse and calls to Carter went unanswered.

She was almost asleep in the truck when she heard a diesel engine. A blue dually pulling a two- horse trailer eased to a stop outside the barn. Molly jumped out and went to meet the driver.

"Are you Molly?" he asked.

"Yes. I was expecting you at eight."

"You were? Well, we had things to take care of at the barn. Sorry about that. Are you ready to load?"

Molly told him she was and dropped the tailgate on her trailer. A liver chestnut mare, looking a lot like the new mare at home, stepped politely out of his trailer. She looked around and snorted. The driver patted her on the neck, then led her onto Molly's trailer. The mare hesitated for a minute before walking up the ramp onto Molly's four horse slant load. The driver snapped her tie rope and Molly pushed the divider toward her, leaving only enough room for the man to slide out.

He helped her lift the tailgate and close the back of the trailer.

"Do you have paperwork for me?" Molly asked.

"Oh, shoot. I left it on the desk. But I'll see that someone mails it to you."

"Can you tell me anything about her?"

"We've only had her a few weeks. But she seems to be a nice enough mare."

"What's her name?"

"I don't know. They just asked me to haul her over here."

The mare was now pawing with impatience, and Molly knew she'd better hit the road. She handed the driver a card with the stable address and climbed in the truck. It roared to life, and she rolled gently down the gravel drive, opening her window and turning off the radio so she could hear any noise from the trailer. The pawing stopped as Molly pulled onto the interstate. When she came to the downgrade, she downshifted and turned on her flashers, creeping down the mountain with occasional braking. When she reached Mt. Airy, she stopped for a restroom and a snack. The mare stood quietly, munching hay.

Forty-five minutes later, she pulled into the farm drive and left the diesel idling. She grabbed a lead shank and opened the tailgate. The horses in the barn were whinnying to the new arrival, and she whinnied back and pawed, eager to be off the trailer.

"Easy mare," Molly said. "I'm coming."

She undid the partition and unsnapped the mare after snapping the lead on her. The horse backed out nicely, if a little fast, and gave a big snort as she looked around. She was tall, at least sixteen hands, probably more, and well made with a fine head and long neck. Her only marking was a small white star on her head, almost a clone of the other new horse, except taller.

After Molly put her in the stall, she dropped and rolled, got up, shook herself and found the waterer, drinking for a long time.

Molly went home to eat and nap briefly before it was time for the afternoon feeding.

Carter called her cell just as she started to drop off to sleep. "Did you get her home? What's she look like?"

Molly fumbled with the phone, irritated at the interruption. "Yeah, but they weren't there at eight or even nine. She looks a lot like the other mare you just got."

Chapter Five

THE NEXT MORNING BROUGHT RAIN and law enforcement. Multiple divisions in three cars parked outside the office as Molly listened to phone messages. A State Bureau of Investigation, SBI, detective, Ethan Bell, was joined by Allison Holmes from DEA and Bert Anderson from ICE. Deputy Sturgis made the introductions. The officers crowded into the small office, and Molly suggested they adjourn to the viewing lounge where they could all sit. Sturgis was out of his depth, and he had sense enough to know it. He sat by the door, scrolling through his phone.

Bell began the questioning. "Ms. Lewis, do you know the legal names of your grooms who live in the trailer outside? And who lives in which room?" Bell wore khakis and a polo shirt. Molly guessed he was in his early thirties, with thick dark hair, trimmed short.

She thought for a minute. "No, I mostly know their

nicknames. Sometimes one of them will get a phone call, asking for them by their real first name, so I know Pedro is really Eduardo, but that's all I know. And I don't have a clue about who sleeps where."

"You don't see their paychecks?" Holmes asked as she made notes on a tablet. She looked up at Molly, her dark brown eyes beaming intelligence. She wore a navy pantsuit with a white top accented by a burgundy scarf. Her nails were beautifully manicured and her make-up was subtle, but perfect. Navy heels had remained unmarred by the rain outside and sawdust in the barn.

Molly looked down at her own muddy boots and dirty jean bottoms and wondered if she had even combed her hair before coming to the barn. She knew she hadn't bothered with make-up—it melted in the heat. "They're paid in cash," she answered, knowing that immigration status would be the next question.

"Do they have green cards or are they citizens?" Holmes asked.

Molly could plead ignorance, because although she thought only one of them was legal, she didn't really know. "I have no idea. My bosses hire them."

When Molly and John had operated their own barn in rural North Carolina, they'd had trouble keeping help. Few locals wanted to do the hard work required. The farm owners wouldn't allow a mobile home on the property, so they couldn't provide housing for workers. Most stables hired Mexican grooms because they were hard working and needed the money. They mostly stayed out of trouble; they didn't want to risk deportation. But now was not the time for a political discussion.

"Have you ever known any of them to use or sell controlled substances?" asked Holmes.

Had they found drugs in the trailer? That would explain the multiple officers. Molly answered honestly. "No. I've seen them drink a beer at a horse show or if we go out for lunch, but that's all. I don't think they could work as hard as they do and be messed up." But maybe the long hours at a horse show required something beyond an energy drink. She didn't know.

Bell had the next question. "Who drives that car out there?"

Molly had seen all the grooms drive it at one time or another, running out for beer or groceries after a hard day's work, but she was pretty sure Lorenzo had a driver's license. He had driven Carter's truck to the horse show. "I guess Pedro and Lorenzo. But I don't know who owns it."

Bell looked at his notes and then back at her. "It's registered to a Richard Landsdowne. That name mean anything to you?"

She had no idea who that was. But Carter's buddies were always coming around, and they all had weird nicknames. There was Worm and Joe-Joe and Royal. Royal was a gambler, and Carter always bet on ballgames and the like with him.

"No. I don't know anyone by that name. But Carter has lots of buddies who come by. I see them, but I don't know their names or maybe I might know their nickname."

Bell continued, "Thing is, the Richard Landsdowne who owns that car has been dead for two years, but the tag on that car was issued to your boss for another car."

Molly wasn't surprised. She'd seen her boss pull trailer tags from one horse trailer to another. And there was no telling where that car had originated. "I don't know anything about it," she said.

Bell said, "We are impounding that car, should be a rollback to pick it up within the hour. We're going to look around, but you can go back to your work."

"Okay, thanks. Let me know if you have any more questions." Molly had a new list of thoughts to ponder. Were there drugs in the car? Or had Freddy been transported in the car? And who was Richard Landsdowne?

She looked over the lesson schedule and planned which horses she would have time to work before she started teaching. She turned Annie loose in the round pen and walked Phil, a big bay gelding who was recovering from a stem cell implant to repair a damaged ligament He seemed to be doing well, walking better each day. By the end of the week, he wouldn't want to only walk. She wondered how soon he could go back to work, and then when he could show.

The arena looked pretty rough, dry and dusty with a rut around the edge. She turned on the sprinkler system for a while, and then she started the four-wheeler in order to drag it. Bingo loved sitting in her lap while she graded the arena. If she didn't let him ride, he would run behind, barking furiously. Normally, Carter graded the arena every morning and again in the late afternoon—he loved chores that involved moving vehicles. Physical labor, not so much.

After putting away the four-wheeler, she called Bingo and walked over to her house for a sandwich. Her lessons started early that afternoon, and she grabbed an apple and a Diet Coke for later. She had just enough time to check messages before her first lesson. An unidentified woman asked for Carter to call her, saying it was important. As Molly left the office, the phone rang again and the same voice asked for Carter.

"I'm sorry, he's not here. Can I help you?"

"I got bidness with him. I need to talk to him."

Molly knew not to give Carter's cell number to an unidentified caller. "Can I give him a message?"

"No, I need t' talk to him. When will he be there?"

Molly told her that Carter would be back in the barn on Monday and hung up quickly.

She hadn't heard from Carter or Ellen yet today. She had tried to call Carter but, as usual, only got voice mail. She would tell him about the car and the law enforcement visit later.

Chapter Six

THE BARN PHONE WAS RINGING when Molly walked in. It was Carter, who wanted to know if everything was okay. She told him about the multiple law enforcement officers. "They said the car was owned by somebody named Landsdown. Who is that?" Molly asked.

"Hell, I don't know. I won that car in a poker game and kept it for the boys to use."

Then she told him about his female caller.

"Don't give her my number," he said. "And for sure don't give her Ellen's number. Is that immigration guy going to come back when we get home?"

"I have no idea, but I'm guessing he will. And DEA was here, too. I think they found drugs in either the trailer or the car." She didn't want to get the guys in trouble, but Carter needed to know if his grooms were using or selling.

"Aw, hell. I'll talk to the boys. Do you know what they

found—I mean a little grass or something else?"

"They didn't confide in me," Molly said, "but I don't think they'd bring in the DEA over a little pot."

She asked how the show was going.

"We don't have anyone showing tonight. But Ronnie and Halleluiah had a heck of a show last night. Got second after a workout, but I thought she'd won it. Heck of a show. You ride that new horse yet? The one you picked up Sunday?"

"No. didn't have time yesterday, and I didn't have anyone around to help. Maybe I'll line her today." Long-lining or ground driving is a safer alternative to riding a strange horse.

"Okay, good, good."

Molly was glad to hear they had a night off at the show. Maybe John would get some rest. Hopefully, he'd call before too late tonight. Carter had been eager to hear about the newest arrival. She decided to long line her as soon as she finished cleaning stalls.

The new mare looked young and acted a bit skittish, drawing up when Molly put the harness on her and waving her back leg when Molly tightened the girth. She had been antsy when Molly wrapped her legs and put on ankle guards. Molly unbuckled her halter and slid it back around her neck in case she tried to escape from the bridle, but the mare dove for the bit, anxiously chomping on it once it was in her mouth.

Molly gathered up the long lines and led her out of the stall. The mare leapt forward, and Molly snatched the rein by her bit. "Easy, mare, you'll get to work in a minute."

The mare danced as Molly secured the round pen gate. She decided not to check her head up very much and let out the lines as soon as she had a loose overcheck in place. The mare took off like a bullet, bucking, leaping, and snorting. Molly used her right hand to steer the mare to the rail, then tried to straighten her head with the inside rein. She lifted the whip up in her hand in case the mare brought those kicking hind legs too close. After a few rounds, she began to settle into her work. She was still going too fast and would occasionally break into a canter or kick up, but she began to go consistently forward in a strong, ground-covering trot, with her knees rising way above level. This was a very nice mare. Molly wondered if she'd been shown and, if so, in what division.

When Molly stopped her to reverse, the mare gave three loud snorts, raised her tail and eagerly took off in the second direction. She was already dripping sweat, but obviously not winded or tired. She might look like the other mare, but she sure didn't act like her. Molly was glad she hadn't tried to ride her first. She wondered how long it had been since the horse had been worked.

Molly yelled, "Whoa," and the mare stopped, snorting once more and looking around to see if anyone had watched her performance. Molly had to laugh. "You're quite full of yourself, aren't you?"

~ * ~

The rest of the day went quickly with one visitor. A busty peroxide blonde walked into the barn, making herself at home, opening doors and looking around.

"Can I help you?" Molly asked.

"Just lookin' for Carter. I need t'see him."

Molly recognized the voice from the phone. "I told you he's out of town at a horse show. I'll tell him, you stopped by… ah, what is your name?"

"Never mind. I'll be back," she said as she sauntered out of the barn and started up a noisy Ford Focus, which backfired once before trailing dust as she sped down the drive. Another of Carter's less than wholesome friends?

Molly taught mostly advanced students that night, and she enjoyed her lessons. The girls were good helpers, too, and by eight-thirty they had all the lesson horses washed and put out in their pastures.

She fed Bingo and thought about trying to call John, but it was now nine o'clock and he might have already gone to bed since he had the night off. She was getting ready to shower when her phone rang.

"Hey," she answered. "I was wondering whether to call or not. Thought you might be in bed."

"No, but I'm going soon. I'm beat, but at least we have an early night. What's happening there?"

She told him about the multiple law officers and the mysterious lady. "So, they must have found drugs," she concluded.

"Yeah, and with today's politics, they'll jump all over any immigrant with a scent of a drug issue. What did Carter say?"

"He's going to talk to the grooms about it. Hope they don't split on you." Then she told him about the wild and exciting new mare.

"Be careful. You probably don't need to ride her until we get back."

"Don't worry. I won't. But I'm eager to see if she's that fired up tomorrow."

"I wish you could be here with us or I could be there to help you. But I am enjoying what little of the show I get to see. Halleluiah was fantastic last night."

"Carter told me. He thought they'd won—what did you think?"

"He broke once, in a corner, but so did the winner. I would have given it to Ronnie, but then we all love her and her horse."

Molly agreed. Ronnie was a genuinely nice woman who loved the sport and her horses. She owned competitive horses and rode them well.

"I miss you, and I wish you didn't have to work so hard. I'll be glad when you get home."

"Me, too. Don't overdo yourself. Love you."

After the phone call, Molly took a shower and crawled under the covers, with Bingo snoring from his bed beside her. But tired as she was, she kept thinking about the drugs. The grooms all sent money home to Mexico and were usually very worried about getting in any kind of trouble. Did one of them have an addiction? They all showed up for work and worked hard all day, but then again that might be evidence they were using some kind of stimulant. They didn't go out much. Was someone delivering drugs? That shouldn't be surprising, considering the questionable characters she'd seen around the barn. And after managing their last barn and dealing with the owner's addicted daughter, she wasn't naïve.

She knew Pedro gambled a lot. He was always betting with Carter about ball games and car races, and he usually won. He would sometimes flash a wad of cash, which wasn't a good sign. But she knew he was building a house for his family in Mexico. She had heard that Royal was a bookie. He came around, also in a golf cart, like poor Freddy. Probably no driver's license. But Royal wasn't a drunk as far as she knew, and he wasn't poor. Someone had said he was an American who didn't file taxes and didn't exist legally. Was he the source of the car? Was he the "dead" owner? Drugs had been the cause of a murder where she previously worked, at Marsa Farm—could this be a drug dispute?

Freddy was an alcoholic, but he didn't seem to have the means or the interest to get into anything else. Could he have witnessed a drug deal? Or for that matter, a hot merchandise deal like the Bobcat? Who knew? She flopped the covers back and picked up a book to take her mind away. And soon, she slept.

~ * ~

The next morning, Molly realized that she hadn't checked Carter and Ellen's mail yesterday. As soon as she finished feeding the horses and cleaning stalls, she drove over to check the mail in their box. A hand addressed envelope showed the return address of a stable in West Virginia. Good, that must be the Coggins and papers for the new mare. She ripped open the envelope and found a copy of the Coggins she already had on the other mare, Pendiana Poppy.

What the hell?

Chapter Seven

MOLLY RECHECKED THE RETURN ADDRESS on the envelope to make sure she wasn't confused. The address was that of the stable in West Virginia who had sent the mare for her to pick up. So how did they have the same Coggins as the mare from the college? Different drivers, originating from different locations with two different horses; had the mares been in the same barn at one point and someone just used the same papers for both?

Molly knew that happened, because the blood tests were expensive and required a vet to pull the blood. Sometimes a last-minute substitute lesson horse would be sent with other horse's Coggins. But who was the real Pendiana Poppy, and what was the other mare's name? The only commonality would seem that they ended up in the same barn and they had the same markings. By design? Nothing would surprise her, and she decided not to ask Carter or Ellen about it until they got home. She didn't want to deal with their dissembling.

She had tried to call Ellen about whether or not to deposit the large check, but she could only reach her voice mail. For whatever reason, her boss had decided to remain incommunicado. Sometimes Molly was supposed to defer to Ellen for every decision and let her communicate with new customers, and sometimes Molly had to take care of everything. Trouble was, she never knew which kind of day it was.

Time to stop thinking and go back to work. The day was progressing well when she answered a desperate call from Pedro wanting to know what the police had found in the car and in the trailer.

"I don't know," she told him, "but whatever it was it caused them to bring in a DEA officer. Pedro, did you have drugs here?"

"Miss Molly, I don't use drugs. You should know that."

"Then why are you asking me these questions?"

"I don't do drugs. But I owe Royal money. He want me to take the car and pick up a package for him and hold for people to pick up and collect the money for him. I did and I give him the money, but one of the customers hadn't come yet. Carter decided to leave half a day earlier for the show. So, I hid it in the car, under the spare tire. The police must find it."

"Oh, Pedro. I guess your fingerprints will be on the package."

"Shit. What am I going to do, Miss Molly? Royal said he would turn me in to immigration if I don't do what he say. I no want to, but I have to. I can't come back, I will have to go somewhere after the show… or do you think they will come here for me?"

"Are your fingerprints on file anywhere?"

"No, Miss Molly. I never been in trouble before."

Molly paced up and down the barn aisle while she thought about it. "Then they can't charge you until they have fingerprints, but if you don't come back, they'll be looking for you. Have you told this to Carter?"

"No. He just asked if we knew anything about Freddy and if we had any drugs in the trailer. I told him no. But Freddy, I think he was around when Royal came last time. I forgot when Carter ask me. Freddy was looking for beer. Maybe he hear Royal talk about something?"

"Could be. I think you need to speak with a lawyer. Ask Carter if you can talk to Sarah's mom, Judy Franklin. She's at the show now, right? She's a lawyer."

"Okay. I gotta go. You believe me, Miss Molly?"

"I think so. Talk to the lawyer."

As Molly hung up, she heard a commotion outside. The horse she had turned out in the outside round pen, Olympus, had rolled and gotten a foot stuck under the fence. He was thrashing around as Molly ran toward him. "Whoa, boy. Let me help you."

By the time she reached him, he had managed to pull the bottom board off the fence and was scrambling to get up. She had wrapped his front legs and put ankle guards on behind, but she could see a bloody scrape below his left ankle guard as he scrambled to his feet. He limped as he moved away from the disaster scene. Molly grabbed the lead line and slowly approached the frightened horse. He snorted and backed away, but then stood.

She led him slowly into the barn and put him in cross ties in the wash rack. He flinched as she took off the ankle guard. He had a splinter of wood stuck to or in his pastern. Turning on the hose, she began to aim the cold water on his hind leg. He lifted it when the cold water hit.

"Easy, fellow, I'm trying to help you here."

Sand and blood fell away, but once the area was clean, it looked better. Molly picked up his hoof and spoke softly as she reached for the wood splinter. He pulled his leg away. "Whoa, darn it. I need to get that out." The second try was a win, and she held a three-inch long fence splinter in her hand. She hosed more and tried to feel around the wound to see if she had gotten it all. It looked clean and the bleeding had almost stopped, so she let him dry while she went in search of first aid supplies. They had taken the medicine trunk to the show, but she always tried to reserve antiseptic and bandages for the horses left at home.

She wondered if a vet was needed and remembered she could take a picture with her phone and send it to the vet. She snapped a few pictures before dousing the area with iodine solution.

She called the veterinary hospital, and the receptionist told her the horse vet they used was out, but to send the picture to his cell. She found newly laundered, but not sterile, bandages and decided she'd better wrap the injury to keep it clean. Then she went to the office to see if she could find his health record. Before Molly came, no one kept up with shots and worming on each horse. She had fixed a binder and tried to keep track of vaccinations, deworming and so forth. When she had time, she needed to computerize the records, but that might be more trouble than it was worth. Yes, he'd had a tetanus shot in March, but she'd ask the vet if he needed a booster.

Olympus stepped gingerly on his injured foot but was able to put most of his weight on it. She put him in his stall and gave him extra hay to munch on.

Her student helpers had arrived and went out to the pastures to catch lesson horses. Sarah and Joey came running into the barn. "There's a golf cart in the shed, and Barney has his foot stuck in it," Sarah yelled.

Molly grabbed an extra lead and followed the kids back out to the pasture. The shed faced away from the barn and horses only seemed to go in when it was very hot out or in winter if it contained a round bale. Sure enough, Barney had stepped into the golf cart and his shoe was hung under the gas pedal. Why on earth…

Then Molly remembered that Freddy usually had peppermints for the horses. Barney had smelled peppermints and stepped in the cart to find them. Talking softly to the tall gelding, she was able to lift his leg enough to release it. He put it on the ground gingerly and walked away. This must be Freddy's golf cart. She tried not to touch it as she climbed out.

She pulled the baling twine off of the round bale outside and tied it across the shed opening. Then she went back to the barn to find something more substantial. She found an old gate which would cover half of the opening and roped off the rest with lunge lines.

Only then, when she knew the horses were safely locked out, did she call the sheriff's office.

Chapter Eight

AFTER LEAVING A MESSAGE FOR Detective
Stearns, Molly decided to call the SBI detective as well. Bell
answered, and she told him about the golf cart. He asked
if she or anyone else had touched it. She explained the
circumstances and that the students had no doubt touched
it. He said he would need to fingerprint them for elimination
purposes.

"I can't let you do that without their parent's permission,"
she said.

"We'll see," he answered, "but make sure no one else
touches it."

That, she could do.

The kids caught the rest of the lesson horses and began
to groom and saddle them. Molly had about thirty minutes
before her lessons started. She debated whether or not to
try to work a horse, but decided she was too distracted. No

work was better than inadvertently teaching a horse the wrong thing. She put boots and leg wraps on the new Poppy mare and turned her out in the indoor round pen. The mare bucked and snorted, flagging her tail, looking like a world champion. She didn't stop until she was dripping wet and Molly hollered, "Whoa, mare."

She walked up to the mare and threaded the lead shank through the halter and over her nose. The mare pranced back to the stall beside her, and Molly put her in cross ties, instructing Sarah to wash her off and then walk her.

Detective Bell and company showed up as the lesson began. She couldn't leave her students, so she asked Joey to take him and his entourage to the golf cart. Joey could tell him where they had touched the cart and possibly eliminate the need for fingerprinting the kids.

As the lesson ended, she saw Sarah standing in the barn aisle, waving her hands and telling the newly arrived students about Barney and the golf cart. *Wonderful. More grist for the rumor mill.* She reminded the girls to bring out the horses for the next lesson. Finally, seven horses and their advanced riders had made it into the ring. Molly had set up cones and directed the riders in a complicated pattern around and through the cones. They ended the lesson with a drill team maneuver, always a popular, if somewhat risky, activity.

When Molly and the students led the lesson horses back to their pastures, she saw lights in the shed. Since it had no electricity, the SBI officers must have brought high powered lanterns. The horses snorted at the unfamiliar activity in the back of their pasture. One of the officers came forward. "Ma'am, could you not put those horses in here now?"

Molly told the students to stop, horses in hand. "Well, this is where they live. But I guess there are enough empty stalls in the barn to put them up for the night."

The officer asked her to do that, and she groaned inwardly, thinking about the extra stall cleaning. Molly and her students found stalls for all the horses who normally lived in that pasture. She told the girls to check the waterers in each stall and give every horse a scoop of grain while she climbed up in the loft to drop hay into their stalls. When she climbed down the ladder, several parents gathered to ask about the state police, the golf cart, and all the activity. Really, she was surprised they had allowed their kids to come ride after all the hubbub. A few had canceled, but not as many as she had expected.

Bingo bounced as she trod wearily home. After feeding the dog, she collapsed with a cold beer in front of the TV. She woke up at midnight, turned off the infomercials, and crawled into bed, sweat and all, setting her alarm to allow time for a shower in the morning. She had to sleep.

The rest of the week flew by. Saturday's lessons ended by three, and with no birthday parties scheduled, she had time to get the stalls ready for the returning horses. None of their horses were showing back in the Saturday night championship classes, so the horses and crew had left early that morning and would be home soon. She made sure they all had hay and that the waterers were clean and working.

She had just started to feed grain to the horses when she heard the tractor-trailer horse van rumbling in the drive. Carter's truck, pulling the gooseneck, followed closely behind, horses pawing and stomping, eager to exit their trailers. John emerged from the dually, and Molly ran to him. He looked dead tired, moving stiffly, but opened his arms to embrace her. Bingo raced up to him, barking and leaping in the air.

"Hey, welcome home. I feel like you've been gone forever."

"Longer," he answered as he squeezed her in a hug.

Molly watched the grooms open the van door and connect the ramp. Pedro threw out the lead shanks from the trailer, and he and the other grooms began unloading the horses.

"Pedro came home?" she asked John.

"You haven't seen him. He will disappear shortly."

Molly grabbed the next horse, and soon all the horses were in their own stalls, happily munching hay. Monday would be soon enough to unload the tack and equipment.

Carter and Ellen were driving their RV home but planned to make stops along the way.

Ed, the other assistant trainer, checked the horses on one side, while John and Molly inspected the other side and the stalls out back. Molly brought John and Ed up to date on the investigation and the discovery of the golf cart out back.

The sound of crunching gravel indicated that a car had pulled up, and Pedro disappeared into the backseat. Molly and John deliberately looked away as the car roared out of the driveway.

Molly had brought her car over to pick up John's luggage. They made it into the house by six. She had ordered pizza and opened wine, knowing she would be too tired to cook.

John revived somewhat after a shower. As he sank into a kitchen chair, Molly noticed deep circles under his green eyes and a defeated expression in the downward turn of his mouth. "There was a murder in his barn, and Carter didn't think he should come right home?" Molly asked, her voice rising, as she poured him a glass of merlot.

John shrugged. "He was going to look at a horse or stop in Hurricane to gamble, who knows? But I don't want to talk or think about Carter or the show right now. When's the pizza coming?"

At that moment, the doorbell rang. Bingo went crazy, and soon they were feasting on a hot veggie pizza, Molly having decided John's horse show diet had probably not included vegetables.

Chapter Nine

THEY BOTH SLEPT LIKE THE dead. Molly and John would do the Sunday morning feeding, and the grooms would feed Sunday night.

Molly tried to explain everything about the two Poppies, the large check, the persistent caller, and the murder investigation while they gulped coffee and John shaved. They quickly fed the horses and dressed for church. After church, they drove to a downtown brunch spot.

John tried to clarify everything she had told him while they waited for their orders. "So, the Bobcat was stolen? It figures. Wonder how long it will take Carter to get a new one?"

Molly sipped her coffee. "I keep thinking about Royal. If he was blackmailing Pedro into dealing drugs, who knows what else he was doing? And Freddy might have been around when he was delivering."

"And the two new horses. Looks like one's supposed to be a ringer, but why?"

"Maybe the good mare doesn't have papers," Molly suggested.

They were interrupted by a server bearing thick, steaming cheese omelets. "Yeah. I could see that. But how did they come with the same Coggins and health certificate from different places?"

"I can't answer that one. Unless Ellen had the papers in advance and duplicated them for the second barn?"

John sputtered his sip of iced tea. "Like she duplicated the horse show passes?" he asked, laughing.

Molly remembered the time Ellen had been caught using counterfeit gate tickets at a large horse show. "I had forgotten that incident."

~ * ~

Monday morning found everyone in the barn working, with a unanimous decision to feed, clean stalls, and unload all the equipment, then quit for the day. With everyone on deck, they made quick progress until Detectives Bell and Stearns arrived. Marco, one of the grooms, took off through the woods but Lorenzo, who had a green card, stayed. No one at the barn had any idea where Pedro might be, but they all agreed he was the last one to use the car.

Stearns and Bell expressed their displeasure that Carter and Ellen had not come home yet. "All this happening on his property and he's not here?" Stearns asked. "Are you sure he's even coming home?"

The thought that Carter might be guilty of murder and

on the run had not occurred to Molly. Other things, yes, but surely not Freddy's death.

John spoke up. "I'm sure he'll be back by tonight or tomorrow. His family's here. This is his property, he wouldn't leave."

Molly nodded her agreement.

After interviewing everyone who had been gone to the show, the law enforcement officers searched the horse van, the dually, and trailers. They told Molly they might be back with a warrant to search Carter and Ellen's house if the couple didn't arrive soon.

Molly tried to call each of them but received no answer.

The barn crew adjourned to the local greasy spoon for a late lunch. "You don't think Carter could have killed Freddy, do you?" Ed asked.

John took a bite out of his hamburger and chewed before answering. "Anything is possible, but I can't see Carter following Freddy into the loft and knocking him out. Was Freddy drunk or do we know?"

Molly shook her head and swallowed. "They haven't shared that information."

Lorenzo asked, "You think the customer for the drugs might come and be mad when he couldn't find Pedro? Maybe he don't know who had the drugs—maybe he kill Freddy?"

John asked, "Did Pedro know who was coming to buy?"

Lorenzo shrugged before answering, "I don't know. I mean, I think he had a code name. But he no tell me."

Molly drained the last of her Diet Coke. "The only one who might know is Royal, and he won't be volunteering any information to the police. Does anyone know where he lives?

I know he has a farm and horses that Jose takes care of, but he doesn't live there, does he?"

No one knew.

When they got back to the barn, Molly found the busty blonde in the office. "Where's Carter?" she screamed at Molly. "You said he would be home today."

"I was wrong. I don't know when he'll be home."

Her anger morphed into desperation. "I need to see him. I have to see him."

Molly realized the woman was choking back sobs. "Look, can I help you?"

"It's too fucking late for that. Can you tell him to call this number when he comes back?" She scrawled her number on a Post-it note and shoved it into Molly's hand before stomping out the office door.

John walked in. "Who was that?"

"She won't tell me. She's been trying to get a hold of Carter. I don't know why, but a few scenarios come to mind."

Chapter Ten

ED HAD LESSONS TO TEACH that afternoon and evening. Molly and John went home to do laundry and shop for groceries.

Tuesday morning, Carter was grading the arena when John and Molly arrived at the barn. Carter's Jack Russell terrier, Pepper, sat in his lap. Bingo went flying after the four-wheeler, barking non-stop, and Carter laughed.

When he came to a stop, Molly asked, "When did you get home?"

"Late last night. Everything okay?"

Molly didn't know where to start. "The state police and Deputy Stearns want to talk to you and probably the woman from DEA and the immigration guy want to see you. And that woman came by again. She gave me her number, wants you to call her. She was really upset."

"Oh, hell. Pedro gone?"

"Yes, and so is Marco. He ran off through the woods when he saw the police cars."

"Call Jose and see if he can work this week." With that, he turned away and went to start up the tractor and pull the spreader into the barn.

Jose didn't answer, but she left a message. Molly did the required thirty minutes of bathroom and lounge cleaning, which Carter expected every morning. She grumbled under her breath, knowing that the woman who cleaned Carter and Ellen's house made a lot more per hour than she did.

When Molly came back to the office, Jose called.

After he agreed to work the rest of the week, Molly asked him where Royal lived. "Not here at the farm. I stay here, but I don't know where he lives. And he no pay me for last week. He usually pay me every Sunday, but he not around. I need to go, I can't find one of his broodmares."

Was Royal on the run, too? Carter came into the office. "I'm going to the sheriff's office. Be back after lunch."

Molly looked up. Carter was red-faced and sweating. The morning was already warm, but all he'd done was drive the tractor and the four-wheeler. "Are you feeling okay?" she asked as he wiped his face with a handkerchief. He mumbled something and stormed out the door.

The next caller was Ellen. She told Molly to go get the large check from the house and deposit it in the show horse account. Molly mentioned that she had duplicate paperwork on the two mares.

Ellen hedged, "You know those haulers do that. They keep a set in case they get caught without any. It was a coincidence—he must have hauled that mare sometime earlier."

Not likely. "Are you coming in?" Molly asked.

"No, I'm actually out of town, visiting my friend. Not sure when I'll be back. Anything else I need to know?"

"Carter went to the sheriff's office. Marco and Pablo are gone, and Carter asked me to get Jose to work. He's coming in tomorrow. Will you be back in time to fix the grooms' payroll on Saturday?"

Molly also wondered about everyone else's paychecks, including her own, but decided this question would work to get the answer.

"I think so, I just need some time." Her last line ended in a sob.

"Ellen, are you okay?"

"No, but I will be."

Clearly, Ellen was in distress; Molly thought about the nameless woman visitor and made her own conclusions. She wasn't sure how to respond, but she finally asked, "Are you getting help?"

"I will," she said, sniffing.

"Take care." Molly hung up the phone and sighed. As angry as she sometimes was with her boss, she did feel sorry for her at the moment. Carter wouldn't be easy to live with in the best of times, but Ellen should have known what she was getting. He had left his last wife for her. Molly walked out to get a Diet Coke and then she checked the lesson schedule to see if she needed to catch any horses for the earliest lessons. She entered last night's payments in the computer and tried to clean the office. Student helpers were catching the horses, but they had left a trail of sticky ice pop wrappers across the floor. Ellen insisted she keep the freezer stocked with the messy things.

She had hardly seen John. He was busy grooming and working horses. He stopped by the office before leaving for the house. "How about I grill burgers tonight? What time do you finish?"

"I should be home by 8:30. Thanks, dear."

Molly helped her students put out the last of the lesson horses and clean the holding area. She checked all the stalls before following the aroma of grilling burgers to the house. John had lighted candles on the small deck and set the table with a glass of wine already poured. An old boom box played soft music. She sank into her chair and kicked off her stinky boots. Bingo had abandoned her when John walked home, but he greeted her eagerly, begging for meat.

John laughed. "I already fed you. Honest, Molly, I did. He lies. Is Jose coming tomorrow?"

"Yep. And he said he hasn't seen Royal all week. Royal owes him money and hasn't been around."

"Well, that might be why, but I guess that's out of character for him?"

"Yeah. From what Jose said. We'll find out more tomorrow." Molly added lettuce and onion to her sizzling hamburger. "Thanks for cooking."

"My pleasure. Where was Carter this afternoon? He never came back, did he?"

"No. He went to the sheriff's office, said he'd be back after lunch. He looked awful. Ellen called. She's somewhere out of state—apparently there's trouble in paradise."

John had followed Molly's earlier description of the busty blonde. "So you think this chick is pregnant? And

Ellen knows?"

"That's my guess." She looked up at John and toasted him, "To us," thinking how rare a good marriage might be.

He smiled and lifted his glass in return.

Molly cleaned the dishes and took a shower. She found John already in bed but awake, waiting for the reunion they had been too tired to have earlier.

Chapter Eleven

ON WEDNESDAY, CARTER WAS BACK at the barn barking out orders when Molly arrived. Jose was cleaning a stall but called her over. He held his pitchfork in one hand while running the other across his black, buzz-cut hair. "Miss Molly, I worry about Royal." He turned, continuing to clean the stall while he talked. "You know I had to find one of the mares when I talk to you? The fence in the woods by the road was broken. I find the horse, but I also see Royal's golf cart in a ditch. There was no one around."

"You need to tell the deputy."

"I can't." Jose looked to see if Carter was watching or listening to the conversation before turning back to Molly. "The police would think I do something to Royal. And I think there is money hidden at the farm. If they find it, they think I kill Royal for the money."

"Why? If you reported it… wait, you're a citizen, aren't you?"

"Yes, but my brother is not. He is a 'Dreamer.' He live with me."

"So, where are your parents?"

"My father got hurt falling off a roof. He could no work. My mother clean for a motel, but she had diabetes, she could no pay for her medicine, and she died. My father go back to Mexico to live with his brother. I send him money, and I buy clothes and books for my brother to go to community college—he had a job but they fire him because he no have papers."

Carter pulled the tractor up to the next stall. As Molly slid out the stall door, she said, "Talk to you later," and headed back to her cleaning chores. She understood why Jose was afraid to go to the authorities, but the longer he waited the worse it would look. She thought about him losing his mother because she couldn't afford insulin. And Molly knew that was happening to poor Americans as well. What was wrong with people? For what some of the customers spent in one month's training, Jose's mother might have lived six months. Yet she knew most of the customers were incredibly generous. They tipped the grooms and rewarded them well at Christmas. It wasn't the fault of those who happened to have money that the whole system was broken.

Carter and Ellen didn't provide health insurance for the grooms, or workmen's comp, but she had heard they paid the bill when a horse kicked one of the grooms and broke his leg.

She tried to think of a way she could go to Royal's farm and accidentally find the golf cart. But maybe that would look even worse.

Carter told her to get the newest Poppy ready for John

to ride. She grabbed a groom box from the tack room and brushed the mare before putting on bell boots and leg guards and wrapping her front legs. The mare not been out for two days, so she hoped John could stay on her. Knowing Pepper and Bingo would add to the excitement, she locked them both in the office.

Molly grabbed Poppy's bridle and the opposite stirrup as John swung up. "I've got her," he said as he shortened the reins, and she took off trotting.

She took a giant leap for joy at the end of the barn aisle, and Carter laughed. "Take her out in the arena," he said.

John slowed her enough to make the turn, and she charged down the aisle into the arena, knees pumping way above level. Molly could see that John was struggling to hold her in the snaffle, but the German martingale gave him leverage. As he bumped and released the rein, she began to yield and put even more energy into her motion.

Carter laughed again. "Yeah, boy, what do you think about that. In a keg shoe?" He looked at Molly. "What kind of tail's she got?"

Molly answered, "I haven't taken it down, but it looks thick." The mare's tail had been tightly braided and wrapped when she arrived, and Molly had neither time nor reason to take it down. The mare carried it up and it appeared to be straight.

"Take it down and wash it this afternoon when you get a chance. I want to know how long it is," Carter said.

John began to serpentine the mare to slow her and get her off the bit. She relaxed and dropped to a jog walk when John asked her to. "Go ahead and canter," Carter said.

Before John could even give her a signal, she took off like she'd been shot out of a starting gate. He managed to grab rein and bring her head back to him, being careful to move his long legs out from her sides. She slowed a bit before the turn and John managed to pull her in a large circle, arena footing flying with her energetic strides. "Easy, mare, easy," he said as he worked the bridle. She had slowed into a normal if somewhat fast canter by the end of the second circle, and Molly thanked God that they hadn't fallen on the turn.

He pulled her back to a walk and cut across the arena to trot in the second direction. John was figuring her out and she was tiring, so by the time he trotted a few more rounds, she came willingly down to almost a flat walk. John gave her the slightest of canter signals, barely turning her head and touching her with his heel. She took off quickly but stayed under his control.

"Lordy, lordy," Carter said, shaking his head. "Put her up."

The mare stood quietly for John to slip down, and Jose grabbed her to take her in, while Ed led out a horse ready to jog.

"Gotta get water," John said, "then I'll help you hitch."

"Look up that mare's show record," Carter told Molly.

"What's her real name?" Molly asked.

"Hell, I don't know. Didn't you get paperwork when she came?"

"Yeah. But I got the same paperwork on both mares. Which is the real Pendiana Poppy?"

Carter mumbled something under his breath then said, "Yeah, that's her name."

Molly went to the office computer and typed in Ellen's

password to the American Saddlebred Association and clicked on horse search. She found a twelve-year-old mare by a horse called Pendiana Chief and out of a mare by Forty-Second Street. Her show record had ended two years ago when she won a few show pleasure classes in Pennsylvania. *Show pleasure, huh, twelve years old—that description fit the first mare, but not this ball of fire.* Before she could puzzle further, Carter strode into the office and looked over her shoulder. She didn't say a word.

"Good, good," was all he said before calling for Pepper and leaving for home.

Molly and John walked home for lunch and kicked off their stinky boots on the deck. The air conditioning felt heavenly. Molly filled large glasses of ice water while she shared what Jose had told her.

She pulled ham and cheese out of the fridge. "These Mexicans work their tails off, but they have to be looking over their shoulders all the time. I don't know how to help him without making things worse."

John washed his hands in the sink and then used a paper towel to mop the sweat off his face. "Maybe we need to go out to Royal's farm and help Jose with a horse tonight. Find the golf cart with him. How late do you teach?"

"My seven o'clock and my six–thirty canceled. I should be able to leave by seven—this time of year it'll still be light."

~ * ~

Thunder boomed as Molly hurried through her end of night chores and rushed home. Lightning flashed across the western sky as she and John drove the twenty miles to

Royal's farm.

Jose was in the barn grooming a horse. "I tell my brother to stay away," he said. He turned the horse loose in its stall and grabbed a flash light. "I show you where I find the golf cart. We better hurry before the storm."

If anything, it was hotter and more humid than it had been during the day. Thunder rumbled from all directions, but the lightning strikes appeared distant. Royal had a pinto stallion turned out with his broodmares. The stud raised his head and looked toward the storm before screaming and then circling his mares, bringing them away from the trees. Molly watched, fascinated. Horses were smarter about storms than cattle, but she'd not seen a stallion react so strongly to impending weather.

"Come, this way," Jose said, pointing to a fenced lane leading off into the woods. The agile groom strode quickly down the grassy lane. Molly swatted at buzzing mosquitos and wiped sweat out of her eyes with her shirt tail. The lane went downhill and opened into a wooded pasture near the interstate. The sweet smell of honeysuckle lingered. They couldn't see the highway but they could hear tractor trailer engines as big rigs downshifted coming down the hill.

Jose turned on his light and walked along the fence by the tree line before stopping and climbing over. John and Molly followed. The golf cart lay on its side against a steep embankment below the roadway.

John asked, "Do you think he met somebody on the highway?"

"Maybe, but why would he turn it over?" Jose answered. "Maybe it fell from up there?" He pointed up to the shoulder of the interstate.

"Don't touch it," Molly cautioned. "Fingerprints. You looked around, right? We have to make sure he isn't lying somewhere injured."

"Yeah. I walk up and down maybe half a mile. Down to the culvert to the right."

"How big is the culvert? Could someone walk through it?" Molly asked as she began to walk that way.

"Pretty big. When it rain hard, a lot of water come through there." With that, the sky opened and a cloudburst began. The rain was as warm as the air had been, but at least it washed off the sweat and bugs.

"Molly, where are you going?" John asked.

"I want to see the culvert. He could have gone in there or crossed under the road. I need the light."

John and Jose caught up with her. Blackberry briars grew between the fence and the bank, and the light was fading fast. "We climb back into the pasture and get around the briars," Jose said. They climbed the three-board fence and hurried through the driving rain to the corner of the pasture. A gate opened onto a path leading down to the culvert. The path was already muddy, and the trio slipped and slid to the bottom. Water gushed under the highway. The culvert was slightly over five feet in height.

"I'll go," Molly said. "I'm the shortest."

"Watch the water," John cautioned. "It's getting deeper."

"No worries, I can swim." Already soaked to the skin, Molly stepped into the torrent of water and pushed against it, the flashlight in her hand. She flashed it around the walls and estimated how many steps would take her to the other side. Without the light, she would have been seriously creeped out.

She was about halfway across when something big and black swooped toward her. She screamed and dropped the light as a stinking, beating wing hit her face. The stench was overpowering.

"Molly, what's happening?" John yelled. "Oh, shit!" A vulture flew at his face, exiting the pipe. "Molly!"

Molly gulped air and tried to get her bearings in the dark tunnel. She turned around and headed back out, noticing the water was deeper and faster. "I'm…"

Something hit her hard in the back of the knee and she went down. Whatever it was pushing her forward and prone in the rushing water. She screamed and tried to move out from under it—a log? The water was now waist high, and she took a deep breath and dove under, trying to escape the weight on top of her. She frog kicked and breast stroked in the churning torrent, her water-filled boots resisting. For the first time, she wondered if she truly was a strong enough swimmer.

Chapter Twelve

JOHN PULLED OUT HIS PHONE and tried to see into the tunnel of water. "Molly!" he yelled again as he bent over, trying to see into the culvert.

Molly broke free enough to raise her head and gulp air before she crashed into John's legs, knocking him into a sitting position. "What the…"

Molly grabbed him around the chest and spit water. "I'm okay, but there's…"

Something flew out of the culvert and hit them hard. Molly screamed again and buried her head against John. He scooted backwards toward the path.

Jose, holding his phone for light, yelled, "Madre de Dios, it's a body!" Jose crossed himself before reaching to help Molly and John out of the water. The rushing water emptied into a stream and Jose pointed his phone toward the bank where the body, or what the vultures had left of it, had been caught by a branch.

"Is it Royal?" Molly asked, gulping back the urge to gag.

Jose crossed himself again. "I think those are his boots." The face was beyond recognition.

John tried to wipe the water off of his glasses with a sodden bandana. "We have to call the police. What county are we in?" John asked, realizing that Royal's farm was likely not in the same county as the show barn.

"This is Mock County. Will you call police?" Jose asked as he handed his phone to John since both he and Molly had lost theirs in the rushing water.

Molly wondered if Royal's death could have been an accident. Did they have to report the death of someone who officially didn't exist?

John held the phone, trying to think.

Molly voiced her thoughts. "Maybe his death was an accident?"

John answered, "If we'd found him near the golf cart, maybe. I guess he could have been injured, walked through the culvert, and then died."

Molly said, "But if he was killed, this may not be the end of it. We have to report this."

John nodded and looked at Jose. "Can your brother stay away for a while?"

"Si, he can stay with friends, and he has nothing with this address. He use a box at the post office."

John dialed 911 and described their situation. The dispatcher told them there had been a pile up on the interstate and that it would be at least an hour before anyone could get to them.

He ended the call and told the others. They decided not

to touch the body but to hope that it would stay snagged on the tree. The deluge continued and they sloshed back up the hill to the barn. Jose's house sat across the driveway, on the other side of their truck. On the porch, they pulled off their wet boots before entering the small but tidy cottage.

Jose offered his shower and clean towels. Molly went first, desperate to get rid of the stinky filth, carrying a pair of Jose's sweat pants and t-shirt. They were too big, but she pulled the drawstring tight on the pants.

John went next, borrowing shorts that were too wide for his waist, but he managed to hold them up with his wet belt. He laid his soaked wallet and contents out on the kitchen table to dry. Molly put her clothes in a garbage bag, thinking she might just throw them out. Jose offered beer, coffee, or tequila. Molly, now warm and dry, chose a beer, and John gulped a shot of tequila with a beer to chase it.

Molly thought she would be too upset to eat, but the faded adrenaline rush left her shaky and hungry. Jose found chips and salsa and put them on the table, along with a bowl of oranges.

Although none of them believed Royal's death was accidental—it could have been. Molly said, "He could have hit his head and wandered through the culvert looking for help and died from his injuries."

John peeled an orange and nodded. "None of us got a good look at the body."

Molly remembered her brief sight of the mutilated face and took a gulp of beer. "There was so much damage from the vultures. Jose, when was the last time you saw him?"

"He usually pay me on Sunday, so a week ago Sunday. But

he no come by every day. He used to come watch the horses work and talk about the mares, but now not so much."

John asked, "How do we explain his connection, if any, to the other murder? We know he was making Pedro do drug transactions, but the police don't know that. Or maybe they do?"

"Maybe DEA was already investigating Royal? Jose, anyone out here looking around?"

"No, Miss Molly, no when I am here. A long time ago, an Arizona car come and a woman meet Royal in the barn, but that was last year, I think. The woman knew Royal, might even be his daughter."

"His daughter? Do you know her name?"

"No. I don't know they were related even, just seemed that way to me." Jose's phone rang, and he handed it to John.

"SBI Detective Bell here, I had a message to call this number."

John said, "You probably want to talk to Molly," as he handed the phone to her and put it on speaker.

"This is Molly Lewis, Detective. I'm afraid we've found another body."

"Where? At the barn? Do you make a hobby out of this?"

Molly answered without thinking, "No, of course not. This is only the third body I've found."

"Third? What? Who else besides Freddy?"

John was shaking his head, trying to suppress a smile.

"One was in another county, a few years ago. But, tonight we were helping Jose, who sometimes works at the barn, look for his boss, who is missing. We found his boss's golf cart and then went to look for him, in case he was injured. There was a cloudburst and this body came out of the culvert, after the vulture, and Jose says it's Royal, his boss."

"Slow down. Where are you?"

Molly looked to Jose, who repeated the address loud enough for Bell to hear.

"I'm on my way. Don't leave."

Chapter Thirteen

BELL SLID TO A STOP in wet gravel, and the trio met him on the porch. The rain had finally stopped, but the night was still cloudy and dark. Another car, the sheriff's department from Mock County, pulled up beside the SBI car.

Molly pulled her squishy boots on over the Mexican's large socks. The police flashlights lit the path as Jose led the group past the barn, into the lane, down the hill and through the gate to the culvert area. The rushing water had subsided, but they could hear it long before they reached it.

"The body washed through the culvert and stuck on a branch over there," Molly said, pointing downstream.

The officers swept bright lights up and down the stream bank. "There, that branch, I think," Molly said, indicating a large branch jutting into the water. But there was no body.

Bell cursed as he slid down the bank, sweeping the light back and forth. "You all saw the body?"

John answered. "Yes. It knocked Molly down. We dropped our phones, didn't know what hit us. But Jose used his phone and saw it was a body. When it lodged on the branch, he saw the boots and knew it was Royal. His face…"

"He'd, he'd been eaten by vultures. It was awful," Molly said, now sobbing.

The Mock County deputy climbed closer. "Look, there's a piece of cloth on the branch. I reckon he was stuck here, but washed farther down."

"You people stay right here," Bell said. "Deputy, come with me." They headed downstream.

"You think he no believe us?" Jose asked.

"I think he does," John said. "But until he finds the body, our story sounds a little far-fetched."

A coyote howled close by, and Molly shivered. John pulled her close to him. "Are you cold?" She shook her head and burrowed into his chest.

They heard the deputy yell, "Over there, see the vultures."

Molly jumped when she heard a gunshot and the flapping of large wings. A sliver of moon peeked through the clouds, and they saw the big birds silhouetted against the sky.

"Is that… holy shit," they heard the detective exclaim. And then the chatter of his radio as he summoned assistance.

He walked back to the group. "I'll need statements from all of you, but not tonight. Jose, you live here, right? And that's your phone number I have?"

"Yes sir, but this week I work at the big stables with them."

"Got it. Nobody leave town. I'll catch up with all of you tomorrow at the barn."

Jose asked John, "Do you think I can come in late?"

John thought a minute. "Yeah. Plan to get there about ten. I'll tell Carter."

They trudged back up the hill and asked Jose for a garbage bag for their wet clothes. John threw the bag in the back of the truck, and they headed home. "Do we call Carter now?"

John looked at the dashboard clock. Two a.m. "I think not. We'll set the alarm for eight and call him then. You hungry?"

"Yeah, but I don't think anything's open. Let's just go home and go to bed."

John tried to wake up when he heard the music from their ancient clock radio.

Molly groaned and rolled out of bed. "We can't call Carter. We don't have a phone."

"Yeah. Good thought. He'll already be pissed we're late. Might as well get dressed and go deal with him."

Molly fixed two peanut butter and jelly sandwiches for breakfast on the go and handed one to John as they walked over to the barn. Carter was grading the arena. He made a show of looking at his watch as he drove toward them. "What kind of time are you all living on, slow time?"

Molly answered, "Didn't-get-any-sleep time. Jose called us. He couldn't find Royal, but he found his golf cart turned over. We went to help him look."

Carter stopped the four-wheeler and looked at them. "Did you find him?"

John answered, "We found his body, partially eaten by vultures."

"What? That ain't no good. Think he fell off the cart and died?"

"We don't know. We told Jose to come in about ten. We

85

couldn't call you since we lost our phones in the water."

"The body washed out of a culvert," Molly answered. "It was awful. The SBI detective will be here to talk to us and Jose after a while."

"Leave it to you to find more trouble. Come on, these stalls won't clean themselves." With that, he walked out to get the tractor and spreader.

Ed and Lorenzo were feeding the horses and missed the conversation. Molly went off to perform her cleaning chores, and John informed Ed and Lorenzo of the night's happenings. Her head ached and she was still starving, despite her hastily gobbled sandwich. She bought a Diet Coke and a candy bar from the machine.

Even Bingo was out of sorts, giving her a dirty look. "You don't know the half of it, fellow," she said, scratching behind the dog's ears.

Jose made it by ten and started right in grooming horses to work. Molly could hear him talking to Lorenzo in Spanish.

Carter left for lunch, and the others were getting ready to go when Detective Bell pulled up. John looked ruefully at Ed and Lorenzo. "You guys go on. We've got to talk to him. But bring us food. We're starving." John handed Ed a twenty, and his stomach growled.

Molly went first, collapsing on the lounge love seat while Bell and his assistant got comfortable on the leather couch. "Okay, Ms. Lewis, just for the record, tell us about the other body you found. The one that's not here."

"John and I used to lease a farm in Barnes county. I found a body on the trail. I ah… ah, helped with the investigation. You can talk to Lt. Macy. Do you know him?"

"Actually, I do. And you can be sure I will. Now tell me how you came to go out to that farm in Mock County and how you found the body."

Molly explained as best she could.

"You know him as Royal, but no last name? Is that right? And you've seen him here?" The detective was recording the conversation and making notes in a notebook. "Was he a friend of the owner, a customer, what?"

Molly had heard he'd boarded training horses at the barn before Carter needed the stalls for additional training horses. In fact, Royal might have even built the outside stalls himself, she wasn't sure. And she knew he was a bookie, but she hadn't personally seen any money change hands when he was around. Should she say anything about Pedro and the drugs? Pedro was in the wind and they already knew there were drugs in the car. But if Royal was murdered, Pedro would be the chief suspect.

"The guys used to bet with him, like a bookie, I guess. They bet on ball games and other sporting events. And I think he sometimes had horses here with Carter. But everyone said he had no official identity—no driver's license, nothing." She looked up at the detective, wondering if he believed her.

"Would he have known Freddy Pedigo?"

"Maybe, but I don't think Freddy had money to gamble. He had a hard enough time buying beer and cigarettes, let alone food and rent."

"Did Pedro bet with him?"

Molly ran her hand through her hair. "Yeah. Pedro was always betting on things. He would brag when he won."

"Ms. Lewis, if you know where Pedro is, you have to tell

me. You could be charged with aiding and abetting a fugitive in a murder case. And there could be more deaths. Anyone here could be in danger. Has anyone heard from him?"

Oops. Before or after he disappeared? Molly tried to think. All that came to mind was, *What a tangled web we weave…* She didn't think Pedro could have killed anybody. but then she hadn't thought he would have sold drugs, either. When people are cornered, they do what they have to. She looked down, up at the window, anywhere but at the detective. "Look, Pedro called. Before the others got home. Said that he owed Royal gambling money, and Royal made him carry out drug transfers and collect the money. He said he didn't want to do it, but Royal would get him deported."

Detective Bell stared at her. "I think you should have told me this before now." He stood up and stretched, circling the room before sitting back down. "Do you have any idea where he might be?"

Molly focused on his face. "No, sir, I really don't know where he is. Someone else may, but I don't." After a few more questions, he told her she could leave and to send Jose in.

John was jogging a road pony in the arena. The Hackney was looking good, knees pumping and feet flying while Jose banged on a piece of metal. "Yeah, man, lookin' good."

Molly sent Jose to the office. "Just tell him the truth and don't volunteer anything he doesn't ask." She helped John unhitch the pony and rolled the jog cart back to the wall. After putting the shafts up, she joined John to tell him about her interview while they hosed off the hot pony. John scraped the water off him and walked him until Ed returned with lunch. They sat on the bench out back, wolfing down soft tacos and chips.

Molly took a breath and leaned back. "I didn't want to make it look worse for Pedro, but I couldn't lie about it."

"No, you shouldn't. Pedro got in over his head, and that's not your fault. But I don't think he killed anyone. And it sounds like Royal was living dangerously. But that doesn't tell us why Freddy died."

She ate the last chip and burped contentedly. It was time to get back to work, so she went into the office to check messages. John followed her. The phone rang, and after a brief conversation she made a lesson rescheduling note. Then she had a thought. "Wait, wouldn't Royal's full name have to be on his property deed?"

John nodded. "Should be. Can you look that up?"

"As soon as I can get on the computer."

She dialed the number to hear the messages and looked up with a frown. "Don't know how to answer this one."

"Who? What?"

"Jean Montrose. Wants to come out and see her new horse."

"Is it the Poppy mare, or rather, one of the Poppy mares? Carter already sold her to someone?"

"I'm guessing so. But Carter needs to handle this. Said she might come by later, just to see the mare in the stall. I know, I'll call her back and tell her we got a few new horses in and that we don't know which one is hers. Which is true enough."

John went out to help Ed and Lorenzo work horses. Molly tried to call Carter and alert him about Jean's call. He didn't answer, so she left a message. Maybe Jean wouldn't come by.

She decided not to call her back. Jose found her in the office. He wiped sweat off his face with a bandana. "He ask about Pedro. I not know what to say. He ask about drugs—I tell him I not know but I hear Pedro say he owe Royal money and has to do something for him. And I tell him I don't know where Pedro is. He say he no believe I don't know Royal's last name. But I even look at a horse papers. It just say 'Horse Inc' is owner of horse. I no think his name is 'horse'."

"I think you did fine," Molly said. "Is he gone?"

"No, he talk to John and then want to talk to Ed and Lorenzo about Pedro."

"Okay. You'd better go help work the horses. Oh, and can you hose off Oscar's foot? He hung it in the round pen, but the vet thinks it will be okay."

"Si, I wonder why he not on the work list."

Molly was dragging. She looked at the lesson list: one beginner and then two groups. She tried to think of a lesson plan. She drew out an equitation pattern and posted it on the bulletin board. She would let her groups try to execute it on their own one at a time and see who figured it out. That would be a good challenge. The beginner was ready to trot on her own in the round pen.

Two student helpers arrived. She sent them out to catch horses and instructed them to tell everyone to look at the pattern she had posted. When she walked back toward the lounge, Bell was walking out. He looked as bad as she felt. He probably hadn't had any sleep either.

"Ms. Lewis, if you see or hear anything, you call me, you hear?" He didn't wait for an answer but turned and walked toward his car. His assistant followed.

Carter called as she walked into the office. "What's going on?" She told him about Jean and that the detective had been there since lunch. "He's got to let you all work. I'll call Jean, don't worry. Tell her to call me if she shows up. Horses working good?"

"I know the road pony looked good, but I haven't had time to see any others."

"Good, good. See you in the morning."

She had thirty minutes before her first student arrived. She turned on the computer and searched for Mock County property records, trying to remember the address of Royal's farm. Maybe she could answer at least one question today.

Chapter Fourteen

AFTER A FEW FALSE STARTS, she found what she thought was Royal's property on a Google map and figured out the address. Mock County tax records indicated the property was owned by Lanin Enterprises. Taxes had been paid on time. The company had no website. She called the tax assessor's office. "I was wondering if I missed the last tax Carter for Lanin Enterprises," she said. "I don't remember getting it. Could you check the address where you sent it?"

After a few minutes, the clerk came back on the line, "We have Post Office Box 223 in Charlotte? Is that still correct?" Thinking fast, Molly asked, "Maybe the zip code is wrong—what do you have?" She wrote it down quickly and thanked the clerk, just as she heard a car pull up outside the office door. She closed out the browser and stuck her notes in her pocket.

The outside door swept open and Ellen appeared, wearing

a loose-flowing top and pants. "Hi, Molly. You might want to get your notebook. I have things to tell you. And I brought you this." She handed Molly a Lexington Junior League Horse Show t-shirt.

Molly thanked her and grabbed a pen and notepad. Ellen went on to list a bevy of upcoming events to schedule: pony rides, festivals, birthday parties, morning camps, and introductory lessons. Molly made notes as fast as she could, trying to look at the calendar at the same time to avoid any conflicts.

Molly pointed out one possible overlap, but Ellen waved it away. "Oh, we'll figure out a way to do both. I promised them we'd be there." Which meant Molly would have to round up enough volunteers to cover both events, not always easy on a Saturday night. She and John were a given asset. Helping with extra events and hosting birthday parties was the price they paid for their housing, but Molly would have to find more help to make this work.

She handed Ellen the duplicate paperwork on the two mares without questioning her. It was easier that way. "Has Carter seen the new horses work?" she asked.

"Yeah, the last one, the one I picked up but not the other mare."

"Show me."

Molly led her to the stall of the younger, hotter mare and slid open the stall door.

"Isn't she something," Ellen said as the mare raised her head in the air, ears pricked forward, almost touching. "I have payroll in the car," she added. Molly walked out to Ellen's car and took the pay envelopes to distribute, glancing at her watch. Good timing. The guys were about to leave and now they would leave happier. She noticed there was an envelope for Pedro. She started to hand it back, but hesitated. Wherever he was, he needed money and maybe Lorenzo could get it to him.

She handed out the payroll and showed Lorenzo the envelope for Pedro. "Can you get this to him?"

"I don't know where he is."

"Okay, but I will have it if you hear from him."

Molly walked through the barn and realized she was late starting her first group. The students and their horses were all in the arena, waiting for her. "Sorry, guys, let's get going." As she helped each student mount, she asked them if they had studied the equitation pattern she had posted.

The answers varied from, "Yeah, got it," to "Saw it but didn't understand it," to "What pattern?" Should be an interesting class. They all thought she would explain it further, but she refused, telling them to do the best they could.

The pattern began in the center of the arena with a double figure eight, first loop trotting, second loop cantering, third loop trotting, and fourth loop cantering. The first rider started on the rail, trotted a circle, cantered a circle, then reversed and repeated. Molly made no comment and asked for the next rider who wandered randomly around the arena doing various gaits, but the third rider, Sarah, nailed it. Thinking, correctly, that Sarah might know what she was doing, the three remaining riders tried to imitate her performance with varying degrees of success.

Molly told the girls, "A few of you studied the pattern carefully and some not so much, and some had difficulty translating it to putting your horse in that space. Visualizing is harder for some people, since we all have our strengths and weaknesses. Everyone, go to the rail and pick up a trot. Next time, we will work on exercises to help you put your horse where you need to. Sarah and Megan did the pattern correctly. Be sure to look at it again when you go in to see if you understand it now."

The six riders headed out to the rail with vigorous encouragement to their horses. "Whop trot," "up here," and clucks could be heard around the arena. Molly called for a walk and then threw them off balance by asking them to reverse and canter. But only one girl had trouble, and soon they were all cantering on the correct lead. She asked for a walk and then a trot, finishing the class with another reverse and canter, before asking them to line up in the center. The girls were sweating as they reached down to pet their horses.

"Good job, girls. You never know what a judge, or life for that matter, is going to throw at you. Be sure to wash all these hot horses." Ellen had promised exhaust and "Big Ass" fans, but so far neither had materialized in the "climate-controlled arena" that Ellen advertised. But at least they now had a gas heater for winter months.

The next group of riders had been watching, so they handled the pattern a bit better, although a few of the lesson horses in this group were less cooperative.

~ * ~

Over dinner, Molly shared her sleuthing results. "All we have is a post office box in Charlotte. I doubt if Royal drove his golf cart to Charlotte to collect his mail, so who really owns the property?"

John chewed his forkful of salad before answering. "He might have had a property management company to handle everything. He had a house somewhere, too. Did you check to see if Lanin Enterprises had any other parcels?"

"No, but Ellen was coming in and I had to give up my search. Maybe this weekend I can do more research from home. I don't know how to find out who rents the PO box, but I guess the police can find that. They have more resources than I do. Surely, they'll check the property records. I wonder who signs the papers when he sells a horse? He couldn't just sign Horse Inc, could he?"

"I guess it depends on how it's set up, but I would think there would have to be an actual person and a contact number," John answered. "But right now, the only mystery I want to solve is how many hours of sleep I'll get tonight."

John headed off to the shower while Molly cleaned the kitchen. She too was exhausted.

~ * ~

Carter met them with an angry scowl when they walked into the barn the next morning. "Which of your students took off these cribbing collars?" he asked, pointing to a pile of cribbing straps on the ground. The leather and metal straps kept horses from swallowing air when they cribbed—chewed wood and sucked air. Cribbing could be dangerous to the horse.

Molly recognized two as belonging to outside lesson horses and two more with fleece tubes that were normally worn by show horses. She could see Lorenzo walking a mare which had apparently tried to colic. Carter continued, "One of the lesson horses pulled the top fence board down, cribbing on it."

Molly fired back. "All of my student helpers know what cribbing collars are for, and I saw Barney and Moose were wearing theirs when they were put out. And they know not to mess with the show horses. My students didn't do this. One of the first things we teach them is that when a horse bites on wood and sucks air, that can cause them to colic. I teach them to fasten the straps tightly so the horse can't swallow air when it's cribbing. Is Honey okay?"

"Somebody did," Carter grumbled. "I found the straps in the top of the trash can. I gave Honey a shot of banamine, and she looks like she's feeling better." He pointed to the mare who now walked briskly beside Lorenzo. "Take her outside and see if she'll nibble on grass," he told the groom.

Molly said, "Is there grain in her stall? I'll take it out."

"Lorenzo didn't hear anything?" John asked.

"No. He said he fell asleep watching a soccer game. Didn't hear a thing."

Molly scooped out the mare's grain and then took a handful of it out to catch the lesson horses who needed their cribbing straps. Carter hammered the fence board back into place. She wondered if any of her student's parents might have seen the collars and thought they were cruel because they fitted so tight. No, surely if they wondered what the straps were for, they would have asked a student or Molly.

Honey recovered without a trip to the vet, and the day rolled on. When Carter left at four, he asked who had night check duty. John answered that it was his turn. "Try to check pretty late tonight, maybe around eleven," Carter told him.

Easy for him to say. Molly knew the trainer was in bed by nine every night. But if someone was coming around to do mischief, the next incident could be worse.

Molly and John went to bed around ten, but they found activities to keep them awake. John called Bingo and walked to the barn at eleven. Bingo was energized by the cool night air and eagerly ran ahead, hoping to find rats to hunt in the barn. All was quiet as John unplugged the fans and checked on each horse. Bingo got one rat and John coaxed it out of his mouth to deposit in the dumpster.

Molly was asleep when John came to bed. He watched her for a minute in the ambient moonlight filtering into their bedroom. Her hair was fanned on the pillow and she looked younger asleep. The worry and stress lines disappeared. He wondered, not for the first time, if their move to Carter Mills Stable had been the right one.

Chapter Fifteen

MOLLY FINISHED HER CLEANING DUTIES and was about to check messages when Ellen swept into the barn. "Can you teach my little Jon-Jon?" she asked. "I have a meeting."

Jon-Jon was due at eleven, and Molly replied, "Sure." His family had been on vacation while Ellen was at the show, but today he would be back. Teaching four-year-olds was sometimes fun, but often frustrating because of their limited attention span. However, Jon-Jon's mother seemed to be in this sport for the long haul, and the boy usually tried hard. Thanks to Molly having filled in on other occasions, the boy could actually post and steer the pony, so Molly didn't need to lead him, but she did need to stay close, running beside him as he trotted.

She had once beaten a friend in a fun run, and her friend asked how that could have happened. Molly didn't even jog.

"I give beginner lessons," she quipped and knew that was what kept her in shape. She went out to catch her favorite lesson pony and noted that Barney and Moose wore their cribbing straps.

Molly played Simon Says and other games with Jon, and he rode very well despite having had two weeks off. At the end, she led the pony and had the boy post with his hands flapping like wings while she held his leg in place. "You're a bird," she told him and then said to his mother, "Look, Mom, no hands." Jon and his mom were both smiling at the end of the lesson. Molly realized she had another lesson at noon and hadn't yet caught the horses. No lunch today. John offered to bring her a sandwich later, but she knew there wouldn't be time to eat it.

Molly scheduled daytime lessons at noon because everyone was usually gone and she could use the arena. But today a show horse customer had come late. As she got her two adults mounted and on the rail in the arena, Carter asked her to take them to the outdoor ring.

She tried to put a positive spin on things and said, "It's not bad outside, you'll enjoy riding outside," as they rode out the arena doors and over to the ring. They had trotted one way and were preparing to canter when Carter and his mounted customer brought her show horse into the ring with a great flourish of yelling and whip popping.

"Maybe you'd better go back to the indoor arena," Carter said.

Molly grabbed Moose, who was reacting to the popping whip, and ran beside the trotting horse, hoping the other horse was under control. She gratefully turned him loose once they entered the arena. "You've got a show horse now," Molly yelled.

"Shorten your reins, sit up and ride." The retired show horse was up in the bridle, pumping his knees and giving his rider a whole new experience. Molly prayed she would stay on. Barney, too, was more alert than usual and just as both horses began to calm down, Carter and the show horse came back into the arena. "Let's stop for the day," Molly said. "I think we've had enough excitement." She asked the two riders to quickly line up in the center and dismount. When Moose's rider hit the ground, Carter picked up a piece of tin and began to bang on it, getting the attention of the show horse, oblivious to the lesson horses in the middle. Molly grabbed Moose and asked Barney's rider to follow her into the barn. "I am so sorry."

Moose's rider, a slender brunette who'd handled her excited horse well, asked, "Is there a better day or time during the day? I'd come at night, but I work."

Molly answered, "No, not really. Usually everyone is gone for lunch, but this customer showed up late."

The other woman spoke, "Aren't we customers too? I don't feel very valued. I know it's not your fault, Molly, but I don't think this is the right barn for us. We'll talk about it."

Molly's day went downhill from there. Two of her four o'clock group didn't show. Ed had a show rider group in the arena and asked her to take her two five o'clock riders outside. The outdoor ring was too large for a beginner group. She had begged Ellen to build a smaller ring for lessons. Not only was the fenced area too large, but it backed up to a row of houses with barking dogs and other distractions. She thought about going to the barn aisle, but someone was hammering siding to enclose the loft.

She led the beginner horses into the ring and gave her riders a leg up. One of them was a fairly heavy young man, but there was no way she could lead two horses out and bring a mounting block. She closed the gate and sent the riders to the rail. Just as the first rider walked to the opposite side, a homeowner started weed-eating along the fence. His horse spooked and the rider hit the ground. The boy got up slowly, but claimed to be unhurt. Molly caught the horse, reassured the other rider, and brought both horses to the middle of the ring where they tried to eat grass. After cautioning both riders not to let their horses get their heads down, she again hoisted the boy onto his horse and confined the lesson to a small circle at the end of the ring away from the weed-eater. The boy didn't want to trot after his fall, and Molly had to run beside him and promise to hold on to the horse. The other horse kept diving for grass. She finally stopped both horses on the edge of the ring and had the riders do exercises in place. She knew she was ending the lesson early, but sometimes it was important to stop before things deteriorated further. She praised the boy for getting back on after his fall and the other boy for coping with the excitement. "You rode 'em, cowboys," she said, hoping they would feel like proud survivors.

She called Ellen at the end of the night as they were always supposed to report any falls or incidents.

"Why were they in the outdoor ring?" she asked.

Molly explained.

"That man shouldn't have started a weed-eater with a rider in the ring. Why didn't you use the barn aisle?"

Molly took a deep breath and explained that it was unavailable. Then she told Ellen about the two students who hadn't shown up and said she was about to call them.

"I actually moved them to Ed's Monday night class. They wanted a change."

Molly hadn't noted any displeasure on the part of those students or their parents, but anything was possible. And the two pre-teen girls might have wanted a young man to teach them. But this wasn't the first time Ellen had moved students without telling her. Did she think Molly wouldn't notice? She told Ellen about the disruptions to the noon lesson and the women's reaction.

"You should have laughed it off. They probably fed off of your attitude."

Now it was Molly's fault they were unhappy? What the hell?

"Was that all you needed?"

Molly tried to keep civil. "Yes. Goodnight, Ellen."

She returned to the holding area to find two horses she hadn't even used, plus one that was tacked up for one of her no-shows still tied; Ed and all of his students were gone. Four-letter words ran through her mind as she put away tack and shoveled manure. She remembered that Lorenzo had night check duty at eleven but decided to check all the stalls before going home. John had gone out with a buddy from church, and she knew he wasn't waiting on her for dinner. Dinner? She had been too upset to realize how hungry she was. She quickly made her rounds and hoped nothing was amiss. One of the automatic waterers was overflowing and she couldn't get it to shut off, so she turned off the valve and put a water bucket in the stall. The guys could fix it tomorrow.

Bingo greeted her with barks and leaps, telling her he had not eaten. She knew he might be fibbing, but she fed him before opening the fridge to see what it contained. She found and ate the remaining half of a block of cheese before moving on to an apple, a beer, and a bowl of ice cream. She needed calcium, right?

John made it home by ten. Molly hit the bed, ready for this day to be over.

Sometime in the middle of the night, Bingo erupted with barks. Molly and John came awake and ran downstairs. Bingo scratched and growled at the back door, trying to get at whatever had woken them.

Chapter Sixteen

JOHN OPENED THE DOOR AND heard thundering hooves and squealing horses. He and Molly ran back upstairs to get clothes and shoved their boots on as they made their way out the door. They could hear Lorenzo shouting, "Whoa, whoa." A horse galloped across their backyard, headed toward the road at the front. Molly yelled and waved her arms, hoping to head it off. Were the lesson horses out? Had something happened to the fence?

Thanks to Molly's efforts, the horse turned back toward the barn and ran by John. He said, "That's not a lesson horse, that's the road pony."

They chased after the pony and heard more loose horses running, a snort, and Lorenzo yelling. "You people no can let horses out. They get hurt."

John sprinted into the barn and turned on the lights. Several stall doors stood open. Molly ran to grab halters and leads and handed them to John and Lorenzo, keeping one of each. She went into the feed room for a bucket of grain. As she rounded the corner, a voice bellowed from the shadows behind the barn. "These horses need to be free," a woman yelled.

Molly answered, "If they get in the road, they'll be dead. And maybe people killed. And you're trespassing."

Somewhere in the distance, a mare squealed and the sound of hoof connecting with horseflesh echoed through the night.

The woman ran off toward the pasture, screaming, "You haven't seen the last of us."

Molly shook her bucket of grain and a horse came out of the dark toward her as she spoke softly. "That's it, have some grain." The horse stuck his head in her bucket and she wrapped the lead line around his neck, then slipped on the halter and led him back into the barn. Lorenzo had captured the road pony, and John had a halter on one of the Poppy mares.

The lesson horses in the pasture had joined the melee and were whinnying and running the fence line. One of the loose show horses charged the fence and crashed through, the pasture horses following as she galloped toward the rear of the field.

Molly ran to the tack room to get a lunge line and tied it across the broken fence. She heard John yelling as he tried to head a horse away from the driveway. The horse galloped back in the barn and leaped into an empty stall. One more captured. John opened the gate to the round pen and another horse trotted in. Molly shut the gate.

"There's a horse loose in the pasture," she called. "She crashed through the fence. I tied the fence up with a lunge line."

Lorenzo brought a bale of hay from the hay shed and began spreading sections along the pasture fence. The lesson horses came toward the forage, leaving the chase. Honey trotted up to the fence and snorted, then dropped her nose to take a bite of hay. Lorenzo took a handful of grain and slowly approached the mare, talking softly. She backed away, then smelled the grain and extended her nose. Lorenzo eased up beside her and slipped on a halter.

"Has anyone called Carter?" Molly asked.

John said, "I was a little busy, but I'll call him now."

There had been ten open stall doors and now nine horses were back where they belonged and one in the round pen. Molly grabbed another halter and lead rope to catch Annie.

She began to check the horses. Honey had an indentation and scrape on her chest where she had charged through the fence. Molly took her to the wash rack for first aid and realized the mare had lost one of her shoes and a chunk of hoof with it. Poppy had an indentation on her hip, no doubt the result of a kick. Annie was limping slightly, but she had no sign of injury yet.

"I couldn't get Carter, so I'm driving over there," John said, shoving his phone in his pocket as he quickly unlocked the office and grabbed the keys to the dually.

"You call police?" Lorenzo asked.

"That's up to Carter. That chick is long gone now. What did you hear?"

"I was asleep, and I wake up because I hear horses running

and squealing. I run out and see stalls open and loose horses everywhere. I know I check barn at eleven and everything was fine."

"I guess that's who took off the cribbing straps the other night. These people know nothing, but they think they know what's best. We're lucky none of the horses got in the road. I wish we had a front gate."

"Yes, we have fence by the road but no gate."

The dually roared in the driveway with Carter at the wheel. "You catch 'em all?" he asked as he stepped out.

"We caught the horses, but not the idiot who let them out. It was a woman who yelled, 'Horses should be free.'"

Carter shook his head. "What was she thinking? Let horses worth thousands of dollars out to get hit by a car or run through a fence."

Lorenzo was at work on the pasture fence, his hammer making rhythmic sounds.

Molly walked Carter down the stalls, showing him the injuries and missing shoes. "I guess I should give Honey a tetanus shot," she said, pointing to the mare's injury.

"Couldn't hurt," Carter agreed. "Lordy, Lordy. We'll wait to see how they are in the morning, might need a vet then. The farrier's coming first of next week, right?"

"Yes, on Tuesday. Are you going to call the sheriff?" Molly asked.

Carter shook his head. "Won't do no good. She's gone now. You say she ran out through the back pasture? Better check the pasture fence, you'll need a flashlight."

"Yeah. Maybe we should alert them tomorrow?"

"You can call them in the morning. There might be

evidence or something," Carter said as he walked toward the truck.

Molly knew they had all touched the stall doors since the intruder had opened them, and she doubted the trespasser had left any trace other than fingerprints, which were probably well smudged by now.

John walked over to Molly and put his arm around her shoulders. "We'd better get back to bed, the morning will be here soon."

"I have to check the pasture fence. No idea where there's a flashlight. I'll get the one from home." They trudged back to the house. Bingo was very excited, having been left behind.

"Need me?" John asked.

"No, one of us ought to get sleep. I'll take Bingo."

Molly spoke to Lorenzo, who was nailing his last fence board before she headed into the pasture. Bingo trotted along beside her. The horses were finishing up the hay that Lorenzo had put out and paid them scant attention.

Molly walked along the fence, wondering how this latest calamity would affect the coming days. Louisville, The Kentucky State Fair Horse Show—The World's Championship for Hackney ponies and American Saddlebred horses—was only three weeks away. At least one Louisville-bound horse had lost a shoe and some foot, and others were also injured. The small farm was mostly surrounded by houses except where she now walked through the woods. The fence was not great, but the horses seldom came to the back of the woods, due to the thick trees and brambles. Molly pushed through the briars and shone her light along the fence of sagging woven wire. The rest of the fence had electric wire, but here in the woods it was always being shorted out by falling branches and rapidly growing vines, so they had routed the electric wire away from this section.

She heard a rustling ahead and froze, shining her light in front of her. Bingo howled. A doe startled and crashed past her, as Molly stifled a scream. She took a deep breath and continued. What if the fanatic woman was hiding in the woods? Was she armed? Molly had heard horror stories about animal rights activists. Her cousin had owned a small circus and had to sell it after activists threatened the lives of his sponsors and their families. His animals were very well treated, mostly rescues, but the protesters would never come on the lot to see that. They would rather make up lies.

Molly resumed her hike. The fence was more or less intact in the woods, and she turned to walk along the section which bordered the backyards of newly built homes. Security lights from the houses provided enough illumination, and she shut off the flashlight for fear of being accused of being a prowler. She stirred up one sleeping dog, Bingo growled, but otherwise everything was quiet. No telling where their own prowler had gone.

She called to Bingo and he followed her home. She let her clothes fall to the floor and crawled into bed beside her snoring husband.

Chapter Seventeen

THE STENCH OF ROTTING MEAT filled her nose, wings beat around her, water rushed toward her. Molly flailed and tried to scream but could make no sound. She clawed at the approaching beast, thrashing and slipping in a raging river, something else was grabbing her…

"Molly, wake up. You're having a nightmare. Ow, dammit, Molly, wake up. I'm here, you're okay."

She opened her eyes to find John holding her wrist and leaning over her.

"I dreamed the vulture was gabbing me, it smelled so bad." She saw a bloody gash on John's cheek. "What happened? Did I do that? Oh my God, I'm sorry."

"You were wild. I couldn't get you to wake up. Are you with me now?" He let go of her wrist and smoothed back her hair before gently kissing her on the forehead. "Did something happen in the pasture? I never heard you come in."

"Only a deer. What time is it? I'll never go back to sleep now."

John turned to look at his watch, sitting on the nightstand. "It's six-thirty. Guess we might as well get up." He rolled out of bed and walked to the mirror over his dresser. "Good heavens, I knew it hurt, but I didn't know you had scarred me for life. What a wildcat." He went to the bathroom to shower and doctor his bloody face.

Molly grabbed a robe before going to start the coffee and take her own shower. They beat Carter, Ed, and Lorenzo to the barn and were feeding the horses when Carter arrived. "How're they looking?" he asked, referring to the injured horses.

"So far they're still alive," John quipped, turning toward Carter.

"Good God, what happened to you?"

"Molly had a nightmare."

"You look like a nightmare. She here?"

Molly emerged from the supply room where she had been trying to find a tetanus shot in the medicine trunk. "I'm here but your tetanus shots aren't. I can go get some or we might need the vet anyway. Please keep your smart remarks to yourself, I feel terrible that I scratched John."

Carter laughed and went out to grade the arena, Bingo barking and bouncing behind him.

Honey was no worse, but Molly put her in the wash rack to hose off her scrapes and spray them with antiseptic.

Carter walked back into the barn. "Go ahead and call the vet, soon as they open. I think he better come out. We need health certificates on the ones going to Louisville, and we'll need vet certificates if we cancel any entries."

He looked at his watch. "But you can clean for thirty minutes before you call."

Molly was most definitely not in the mood for cleaning. She ducked her head and turned away before she was tempted to tell him what to do with his toilets.

Ed came in late and John filled him in. He walked toward the men's room as Molly walked out. "Guess I missed all the excitement. Was it really a nightmare or did John piss you off? Uh, maybe you need to trim those claws."

"Watch it. I'm not in the mood for humor."

She walked out to dump the dirty mop water in the barn aisle as John rounded the corner, splashing most of it on his jeans. "Oh, no. I'm so sorry, honey."

She felt horrible. First, she disfigured him and now she covered him in dirty water. But a giggle surfaced and then they were both laughing, soon laughing so hard she couldn't breathe.

Ed walked out to find them both collapsed in hysterical laughter. "What's up with you guys today?"

Molly laughed harder and finally gasped out, "No sleep."

Dr. Haynes arrived at eleven with his vet tech. The horse specialist made frequent visits to the barn and over time had managed to diagnose and cure several lameness issues. To be on the safe side, Carter told him to look at all the horses that had been let out. He x-rayed two of the injured with his portable machine and gave Molly more medicine and silver spray to use on the cuts and scrapes. He told them at least one of the Louisville horses would likely have to be scratched from the competition. He would wait and see on the others.

Carter went in the office to call customers. Molly checked over the list for the blacksmith coming Tuesday. She made a note to herself to examine all the school horses. A different farrier shod them, and some may have lost shoes while galloping around the pasture.

She hadn't yet called the sheriff's office, so she did and finally tracked down a deputy. He said he'd be out in an hour.

Deputy Horne drove in and asked for Carter. They found him still on the phone in the office. He held up a finger and indicated he would be out shortly.

"Some woman let a bunch of horses loose last night," Carter said. "She shouted something about how they should be free. I didn't see anyone, talk to Molly."

Molly described what happened, but other than hearing the woman, she couldn't tell the officer much about her. "I think I would recognize her voice, though."

The deputy didn't really understand the scope of the damage. Molly told him, "Owners can spend thousands of dollars competing their horses and hoping for a good ribbon at our championship, not to mention what they spent to purchase the horse. Now their horse may not be able to show or may not perform as well, not to mention the extra shoeing and vet bills."

"What do these horses cost?"

"Anywhere from a few thousand to several hundred thousand dollars. Depends on their age, what they've done in the show ring, and most of all, how badly someone wants to buy them. I don't know the purchase price unless I happen to get a commission, and even then, I don't know for sure.

"And the lesson horses may have been cheap or even free,

but their value to the lesson program is enormous. We can't just go out and easily find a replacement." Molly pointed to the school horses out in the pasture before walking back into the barn.

"Are they insured?" he asked.

"I'd say most of the show horses are, but they may not be insured against loss of use or diminished value due to injury."

"So, you don't think any customer would do this to try to collect on insurance?"

Molly hadn't thought of that. Most of their customers truly loved their horses. And in order to collect insurance, the horse would have to die. Turning a bunch loose might accomplish that, but it was too uncertain a method to kill a specific horse. After hesitating a minute, she explained her thoughts.

He nodded. "Makes sense. Any enemies of Carter or his wife or someone who'd want to hurt the business? Dissatisfied customers?"

"Possibly, but most horse people would never want to hurt a horse, any horse. Sounded more like an animal rights activist, but of course that could be what they want us to think."

"We'll try to make a few patrols by here at night, but it would help if you had a locked gate."

"Wouldn't it though? Thanks for coming out."

George Adams, their blacksmith, came Tuesday. Molly loved to watch him work. He could watch a horse perform and almost always shoe the horse to work better. Although Molly knew a lot about conformation and way of going, she always learned from George. He managed to replace all the missing shoes and with careful use of filler and pad, was able to get the horses who had lost part of their hooves looking level and moving evenly. "Hell of a thing," George said, "someone letting them out like that. Carter piss anybody off lately? Besides Ellen, I mean."

Molly giggled. "Who knows?"

The work schedule increased for all the Louisville horses. They worked every day. The scrapes and abrasions were healing, and only one horse had to be scratched from the competition. Fortunately, that owner had two horses and would be able to compete on the remaining horse.

Lessons tended to drop off at the end of August. Kids were getting ready to go back to school or taking one last vacation trip. The lull gave Molly time to help organize health certificates, Coggins, and other paperwork needed for the big show. The washing machine ran non-stop, laundering towels, leg wraps, and show sheets. She and John would help load the horses, which left on Thursday before the show started on Saturday, then stay and take care of things until midweek, when Carter's brother would take over feeding and stall cleaning for a few days so John and Molly could travel to the show.

The entourage pulled out at four a.m. Molly wondered what they had forgotten this time. Usually, they called once they arrived at the show, and she would need to draft a customer to bring a few more items.

John and Molly collapsed in the lounge and promptly fell asleep. Bingo woke them around seven. They got up, fed the horses, cleaned the stalls, and took off for a late breakfast. Then Molly helped John work the horses. She had a few lessons that night, and they went to bed early.

Jose came out the next day to help. "Hey, Jose, any news about Royal?" John asked.

He told them no one knew his real name and if he had a will or relatives. The deputy said the medical examiner thought Royal had suffered a heart attack and might have wandered through the culvert looking for help. They were waiting on tox screens, but leaning toward the idea of an accidental death.

"Really," Molly said. "We know Freddy's death wasn't an accident, or at least we think we do, so I'm glad to hear Royal wasn't murdered. I mean, I'm still sorry he's dead, but what about you? Will you be able to stay at Royal's farm?"

"Si." He went on to tell them that a trust had been set up to pay Jose and care for the horses, at least for a year. But the most amazing thing, he told them, was that Ace had no fingerprints.

Who was Royal? Molly wondered. Witness protection program or master criminal? And would they ever know?

Chapter Eighteen

MOLLY TRIED TO CATCH UP on paperwork and draft volunteers for various upcoming events. In mid-September they were having a Fall Fun Show for the riding students, and she needed to recruit both entrants and volunteers. She thought Ellen had already hired a judge, but she wasn't sure. They usually made the show a fundraiser for a cause, and a portion of the fall show proceeds went to horse rescue. But Molly couldn't say what portion because she never knew.

They had been following show results from Kentucky, and many of the horses had done well. The road pony won the under-saddle class, thanks to the good riding kid who owned him. Both Carter and Ed earned top ribbons in qualifying classes on young horses. Annie was a reserve champion in the country pleasure division. In fact, everyone earned a ribbon in their qualifier and thus could show back in their championship class.

Molly and John worked hard, and soon it was time to sort through their closet for suitable attire to pack for the show. They needed to take their truck and trailer and drop a horse off in West Virginia on the way and might have to haul one home. Horses were often bought and sold at the show.

It was a relief to be on the road and not doing physical work. The show was always exciting, and they would get to catch up with horse friends from throughout the country.

Molly and John arrived at the fairgrounds on Thursday night and helped with last minute grooming. Then they went to buy tickets. They couldn't afford the box seats where the customers and Carter and Ellen sat, although they could often find open box seats for the free daytime sessions.

As they walked from the barn to the show arena, Molly heard a familiar voice. "Molly, John, how are you? When did you get here?" Jean Montrose was decked out to the nines in a black dress with a large, gold horse necklace. She brought her golf cart to a stop beside the couple. Before Molly could answer, she continued, "I'm so excited about my new horse. Too bad we missed the entry deadline. Carter showed me a video before we bought her, but I had to leave town and I haven't had a chance to get out and see her. I can't remember where Carter said he found her. Do you know? I know she arrived during the Junior League Show when you were taking care of things. Who delivered her?"

This could be a heap of trouble. There was no right answer.

Molly looked away, trying to frame her reply.

John gazed into the distance and saw Ed riding Annie to the make-up ring. "There's Annie, we'd better go with them."

"Good to see you, Jean," Molly said as she followed John.

They made a beeline toward Annie as she entered the warm-up aisle known as Stopher Walk. They followed Annie to the paddock area and then entered Freedom Hall to find food and their seats. They would have to avoid Jean for the rest of the show or ask what they were supposed to say.

With a sigh of deep satisfaction, Molly sank into her seat, being careful not to drop her pork burger or spill her beer. The sandwich, sold by the Kentucky Pork Producers, was a treat she enjoyed every year. In many ways, the State Fair was a distraction from the horse show and caused exhibitors and spectators parking and traffic problems, but Molly also enjoyed seeing the art, crafts, and other fair entries.

She and John knew most of the exhibitors by name, even if not in person. The Saddlebred world was relatively small. Exhibitors from all over the country and a few from Europe, South Africa, and Canada often spent thousands of dollars on advertising and promoting their horses before the big event. It was interesting to see the West coast winners take on the Kentucky and Midwestern contingents. But shows were not as regional as they used to be. Horses from Texas and Florida might spend the summer in Kentucky, and New England stables often shipped south for the spring shows.

The show began with a ladies' three-gaited class, the high trotting entries showing at a walk, trot, and canter, set off by the colorful silk coats or formal habits and top hats worn by their riders. A three-gaited horse should possess high balanced action at the trot, an elegant headset and a fine neck and head, accented by their roached manes. The footing in Freedom Hall was sprayed green for the show. Green shavings flew in the air as high-trotting horses entered the ring, sometimes leaping off their feet in the excitement of the moment.

Soon the class was underway, and the three judges watched intently as the horses strutted their stuff. Lady Charming, an elegant bay mare, had won the class last year and looked like she would take it again. In a ladies' class, both amateurs and professionals competed. There was often no difference in the ability of the riders between the two, only what they did for a living. The judging criteria emphasized manners as well as quality.

The horse show organist chose his music to coordinate with the tempo of the horses at various gaits, and a few horses appeared to dance to the music. The work ended and the twenty horses were lined up for close inspection. Spectators yelled for their favorites as the judges walked the line. Lady Charming won, and the crowd clapped and yelled approval. Every ribbon winner was recognized, and in this class at least, the crowd and the judges were in agreement. That was not always true, of course, and Molly, who had judged previously, understood why. The view from the stands was not the same as the ground level view of a horse passing by or coming toward the judge. And no one could see all the horses all the time, hence the three-judge system for the largest shows.

Annie showed next, in a country pleasure class for riders thirty-five and over. Her owner, Leslie, was a pretty and competent rider, although not always confident. She was a genuinely nice woman, and Molly wished her well. John had a groom's pass and made his way to the rail to help coach her. Annie was a golden chestnut with a flaxen mane and tail. Leslie had chosen medium brown jodhpurs, and a light coat, a brown derby, and a tan vest. Molly thought the combination was a perfect accent to the mare's coloration.

Annie broke into a canter as she came down the ramp, but Leslie bumped her gently with the snaffle rein and the mare settled into a trot. She made a few nice passes, but it was a large class. Molly hoped she would be seen. The call judge asked for a halt. This was the undoing of many horses when they showed at this level. They were expected to trot with animation and brilliance and then stop and stand quietly. The rider's and/or the horse's nerves often prevented that. But Annie stopped and raised her head to gaze at the crowd. Leslie reached down and petted her neck. The call judge asked for a canter. Leslie waited until a mob of horses had passed her and calmly moved her right leg back to signal a canter. She remembered to sit back and keep her lower legs away from the horse. Annie cantered slowly in form, a pretty picture indeed.

The pair performed equally well in the reverse direction, although Leslie was often covered up by more aggressive riders. After coming down to the walk, the announcer asked for one last trot. Leslie cut across from the corner, pushing her horse into an impressive extended trot, coming right in front of one of the judges before the class was called to line up. Molly saw the judge look up and note Leslie's back number. Good one.

Leslie's number was called for third place and the woman was ecstatic. Molly teared up, knowing how hard Leslie had worked for this.

Ed was showing the other entry for the night, a young, five-gaited horse who had lost a shoe and part of his foot on the night of the vandalism. Five-gaited horses are shown at five different gaits, with speed, action, and collection all being important. Cat, as they called him, entered the ring bucking and leaping, but fortunately the class was not judged until the gate closed. Then he wanted to rack instead of trot, but Ed touched him on the neck, turned him loose, and the horse dropped into a trot, only breaking into a canter once on a corner. He stepped right up into a collected true slow gait with a hesitation, a gait that many horses didn't do these days—they racked, moving fast in four even beats, for both the slow gait and the rack. When the announcer called for them to move into a rack, the little chestnut settled into an impressive ground-covering gait, his four feet hitting an even one-two-three-four, as they should. He took his canter on the second try. When it came time to reverse, a horse blew by him and cut him off, causing him to stumble and almost go down. The crowd gasped. He recovered, Ed stayed on, but his next step was a limp. He had cast a shoe.

Knowing how hard their farrier had worked to patch him back together, Molly hoped it wasn't the same foot. The show farrier had five minutes from the time he picked up the foot to reattach the shoe. Carter walked into the ring as the announcer called a time out. Ed dismounted and led Cat to the center ring. The farrier walked out to the horse, but Molly could see both he and Carter shaking their heads. This would not be a five-minute job. Ed and Cat were excused and received a loud ovation; the colt had performed well.

Chapter Nineteen

THE EVENING'S SHOW WAS ALMOST over, so John and Molly decided to walk back to the barn to congratulate Leslie and commiserate with Ed. It was not his fault, but he would likely blame himself. He was young and working really hard to learn all that he could. They made their way back to the barn, dodging between horses and golf carts festooned with streamers and other gaudy décor.

Molly hugged Ed. "Tough break, but Cat looked great."

"Thanks, Molly, but maybe if I had turned him the other way or—"

Molly interrupted, "Stop. You made a good show. We all knew the shoe was iffy. And look, I think that trainer is asking Carter about the horse, now."

Leslie was still in her riding habit, enjoying a cold drink. "Molly, I'm so happy. I never thought I would do that well with all those nice horses."

"You rode well and the mare was beautiful. Your hard work paid off. Congratulations."

Leslie's gratitude was genuine. They'd had other riders who sobbed after a second or third place, let alone not getting a ribbon. Molly never had the opportunity to show at Louisville, since they never owned a horse who would be competitive at that level, nor had a customer with the money to compete at Louisville when they managed their own barn.

Ellen walked up. "Are you two enjoying the show?"

Molly said, "Of course. Leslie rode so well and so did Ed. Listen, I saw Jean Montrose, and she asked me where her new horse came from and who delivered it. I didn't know what to tell her. It's the nicer Poppy mare, right?"

"You let me handle that. Just say you don't know."

~ * ~

The night's performance had ended, but the trainers weren't leaving. Now was the time they worked horses or tried out horses for customers. The work rings were full, and Molly always enjoyed the spectacle. Two women brought out a nervous horse and a mounting block. The horse swung all the way around the mounting block and then flew backwards, not wanting any part of anyone getting on him. One of the women left and shortly came back with another bridle, trading his full bridle for a snaffle. This should be interesting. They changed bridles, almost losing the horse in the process. Again, the horse pulled back and away. Was this their horse? Finally, they gave up and led the horse out of the ring.

Meanwhile, several accomplished riders were trying out a few of the talented horses.

John and Molly helped clean up the tack room and put things away before leaving for the evening. As they left the barn, Molly heard someone calling her from another barn.

John and Molly looked around but saw no one familiar. "Over here," hissed a voice from a stall.

"Pedro. Have you been here all week?"

"Si. I get a job with barn from Wisconsin. They don't know me. Did the police find the murderer?"

"No. And I'm sure they're still looking for you. And Royal is dead."

"Royal dead? He can no more make me sell drugs."

"True," John said, "but you have bigger problems than that. We don't know for sure if it was an accident or if someone killed him, but you would be a top suspect."

Molly remembered the envelope in her purse. "Here, Pedro. Ellen gave me your pay after Lexington." She handed him the envelope.

Pedro opened it and counted the cash. "I get paid tomorrow, and I can catch a Mexico bus. I think I need to leave."

Molly hugged him. "Be safe, Pedro, and stay out of trouble. No more gambling."

He stared at the ground before answering, "Si, I learn my lesson. I hope I come back some day."

John shook his hand. "We hope you can."

~ * ~

Mills Stable finished their classes on Friday night, with no one competing in the big grand championship classes on Saturday. Carter was bent on leaving Saturday morning and had managed to pull the tractor trailer up to the stalls sometime during the early morning hours. Molly and John arrived at seven and helped tear down stall curtains and load equipment.

Ellen drove up in her golf cart, festooned with pink tulle and sequined pompoms, and asked Molly if she and John would like to use their box seats for the night.

"Sure, thanks," Molly answered. "We'll need your armband."

"Oh, I think I left it in the motor home, but just tell them you're using my seats, shouldn't be a problem."

Ellen drove off and Molly began taking down water buckets and stacking them together. By noon, they were ready to start loading horses. Twelve horses were on the trailer, but one was still in a stall.

"Oh, hell," Carter said. "I forgot one of them came with someone else. But you have your trailer, right, John?"

"Yeah. But we weren't planning to leave until tomorrow."

"That's fine. Just be sure to save enough hay to feed tonight. And I might need you to haul another horse, too. I'll let you know in a bit."

Molly scurried onto the trailer and dug out a water bucket before the driver started to make his way out of the gridlock of trailers, horses, golf carts, and people.

The remaining horse was not happy to be left behind. He whinnied piteously when he saw his stable companions pull away. As Molly and John were leaving the fairgrounds to eat and dress for the evening show, Carter called. "I bought a mare from Kenny. You might want to go get her and put her beside the other horse."

"Kenny who?" John asked. "And where is he stabled?"

"Oh, you know Kenny."

Through a series of questions and answers, John was able to figure out who Carter was talking about and guessed at the location of his stall. He went to find Kenny or one of his grooms while Molly hiked across the fairgrounds to their trailer to find another bucket.

John found Kenny's stable but no one was around. They'd have to meet up with him when they returned for the evening show.

They made it to their motel with only an hour until show time. Molly showered first and pulled out one of her few dressy outfits, a simple black dress with a cowl neckline. John wore khakis and a blue blazer.

They walked to Kenny's barn and found out which horse they were supposed to take. A groom dug out the Coggins and release form for the horse. John led the mare back to their stalls and put her in the stall beside the lonesome gelding. He tossed them hay before they hurried to Freedom Hall.

Molly's dress sandals were now covered in mud and shavings. She tried to hurry despite her heels. When they arrived at the box seats, they noticed Jean Montrose and her husband were already sitting in Carter and Ellen's seats. Since John and Molly already had general admission seat tickets, they grabbed drinks and hiked up the ramp to the upper level.

The Saturday night show was as wonderful as always. Seeing the best of the best was always a thrill, and the open stake classes were well populated. Before they knew it, the organist was playing "My Old Kentucky Home" and everyone was on their feet for the entrance of the Five-Gaited World Championship contenders. Eight horses entered the ring, one at a time, each garnering a spotlight and applause from the crowd.

The class was underway. A friend of theirs from North Carolina was showing the winner from the mare class. She ate up the ground with her bold trot. The stallion winner had trouble, wanting to rack instead of trot. Everyone worked hard, cutting to the inside to show off their horse to each judge. Then they slow-gaited, at least a few of them, although most were already racking. But one of the geldings came down the stretch with a smooth, magnificent slow gait, a slow four-beat gait with hesitation. The crowd went wild.

Now they were all racking or breaking, but their riders quickly brought them back under control. One horse refused to canter, preferring to continue to rack. They reversed and trotted their hearts out in the second direction. By the second slow gait, a few were tiring and losing their form. When they moved into the rack, the gelding with the good slow gait settled and flew around the ring, perfectly in collected. Everyone got their last canter and the line-up was called. The steaming horses parked out as their riders dismounted and saddles came off for conformation judging. Molly couldn't fault any of them, although the stallion winner was a bit coarse in the neck and head. The mare and one of the geldings had really long, fine necks and beautiful, delicate heads.

Everyone remounted and the announcer said, "Anybody want to see more?"

The crowd yelled their approval of the workout and the four best horses were back on the rail at a trot. The good gelding didn't look a bit tired and made one brilliant pass after another. When he picked up his slow gait, the stallion winner came alongside, and the commotion in the stands raised to a fever pitch.

"Rack on." And they did. Flying down the straightaway, one breaking in the turn but settling for his next pass. No canter this time. They reversed at the trot, each trying to outdo the other. By the second slow gait, one horse had had enough and lost all form and composure. The gelding kept his brilliance and moved into his flawless rack. Time to line up.

Chapter Twenty

NO ONE WAS SURPRISED WHEN the fifteen-year-old gelding was chosen as the World Champion for the second year in a row. The crowd applauded every one of the eight contenders when their numbers were called for their ribbons.

John and Molly checked on their horses and headed out of the fairgrounds. It was already too crowded in the stable area to try to hitch and pull the trailer close to their stalls, and they needed the truck to get to their outlying motel.

~ * ~

They took their time the next morning, knowing the stable area would be in gridlock. Finally, they were able to pull the trailer into an aisle not too far away. Molly took down the water buckets and stowed them in the trailer tack room. They had two lead lines, and they each grabbed a horse to lead to their trailer. Molly took Cat and John grabbed the new mare.

Cat walked up the ramp and into the slant load trailer, eager to go home. Molly hitched him on both sides and swung the partition to lock into place.

The new mare was not so cooperative. She took one look at the ramp and locked her feet in place. John held her firmly and Molly lifted one hoof up onto the ramp. She politely removed it. John walked her in a circle away from the trailer while Molly got a broom out of the tack room. Once John had her moving forward, Molly clucked from the rear and tapped the mare on the butt with the broom. She hesitated, then jumped onto the ramp and into the trailer. Molly dropped the broom and quickly brought the ramp up, before the contrary mare could change her mind. When she saw the hay bag she stepped forward, and John was able to hitch her and swing the partition against her. John ducked under, locked it in place and made sure everything was secure. Molly let the ramp down to let him out and they secured it for the ride home.

They dropped the back two windows for air and made sure the roof vents and sliding windows in front of the horses were open. John started the diesel, and they wound their way out of the barn area to the Watterson Expressway and then Interstate 64. The horses quietly munched hay, headed for North Carolina.

They were fueling up in a truck stop near Charleston when Carter called. "Where are you? You should be home by now."

"Yeah, well not if you have to wait an hour to get out of the barn area," John answered. "We just stopped for diesel in Charleston."

"Okay. See you later," Carter said, hanging up.

Molly relieved John at the wheel, and the next several miles of West Virginia Turnpike required all of her attention with the curves, toll booths and hills, not to mention the tractor-trailers which crept up every incline and sped down the downgrades. They stopped again where I-77 left I-81, and John took over for the drive down from Fancy Gap. Molly fell asleep and didn't wake until they exited the interstate.

At last back home, they pulled in behind the tractor-trailer and unloaded the two eager horses. Making sure the new arrivals had water and hay, Molly and John turned the horses loose in their stalls and trudged to the house, pulling their luggage.

~ * ~

Ellen arrived at the barn around ten. She carried boxes and folders from her car, trying not to drop anything. Molly saw her and ran to grab a falling box. "Thanks, Molly, I was about to lose that."

She was full of ideas for the fall fun show, scheduled for a mere two weeks away. Together, they made lists of everything that needed to be done. Molly's first job was to count the ribbons and make sure they had enough for all the classes. Done. The sign-up sheet had been posted for a few weeks, but few students had signed up. Molly was to contact students, either during their lesson or by phone, and encourage them to enter. The fun shows were always advertised as fundraisers for various charities, but it was never clear what percentage the charity would receive. Ellen had found a judge, and Molly needed to recruit an announcer and a ringmaster as well as students and parents to help with the event.

Freddy's murder lingered in her mind, like a bad dream, but she was too busy with day-to-day work to give it much thought. Detective Bell came out to talk with both Carter and Lorenzo again. Molly wondered if he asked them about Pedro and if either of them had seen him in Louisville. So far, no one had asked her.

The week of the show, Molly organized the classes, but Ellen changed them to make sure that certain students might be more likely to win. That always happened, but Molly hated it. This was supposed to be a "fun" show. This would be as close to a real horse show as a few of her students would ever be able to enter. Ellen had ordered big banners to be erected at the farm entrance, promoting the show. She wanted to offer free pony rides as well, but Molly convinced her that the horses and ponies would be too busy competing in the show, and the staff and volunteers would also have their hands full.

Once lessons ended on Friday night, Molly, John, and Ed were all at work cleaning the arena, the holding area, the lounge, and everything that needed cleaning. Electric clippers ran non-stop, trimming bridle paths (the area behind the ears where the bridle fits) and ears. A September thunderstorm roared through, with cloudbursts dumping inches of rain. The lesson horses would be muddy messes.

Show horse customers were still coming Saturday morning, and Ellen had wanted Molly to reschedule her afternoon lessons for the morning before the show, but there was no place to do that, and too much to do.

Molly and John were in the barn by seven on Saturday, and she began bringing in the filthy horses. As soon as any helpers arrived, she put them to work, hosing off feet and legs and curry combing the dried mud off the rest of their bodies. She had begged to keep two horses in the only two empty stalls and leave another in the indoor round pen, but Carter had insisted they all go out.

By noon, the customer horses were worked, and Carter was grading the arena before roping off part of it for spectators. Molly was filthy and ran home to change before the one o'clock show. As she walked toward the house, she noticed a commotion at the front entrance to the farm. The animal rights folks were out in force, holding up signs and heckling anyone who tried to turn into the driveway.

She walked that way as they chanted, "Free the horses, let them be wild."

Chapter Twenty-One

MOLLY PULLED OUT HER PHONE to call Ellen, but it went straight to voice mail. She walked over to the group. "You can't block our drive. This is private property. Children and parents are coming for an event."

"Horses shouldn't have to perform for people or carry them around. They should be free."

"Free where?" Molly asked. "Even the wild horses are being rounded up out west. If you have a couple of hundred acres sitting around, all properly fenced, and you want to buy horses and set them free, have at it. But horses have been domesticated for thousands of years. We provide food, shelter, and protection when needed, and they help us. These horses are privately owned, and you are trespassing."

"We've heard Carter Mills hires illegal aliens and brings them to our city. That's unsafe."

Molly thought she recognized the voice. "What does that

have to do with animal cruelty?"

"It shows what kind of people you are," answered another protestor.

Molly walked away and tried to call Ellen, getting only a recording, then Carter, who answered. She explained what was happening. As she watched, a few cars went by, one turned around in the driveway and left.

Carter said, "Call the sheriff's office. Get rid of them."

A car came around the corner at speed and slammed on the brakes, barely making it to a stop behind the line of traffic. Drivers exited their cars to take pictures. Molly called 911 and explained the situation, then she ran for the barn and the horse holding area. Finding Spirit, a tall black gelding that was already tacked up, she led him outside and mounted, a whip in her hand.

She trotted down the gravel drive and approached the protesters who were now blocking the driveway. "We need you all to please move. You're blocking our driveway."

No one moved. They merely turned toward her and continued to chant.

Molly swung her horse into the crowd. "Head's up," she yelled. "Clear the entrance."

As mounted police officers know, a horse can move a crowd much better than anyone on foot. A protester turned and then jumped out of the way. Molly rode through the opening, pivoted and, using her legs, asked the horse to sidestep into the crowd. A woman screamed as the horse stepped on her bare toe. Protesters scattered. One woman was pushing a baby stroller. Molly turned the horse away from her and said, "Please, get your children out of the way."

At that point, John walked out of the house with Bingo, who immediately ran for the excitement, barking as loudly as he could.

One of the people grabbed Molly's leg and tried to pull her off. She wheeled again, whip in hand, smacking the arm grabbing for her. A man latched onto her rein and jerked it. Growling, Bingo jumped for his hand. Spirit reared.

"Let go, you fool," Molly shouted. She stayed on and turned toward the man, loosening her reins and urging her horse forward. Sirens screamed in the distance. The man let go of the rein as he fell back. She squeezed the horse with her heels, and he jumped the man's fallen body. Bingo stood his ground, growling at the fallen form.

Spirit needed no encouragement to flee the melee. Molly rode fifty feet in the drive and halted, her horse snorting. She called Bingo, and he reluctantly ducked his tail and followed her.

John ran up to her and put his hand on her thigh. "Are you all right? What's going on?"

Molly reached down and touched his hand. "Spirit and I were clearing the blocked drive. Someone grabbed Spirit and jerked. He went up. But I think we got the job done."

She turned to face the protestors as two police cars squealed to a stop. Carter roared out the driveway in the four-wheeler with Pepper in his lap, passing her and stopping at the entrance.

"She attacked us," one woman screamed. Another shouted, "They hire illegal aliens and there was a murder here."

Pepper began barking at everyone.

Carter grimaced as he looked over to see that they had covered his large stable sign with "Free the horses" posters.

He strode among the protestors and began ripping the offending slogans off the sign and the adjoining fence.

One of the women walked up and pointed to Molly's horse. "Look. His tail is broken, it's all bandaged." Molly shook her head, dismounted, handed her reins to John before walking back to unwrap Spirit's tail braid. After removing the vet wrap, she began to unbraid the thick, beautiful hair. Another woman walked close, sure to find signs of cruelty. "They can't swish their tails, you know," she said. Molly let go of the tail and Spirit got the protestor right in the eyes as he swished off a fly.

Meanwhile, the sheriff's deputies had arrived. Protestors pointed at Molly and said, "She attacked us."

One of deputies walked up to Molly, a small smile playing at his lips. She told him, "Officer, these protesters were blocking access to private property, to our business. I asked them to move, but they wouldn't, so Spirit and I asked them to move."

Most of the crowd was dispersing, with only a few hardcore activists remaining. One of them yelled, "They put tight collars on them to starve them."

Carter turned toward her. "You stupid bitch. Those are cribbing collars. You took them off, and one of my horses almost died from colic. Those straps keep them from swallowing air when they bite on wood and suck air."

Molly told the deputy, "I recognized the voice of the woman who let the horses out, but now I can't tell which one she was."

The other deputy spoke to the remaining crowd. "You folks are trespassing on private property. I suggest you go home and stay away from this stable."

"Make them turn the horses loose!" The cry came from the rear.

The deputy answered, "So they can tear up yards and be hit by cars and cause accidents? Are you crazy? This horse looks well cared for to me."

One woman came toward the deputy, her arms outstretched in front of her. "Go ahead, arrest me, for trying to make life better for these poor creatures." Molly saw others videoing the event.

The deputy held up his hand. "Ma'am we have real crimes to solve. Please go home before we have to arrest all of you." He walked over to Carter. "You okay with not pressing charges if these folks go home now?"

Carter took a deep breath and looked around. "They'd better not come on the property again."

Chapter Twenty-Two

THE SHOW WENT ON. A few of the expected entries were not there, but Molly didn't know if the protests kept them away or if they had other conflicts. The audience was a bit smaller than usual. Casual spectators had probably decided against coming when they saw the commotion.

Molly had never gotten back to the house to clean up, but she found a clean t-shirt in the office and pulled it on above her filthy jods. She washed her hands and face and slicked her hair under a Miles Stables cap.

She sneaked a hot dog out of the concession stand before she passed out from hunger, and the marathon continued as horses, riders, and appropriately sized saddles were switched and sent into the ring, class after class.

At the end of the show, Molly was starting to clean up when Ellen called Ed and John to the center ring. She brought out a huge make-up box and said to the riding students, "Now's your chance, girls. Let's make Mr. John and Mr. Ed beautiful. Use lots of eyeshadow and lipstick."

Molly was horrified. The girls were in the guys' faces, smearing makeup everywhere. Ellen took pictures and hooted with laughter, but John and Ed were not getting in the spirit of things.

Molly called, "Hey guys, we need help to put these horses away," as she tried to lead the kids into the holding area away from the debacle in the center ring.

Molly continued to steam. Ellen wouldn't have done that to Carter, so what gave her the right to do it to her employees?

Most parents were eager to leave, and the arena quickly cleared out. Molly brought a trash bag and picked up debris, while John and Ed put tables and chairs back into storage. After the last of the supplies were back in the office, they checked on the horses and headed home.

After a shower, Molly threw on clean jeans and a sweater. "We're going out. Somewhere we've never been."

John yelled from the bathroom, "How do I get this damn mascara off?"

Molly snorted and gave him a bottle of make-up remover. Soon, they were headed to a downtown bistro known for fresh, local food. After a much-needed sip of wine, Molly ordered coastal red snapper and new potatoes, along with grilled broccoli. John had a grass-fed steak and baked potato, as well as a huge salad. She noticed someone in the bar area pointing at the television. Expecting to see a sporting event, she was shocked to see a wild looking woman on a black horse yelling, "Head's up, clear the driveway."

John almost choked on his sip of water and burst into

hysterical laughter. "Shut up," she hissed. "Maybe they have a video of the make-up session." She turned her face toward the wall and tried to pull her short hair over part of her face. Then she reached into her purse and took out her sunglasses and put them on. This made John laugh even harder. Molly, too, realizing the absurdity of it all, began to laugh. Carter could be seen pulling banners and signs off of his billboard and fence.

No one recognized them as they finished their very good, albeit expensive dinner. They went home and consoled themselves as only two kindred souls could.

~ * ~

Monday morning, Molly woke up with cramps and the period from hell. She gulped Motrin for breakfast and stuffed her purse with necessary supplies before dragging herself to the barn.

Mid-morning brought Ellen storming into the office and closing the door. "What made you decide to pull a stunt like that with the protestors?"

Molly dropped the pen she was using to make notes and looked up. "They were blocking the driveway and causing a traffic jam, not to mention maligning your stable. Carter told me to get rid of them. I started with politely asking them to clear out, but they wouldn't."

"You've embarrassed us on local television. I'm not sure if you can continue to work here. You need to apologize to Carter as well. And using a whip. When they are accusing us of animal cruelty."

Molly bit off her next words as she stood to face her boss.

"I used the whip on people, not the horse. People who were trying to hurt me." All Molly could think of was Ellen's latest safety training, telling the helpers to carry a whip when they went out to catch a horse—not always a successful ploy.

"Talk to Carter, and then we'll talk." With that, she marched out to her car and left.

Carter had just finished grading the arena. Molly walked up to him. "Ellen says I owe you an apology for using the horse to clear the protestors."

He stared at her. "What? I thought it was perfect. Sent those idiots scrambling for cover. I guess she thinks you were rude to them, but hell, they needed rude."

Molly took a deep breath. "I asked nicely at first, but it didn't do any good. And then that guy grabbed Spirit and things went downhill."

"Don't worry about Ellen. She's just embarrassed. I didn't see it on TV. Did they show the part where I called 'em 'stupid bitches'?"

Molly giggled. "I don't think so, but it did show you ripping down their signs."

~ * ~

The fall went on. John left to set up stalls and tack rooms for the Raleigh show. The horses would leave the next morning. Carter walked in the office and told Molly he needed her to deliver a horse. "You know that mare that came when we were in Louisville."

"The first Pendiana Poppy?" she asked. "She's a great lesson horse. Don't tell me she's leaving."

"I'm selling her. Too confusing with the other mare. You

need to take her to Hickory. And that big gelding, the one that's lame. Take him too."

"When?"

"Tomorrow morning. You'll need to leave about six. Take my three-horse trailer and your truck."

"I'll get their paperwork…"

"No paperwork. You just drop them at that sale barn."

"But don't they need Coggins…"

"I said no paperwork. Got it?"

"Yes, sir."

Molly filled up the truck with diesel and started to hitch it to the trailer when Ed stopped her with a wave.

"I've got to pick up a load of hay in the next county. Carter said to use your truck since John has his. Sorry," he said as he gave her a lopsided grin.

She sighed and handed him the keys before going to inspect the trailer. When she checked the tires, she realized one was a different size. She asked Lorenzo about it.

"The tire place, they no have other size. Carter say okay for now. Just don't go too fast."

Lovely, thought Molly. She brought the two horses in and clipped and groomed them. Everyone had left, enabling her to put them in the round pen with hay and a bucket of water, so she wouldn't have to catch them in the dark.

She set the alarm and arrived at the barn by five-thirty. She started the truck and went to hitch the trailer. The fuel was down to a fourth of a tank. Darn, she'd have to stop on the way. Poppy walked right on the trailer, but the gelding wasn't having any. She put him in crossties and went to bang on Lorenzo's door. He opened the door, wearing only baggy shorts.

"Sorry, but I can't load this horse by myself."

"I come. Just a minute."

And in less than five minutes, Lorenzo walked into the barn, fully dressed in a t-shirt, jeans, and boots. He picked up a whip and Molly got the grain. "I take the horse, you go behind." Lorenzo said, trading the whip for the handful of grain.

The gelding halted at the trailer and tried to pull back. Lorenzo offered the grain and Molly tapped the horse gently from the rear. Molly clucked and tapped again. He jumped on and Molly hooked the back chain and swung the gate closed.

"Thanks, buddy, I owe you."

"You be careful with the tire, Miss Molly."

Molly crept down the drive and headed for the interstate.

Chapter Twenty-Three

THE TRAILER PULLED A LITTLE oddly, but then bumper hitch trailers were not Molly's favorite. She much preferred a goose-neck with the weight centered on the truck bed. She accelerated onto I-40 and kept her speed just below sixty. Everyone passed her, of course, but she was afraid to go any faster. All was well until she hit a wide curve a few miles outside of Hickory. As she rounded the curve, the trailer jolted and then began to jackknife. She was out of control. Brake or no brake? She swung the wheel wildly, trying to keep the vehicle on the road. Her foot off the gas, she braked briefly and attempted to downshift. The engine roared as she shifted into third, still steering back and forth as the trailer swung from side to side. A ravine loomed to the right as she fought the swinging rig. The truck slowed a bit, and she downshifted again, the engine roaring louder. Finally, the trailer straightened behind her. She began to brake and pulled to the shoulder.

Shaking all over, she climbed out of the truck and walked around, expecting to see the smaller tire blown, but it wasn't. The big gelding stomped and swung his weight against the trailer wall. He must have thrown the trailer off balance. She opened the walk-in door. Poppy stood frozen, breathing hard. Molly yelled at the gelding, "Whoa, stand up here."

She called Carter to tell him what had happened, but there was only voice mail. She tried Ellen.

"You just drive slowly and take the horses where they're supposed to go. I'll tell Carter, and he'll see about getting you another tire when you get there. Be careful."

Her hands still shaking, Molly pulled the rig back onto the road, this time never topping fifty miles per hour. By the time she pulled into the sale grounds, she had tunnel vision. Adrenalin spent, she was about to pass out. She stopped the truck, let it run, and stumbled to a concession stand. The only food available was a hot dog, destined to be reheated for lunch customers, but Molly insisted she needed it now.

Shaking his head, the vendor stuck it in the microwave. Molly almost gagged but wolfed it down, knowing that she had to have food.

Only then did she pull up to what seemed to be the unloading area. She waited for someone to tell her what to do. Finally, a skinny cowboy with a wish of a mustache doffed his hat to her. "Morning, ma'am, what'cha got?"

"Two horses from Carter Mills Stables."

"Can I see your Coggins or any papers?"

"I don't have any. My boss had me bring them here, that's all."

"Well, you can't unload without Coggins. Go park over there and call your boss."

Wanting to scream, Molly eased the truck into gear and drove over to the parking area on the outskirts of the sale grounds. Horse traders were looking into the trailers as they drove up, trying to get a good buy before the sale.

She recognized a local trader, Ralph Loomis, who had sold them a few lesson horses over the years.

"Hi, Molly. What did you bring me?" he asked as he sauntered over to her truck.

"Was I supposed to bring them to you? Carter told me to bring these horses here and wouldn't give me any paperwork."

The trader walked back to the trailer and opened the walk-in door. Molly exited the truck and followed him. "They sound?"

"The mare is, the gelding's lame if you use him very much. But the mare is wonderful. I hate to lose her."

"So, why's he selling her?" he asked as he closed the door and turned to face her, his shrewd blue eyes looking intently at her through horned-rimmed glasses.

Molly had an idea which she kept to herself. "Don't know. I'm doing what I was told."

"Another lesson program could use her, right?" he asked, rubbing his chin.

"Sure. She's sound and broke to death."

"How about I give you $1000 for both, cash?"

"I need to call Carter."

"You do that. I'll get coffee and be back in a few minutes."

Molly climbed back into the warmth of the truck to call, and thankfully, Carter answered. "Hey, you made it there okay?"

"Not really." She explained about the small tire and the jackknifing. And that she couldn't unload without Coggins.

"Ah, hell. That ain't no good. Anybody show any interest in the horses?"

"Yeah. Ralph Loomis is here. Offered me $1,000 cash for both."

"Tell him $1,500 and it's a deal," Carter answered.

"What if he won't pay that much?"

"What kind of a dealer are you? Get as much as you can."

"What about the tire? I don't want to drive home with it like that."

"You got a credit card with you? Find someplace to buy a tire the right size."

Ralph walked back toward the truck with two coffees. "Here, I figure you could use one. Probably could use something stronger, working for Carter."

Molly thanked him and told him Carter's price. The gelding began to paw and stomp.

"Reckon I could get papers on that mare, with a DNA test?" He watched her while he took a sip of coffee.

Molly knew that would not suit Carter and Ellen's plan. "How about $1,200 but no DNA test?"

"It's like that, is it? Did he steal her or is she a ringer for another horse?"

"That's not for me to say."

Ralph laughed. "That Carter is a corker. Or was this Ellen's idea?"

Molly grew increasingly more uncomfortable. She felt slimy, and she hated being associated with such deals. She looked at the steering wheel, saying nothing.

"Okay. Let's get them off the trailer. It's not your fault."

Molly slid out of the truck and followed him to the back of

the trailer. They opened the back gate, and Molly unhitched the gelding. He flew out backwards, but Molly managed to hold the lead. The mare backed out like a perfect lady. "We'll put them on my stock trailer. Reckon he needs Ace?"

"Yeah. Wish I'd had some earlier."

Ralph led the way to a long stock trailer. He traded with Molly and loaded the mare, then brought a bottle of Ace and a syringe, so he could give the gelding a shot of the tranquilizer. He set the bottle back in his truck and dug a roll of cash out of his pocket. "Here you go. Be safe, Molly. Tell him I only gave you a grand."

Molly shook her head. "I try to be honest."

Two tire stores later, Molly drank another cup of coffee while they put a matching tire on the trailer. She munched a candy bar from a machine before the tire was installed. She paid and walked to the truck, noticing it was close to noon. She shifted into first and eased the dually out of the parking lot, headed for home.

She had pulled onto the interstate when Jose called to tell her the police were now saying Ace was drugged, giving him a heart attack. They were searching for the drug.

"Did they say what drug?"

"No, but we have a lot of drugs for the horses. And maybe there are illegal drugs here, too. I no find, but maybe here."

"Do they have a search warrant?"

"I think so. They showed me a paper. I think I need a lawyer, but I don't know one."

"I'll try to find you one. Call me if they arrest you. But I'm on the road. I'll call when I get back to the barn."

Molly's head was spinning. She cranked up the radio and

tried to concentrate on the road and the traffic around her. When she pulled into the driveway, she realized Jose was probably her only help for the week since everyone else had gone to the show. She pulled behind the barn and turned the trailer around before backing it into its parking spot.

At least they had cleaned the stalls before they left, she noted. She walked home to let Bingo out and find a late lunch before her lessons began.

When she came back to the barn, she looked up the phone number for Sarah's mother, Judy Franklin, the attorney. She called her office, but the lawyer was in court. She left a message asking her to call. Molly was in the loft throwing down hay when Judy returned her call. Molly explained about Jose.

"I don't handle criminal cases," Judy said. "If he's arrested, a public defender can see about bond. Does he have any money to hire an attorney?"

"Doubtful," Molly answered as she cut the strings on the next bale of hay. "Are the public defenders here any good?"

"Some of them are. Let me know what happens, and I'll see what I can find out."

Molly thanked her and continued her chores. Jose called at five o'clock. "They arrested me, Miss Molly. They find a drug that could give a heart attack. I know my fingerprints are on it because I use it on horse. Also, can you tell my brother, Juan? He can feed horses. I erase his phone number so they don't find him. You can see him at school. Night class at seven. Biology."

Chapter Twenty-Four

MOLLY CALLED JUDY BACK. "THEY'RE arresting Jose. What can I do?"

"You might call Carter and ask if he would put up money for a defense attorney, but since Jose isn't a regular employee, I doubt that he would. But they'll assign a public defender. I haven't heard anything about the case. Isn't Carter friends with Larry Sommers, one of the assistant DAs?"

"Oh, yeah. He's been out to the barn several times. I'll call him. Thanks."

That would have to wait until another day, since it was too late to call. She finished her chores and went to lock the office for the night. As Molly shut down the computer, the barn phone rang. She was tempted to let it go to voicemail, but with so much happening, she decided to answer it.

"Who is this?" asked an unknown female voice. "Are you, by any chance, Molly?"

"I am. How can I help you?"

"You don't know me, but I'm Freddy's sister. Freddy Pedigo. We're going to have a memorial service for Freddy and since you knew him, and you… you found him and all, we wanted to invite you."

Molly hesitated, feeling awkward, before answering, "I'm so sorry for your loss. Yes, of course I'll come. When is it?"

The service was scheduled for late Saturday afternoon at a small Baptist Church down the road. Molly explained that everyone else was in Raleigh, but she would come. She wondered if Detective Bell knew. Did law enforcement officers really go to funerals of victims like they did in the movies?

After locking the office, she whistled for Bingo and hurried home. She fed the dog and took a shower before throwing on clean jeans and driving their Toyota to Mock County Community College. No sense taking the truck, and anyway, it was still parked at the barn. Assuming it was a two-hour class, Juan should be getting out about nine. She could make it by eight-thirty.

North Carolina had an impressive system of community colleges. All the campuses that Molly had seen appeared fairly new and well maintained. The Mock campus was small, with two buildings apparently in use for the night's classes. Molly found an office, and a woman inside directed her to the science wing in the next building.

Molly found a chair near Juan's classroom and sat down to wait. She had thought to bring a book, and she started reading the latest Rita Mae Brown mystery from the library. Maybe it would help her solve the mysteries around her. But she found herself unable to concentrate and closed the book after reading the same page twice. She tried to call Detective Bell, but his phone went to voicemail.

A little before nine, she heard chairs scuffling and students talking as the class ended. She had never met Juan, but she assumed someone ought to be able to point him out to her. As the students exited, she started to ask the girl who came out first, but then she saw a young man who greatly favored Jose. She hurried up to him. "Juan," she said, "I'm Molly, from Carter Mills Stables. I have a message from your brother."

Juan walked out of the flow of traffic over to the side of the hall. "Is he okay? Are the police back? Do I need to stay away?"

Molly whispered, "They arrested him. They think he drugged Royal and that is what caused his heart attack."

Juan raised his voice and said, "He would never do that. Anyway, like Royal would let him? No one would let you drug them. Why would they—"

"Shh," Molly said. "I'm trying to find out more, but Jose needs you to take care of the horses. But you'll have to be careful. I don't know if anyone is watching the place."

"Okay. I can do that."

Mission accomplished. Molly drove home, her mind swirling.

Too wired to sleep, yet exhausted, she sat down to read. She woke up with her book on the floor beside her chair and Bingo nestled in her lap. Her phone told her it was after eleven. Better do the barn check and then get to bed. The night had cooled. After stepping outside, Molly returned for a sweatshirt and followed Bingo as he bounced across the grass.

All was well, and Bingo helped by killing one rat. Molly put on gloves and carried the dead rodent to the dumpster out back. Seeing the truck behind the barn, she decided to drive it home. When she started it, she saw she was low on diesel. Might as well go fill it up now, before she needed it for who knows what. She was wide awake and cranked the radio up, singing along with Meatloaf on the oldies station.

She filled the tank at an all-night service station and turned around to head for home. When she got to the four-way-stop, she saw a car waiting to her right. She downshifted and hit the brakes, only to have the brake pedal go to the floor with no affect. The big truck continued into the intersection as the car began to cross. She turned the wheel hard to the right and accelerated, squealing tires in a sloppy righthand turn. Bingo hit the floor and yelped. Straightening out, she drove up the hill and turned into a large church parking lot. She let off the accelerator and circled the lot. As she slowed, clutch out, she stalled and stopped dead.

Turning off the ignition, she sat shaking and tried to comprehend what had happened. Thank God it hadn't happened when she was pulling the trailer. Her brakes were fine earlier. She could call Triple A, but at this hour it would probably be a long wait. And was this mechanical failure or sabotage? She tried to call Detective Bell, but once again the call went to voicemail. She left a message, detailing what had happened and that she would walk home. He could call her in the morning. She threw her keys in her purse, preparing to walk.

When she opened the door, she spied baling twine in the

back seat that would work as a lead for Bingo. She tied it around his collar and pulled her purse up on her shoulder. She was only about a mile from home. After locking the dually, she headed down the road, facing traffic and trying to keep as far off the road as possible. When no cars were coming, she walked along the gravel shoulder, but as soon as she saw headlights, she pulled the dog over into the grass. She stumbled once, over a downed limb, and then into a drainage ditch, landing on her hands and knees in the pitch-dark night. She had turned her phone off because the battery was almost dead. Tripping and cussing, she took heart when she saw her security light up ahead.

Her hike warmed her; she was sweating by the time she gratefully unlocked her back door. Her face stung. A look in the mirror showed her she'd had a close encounter with a briar or a sharp twig. She took another hot shower and found herself weak and shaky when she emerged. Throwing on her warmest robe, she descended to the kitchen and put the tea kettle on to heat. Finding an almost empty bottle of port, she poured the remains into a mug and topped it with hot water, a slice of orange, and cinnamon. The hot drink soothed her, and she climbed upstairs to crawl under the covers.

The ringtone from her phone woke her at seven with Detective Bell on the line. He told her not to call Triple A until he could have someone inspect her truck.

She tried to explain why she didn't think Jose would kill Royal. "Royal was his meal ticket. He'd have no reason to hurt him."

Bell said, "He was guaranteed a home and a paycheck for a period of time with no hassle. That might be reason enough.

But I get what you're saying. Anyway, could you stay at home with the doors locked for the day?"

Molly laughed. "Yeah, and the horses will feed themselves and clean their stalls and I will cancel all my lessons. I don't think so. Everyone's at the show except Jose, and he's in jail."

"Look, be careful and don't take off in any other vehicle until we have a chance to inspect it. And keep your phone with you. Don't hesitate to call if you see anything that seems off."

"Got it. Are you coming to the memorial service for Freddy?"

"Don't know. We'll see what Saturday brings."

Molly saw that John had tried to call while she was on the phone. She started to call him back, but thought better of it. She didn't want to tell him about the truck brakes because he would worry, and she wouldn't be able to hide her current emotional state.

Chapter Twenty-Five

THE FIRST THING FRIDAY MORNING, she called Carter's brother to ask for help with the farm.

"They leave you alone again?" he asked. "Can't you get Jose?"

"He's in jail." She explained the situation as best she could. "If you could help me clean stalls, then I'm good. My student helpers will come after school."

"Yeah. I need to finish something. I'll be there in an hour. You feed, but leave the stalls to me."

"Thanks, Jim, you're the best."

Detective Bell walked into the office, his jeans and boots covered in dust. "They showed me where your brake lines were cut. Before last night, when had you driven it?"

Molly explained her trip to Hickory and told him her brakes were fine when she unhitched the trailer. "The truck sat here behind the barn until I did barn check at ten."

"You can call Triple A, but you'd best call your insurance agency because you'll need new brake lines."

Molly mumbled a curse word before making notes on a piece of scrap paper.

"That's your car over by your house, right?" He pointed. "We'll check it out before we go."

She thanked him and went out to feed the noisy horses.

Sarah and Joey ran into her office when they arrived at ten. "We saw you on TV. That was so cool. You and Spirit showed them a thing or two. We were in the back getting horses ready, we didn't even know all that was going on."

Molly couldn't help but smile. "Mm, not sure that was the best example to set…"

Joey said, "My dad loved it. He said, 'Way to go, Molly.'"

Sarah was more serious. "I was afraid Spirit might go over backwards when that guy pulled on him, but I saw how you handled it. You turned him loose like you tell us to. It made me realize what could happen."

Molly looked at Sarah's earnest face, framed by reddish-blonde curls. The girl would be a knockout one day, and Molly was so proud of her riding and her attitude. Judy and her husband were good parents. Molly truly loved this child.

Molly called and arranged to have the truck towed to a garage that could replace the brake lines. She wasn't sure how much it would cost after the insurance deductible.

The kids went out to catch horses. Judy walked in, looking at her phone before sliding it into her pocket. "Hi Molly, how are you doing? None of this can be easy on you. I brought you something." She handed Molly an ice cold can of Diet Coke and a large chocolate chip cookie.

"Thank you so much. You don't know the half of it. But I'm still here. Did you find out anything about Jose's case? I haven't had time to call the assistant DA yet."

"No. But there's something else you need to know. I have a good friend I grew up with in Pennsylvania. She's at the show in Raleigh. She saw that new mare show. Said she was fantastic. But the thing is, she used to own Pendiana Poppy, and she said it isn't the same horse."

"What? I mean, how does she know? She matches the markings on her papers. Horses can change a lot over the years."

"Her mare had an injury. Nothing much, but she rubbed the hair off under her tummy and it grew back white. She went into the stall to visit and this mare had no white hair. And she swore her old mare would know her, and this mare didn't."

Molly had washed the first Poppy mare, but she hadn't looked for white hair underneath. She now knew for sure what she had suspected was true. That's why the other mare had to go. "I don't know what to say."

Judy turned away and ran a hand through her stylish short blonde hair. "I know it has nothing to do with you, Molly. And Sarah adores you. But I keep hearing things about Carter and Ellen. You know, I'd love for Sarah to have a show horse, but I don't trust your bosses. By the way, Ellen told me that she thought Ed would be a better teacher for Sarah. I told her I was not interested in making a change. I thought you should know that."

Molly felt her face heat up. She tried not to let her anger show. "Sarah is wonderful. She works so hard, and she's really riding well. I'd hate to lose her."

"She loves it here. But I have to think about the total picture. I won't do anything without talking to you."

"Thanks. And thanks for telling me all of that. Are you going to bring it up to Ellen or Carter?"

"Don't know yet. Tell Sarah to call me when she's finished tonight. And Molly, thanks for all you do."

Molly stood up to walk her to the door, trying not to let Judy see the tears in her eyes. As soon as she left, Molly looked up the DA's office number and put in a call to Larry Sommers.

"Hey, Molly, I know who you are. How's it going out there?"

She explained that she was asking about Jose, that she wanted to make sure he had an attorney.

"Not my case. And I can't really discuss it. But we try to follow due process," Larry said.

"I know."

"What's Carter saying about all this?"

"I don't think he knows about Jose yet, but in any case, I can't really discuss it. Thanks."

Larry hadn't been rude. But he hadn't been helpful either. And Molly was not in the best of moods. She ate her cookie and opened her Diet Coke while planning her evening lessons.

~ * ~

John called as she was kicking her boots off on the deck. "Hang on a sec, hon," she said as she ditched the boots and unlocked the door, ushering Bingo inside. "Heard you had an awesome ride on Poppy."

"Yeah, she is really hot stuff. But I met her former owner who says it's not Poppy."

"Heard about that, too. Did she say anything to Carter or any of the other customers?" Molly asked as she sank into a kitchen chair and began peeling a banana from the fruit bowl on the kitchen table.

"No. I was in the stall putting the mare's blanket on when she came by. How did you know?"

"Turns out she's a friend of Judy's. They grew up together. She knew Judy's daughter rode with us, so she called to get her take on the situation."

"What did you say?"

Molly chewed a bite of banana before answering. "I said the mare's markings matched her papers. Which is true as far as it goes."

"Do you think Sarah told her mother about the other liver chestnut mare?"

"She rode her, so I'm sure she did. But since she was a lesson horse and the other a show horse, I'm not sure Sarah would have made the connection on the similarity."

John sighed. "Why are we even worrying about this? We aren't culpable."

Molly laughed and said, "You sound like Judy. Problem is, we'll go down with the ship. And we still have three horses in boarding barns." Molly thought about the two yearlings and one retired mare they had farmed out around the county. Carter didn't have room for them, not when high paying customer horses could occupy his stalls.

"Don't remind me. And we can't go rent a barn and do

our own thing within forty miles because we signed a Non-Compete agreement."

"Not to mention, we'd have nowhere to live. I'm thinking we might need to buy property if we can. I mean, just for us and the horses we own. Something to think about. How's the rest of the show going?"

"Ed and Cat won. Annie was second to the same horse that won at Louisville, so Leslie was happy. Is Jose helping you?"

"No. I meant to tell you, they arrested him."

"What? When?"

"Yesterday. They think he gave Royal a horse drug that caused his heart attack. Judy says most of the local public defenders are pretty good. I hope he gets a decent one."

"Lots to think about. But we'd better both get to bed. Miss you."

"Me, too. Good night."

Chapter Twenty-Six

MOLLY HAD NEVER GONE TO funerals as a child and, as an adult, she always felt awkward. She had no idea what she could say to Freddy's family members, but they had wanted her to come, so she did.

The church was white clapboard with black shutters, set in a clearing surrounded by large oak trees. It looked old but well kept. Molly parked beside the twenty or so cars in the gravel lot and made her way to the door. She slipped into a pew at the back shortly before the service began.

The preacher was kind, bringing comfort to the family, saying that Freddy had perhaps lost his way in life, but remained a caring friend and loving family member. A large woman in a gray dress stood up to perform a beautiful solo of Amazing Grace. The family made their way to the church basement where attendees were asked to gather for refreshments.

Jim Mills walked up to her. "I meant to ask if you were

coming. I knew they wanted you to be here." Wearing khakis and a sport coat, and minus his cap, Jim looked totally different. His snow-white hair was neatly combed, and Molly realized he was a good-looking guy.

"Is that his sister?" Molly asked, indicating a brunette who was speaking with the preacher.

"Yeah, Doris Swanson. I'll introduce you."

A receiving line had formed. Jim and Molly walked to the back. A very slender man with a beard stood beside Doris. Molly noted the resemblance to Freddy, and Jim confirmed that this was Freddy's brother. A tall woman in jeans and sandals stepped in line behind them. They made their way to the family.

Jim said, "Doris, I'm so sorry. I want you to meet Molly Lewis."

Molly reached for her hand, and Doris clasped her fingers with both hands. "Thank you for coming, thank you for finding him."

"I—I'm sorry I couldn't do anything to help him, but it was too late."

"Honey, no one's been able to help him for a long time. You all go get yourself some food."

Freddy's brother, Tim, shook her hand and thanked her for coming. Jim gave hugs to both siblings before walking over to the food table. Molly wasn't hungry, but she didn't want to appear unsociable. She picked up a finger sandwich and a few carrot sticks.

Jim filled his plate with ham sandwiches, potato salad, deviled eggs and a piece of pecan pie before leading Molly to a table. As they sat down, they saw the tall woman having an intense, whispered conversation with Doris. Doris looked upset, and Tim finally took the woman's arm and led her to the door.

"Wonder what that's about?" asked Jim.

Tim came over and sat down beside Jim. "Some people have a lot of nerve. That hussy came in here to tell Doris it was to be expected bad things would happen to anyone who hung around Mills Stables. Sorry, guys. She's a piece of work. She used to work at the factory with Doris. Always going on about animal rights."

Molly wished she had heard the woman's voice. Could she be their mischief maker? "What's her name?" Molly asked.

"I don't rightly know, and I don't want to ask Doris right now. But I'll find out and let you guys know later."

Molly made her excuses and left for home. When she stopped by to check the barn, there was a message on the answering machine from Juan. He had taken care of the horses and all was well. He wondered if she knew any more about Jose's situation. He decided to stay with friends but come by and feed the horses on Royal's farm once a day.

Since she didn't have anything to tell him, she didn't call back. She went home and let Bingo out before changing into sweats. John was showing Poppy, or whoever she was, back in the park championship tonight. She wished she could see him show, but with everything that had been going on, she didn't feel comfortable leaving the barn to drive to Raleigh for the evening. She offered a prayer for his safety and success before brewing a cup of tea and curling up with her book.

She had gone to bed and was sleeping deeply when she heard Bingo bark, then John's voice. She had been too tired to wait up.

"Hey there," she said softly, "how did tonight's show go?"

"You mean last night?" asked John, looking at his watch. "Something on the rail spooked her and she switched canter leads right in front of the judge. But I still got second. Good to be home."

John undressed and they snuggled before falling asleep.

The next morning, she had another message from Juan. "Miss Molly, someone broke into my brother's house. All the drawers are dumped out, the couch and mattresses are cut, the barn is messed up too. They broke the lock on the tack room and everything."

Chapter Twenty-Seven

JOHN WAS STILL ASLEEP. MOLLY thought for a minute. Juan wouldn't want to call the police because he had no papers. She could go out to check on Royal's horses and report the break-in. She scribbled a note for John and walked over to the barn to feed the horses. As soon as she finished, she drove her car to Mock County. Donning a pair of work gloves, she checked out the barn and then walked up to Jose's house. She saw the door was unlocked and standing open. She looked in. If anything, Juan had underestimated the damage.

She walked to back to the barn and called the Mock County Sheriff's office as well as Detective Bell, explaining that she had come out to see to the horses and found the damage. Mock County would send a deputy and Bell said he was on his way, to please wait for him.

Molly grabbed a hose and began to fill a water tank for the pasture horses. The deputy arrived first and then Bell. He asked her if she had gone into the house.

Molly kept her eyes on the running water. "When I saw the damage at the barn, I walked up to see if his house was okay. The door was ajar. I looked in but I didn't go inside. I shut the door and called you." Molly knew she wasn't a good liar. She hadn't actually lied, but there was a lot of omission in her statement.

Bell made some notes, then stood, looking at her. "There's something you're not telling me. If you did this to make things look better for Jose, you are in big trouble. Or if you know who did this. I mean it."

Molly looked into his stern blue eyes. "I promise, I don't know who did this. But I thought you needed to know about it."

Bell walked away to make a call. After he finished, he strode to where Molly was dipping grain out of a bin. "We know about Jose's brother. And sooner or later we need to talk to him. I could have him picked up at school. But I don't want to do that. You need to tell him to call me."

Molly said nothing, but finally nodded. "Am I free to go?"

"Yes, unless there's anything else you would like to tell me."

She shook her head and walked to her car.

John was up and reading the Sunday paper when she returned home. Molly joined him on the couch.

"Where's the truck? I didn't see it at the barn last night when we got back."

"In the shop. There was a problem with the brakes."

John looked up from the sports section. "What kind of problem? We bought new brake pads last spring."

Molly hesitated. John wouldn't take the news well. "It wasn't that. Someone cut the brake lines after I got back from the auction on Thursday."

He turned to face her. "Oh my God, Molly, why didn't you tell me? Did you have a wreck?"

"No, I slid through a stop sign but no damage. Detective Bell had someone look at it. And he inspected the car before I could drive it." Molly changed the subject before he could lecture her on staying out of the investigation. "But let me tell you about Royal's farm. Juan called me so I went out there. The tack room, the feed room, and Jose's house were torn up. Might have been local druggies looking for loot or a score, or it might have been whoever was supplying Royal with drugs or betting capital or someone he owed."

"I keep thinking about him being drugged. I mean, how would he let that happen? Maybe he was being chased, and he turned over the golf cart and was injured, then whoever it was drugged him."

Molly jumped up. "That makes sense. I wonder if they found what they were looking for or if he had it with him."

John thought for a minute. "If he had it with him, whoever drugged him would have gotten it. Wait—unless he had time to hide it first. The evidence techs searched the culvert area, but did they look for hiding places? You know, like a hole in a tree or a fence post?"

Molly joined in the speculation. "Or under a rock on the bank. I think we need to go back out there."

"We need to rest. Are you taking your day off tomorrow?"

"You bet. I have a doctor's appointment in the morning."

"Oh. Routine? I didn't know you'd found a new doctor yet."

"Female stuff. Routine."

Chapter Twenty-Eight

MOLLY HATED GOING TO THE doctor. Thinking about it made her nervous. But she knew enough biology to know she needed to take care of her body.

Dr. Lu was a slender Asian woman, probably in her fifties. Molly had filled out scores of paperwork, and the woman studied it carefully. "You had a miscarriage and a stillbirth?" she asked. "That must have been terrible. I'm so sorry. Then you had a tubal ligation?"

Molly nodded. "I was forty by then and we couldn't go through everything again. I guess we waited too late to start. And we work with a lot of kids who need attention. We decided that was enough."

"Your blood test shows you're anemic. Are you taking iron?"

"Most of the time. When I have time for breakfast."

She looked closely at Molly. "How many hours a day are you working?"

"It's supposed to be seven or eight, but more often ten to twelve."

A smile played around her lips. "And this is your chosen career?"

Molly laughed. "The horses, yes. My present employer? Maybe not so much."

"I'd like to see you take two weeks off. But I'm guessing that's not likely."

"I get one-week paid vacation plus holidays. Sick leave was never discussed. A day or two would be okay but not sure how two weeks, even without pay, would fly."

"Did you talk about surgery with your last doctor?"

"I had a D&C, but it didn't help. I don't want a hysterectomy. I've researched laser ablation. Seems like that would work."

Dr. Lu nodded. "I've had patients who did well with that. I can refer you to a specialist. Would you want to do it soon?"

Molly asked, "How much down time?"

"If you had the procedure on a Friday, you could probably go back to work by Monday, but no lifting. Think about it and let me know."

Molly thought if she waited for right before or after Christmas that might work. However, now was not the time to ask her boss.

~ * ~

When Molly arrived home, she and John decided to drive to Royal's farm and search the area around the culvert. The police had probably already done that, but it couldn't hurt. And it was a nice day. They called Bingo and set out in the car.

No one was around at Royal's farm. They parked and

headed down a hill to the culvert area. Molly dreaded stepping into the culvert, even though it was dry and she could see daylight on the other end. John realized the reason for her hesitation and took her hand. "You don't have to go in there, but I think it might help you."

She turned to him and smiled. "I'm sure you're right." She stopped at the edge, took a deep breath, tried to shrug off the fear, and then forged ahead. John had to duck. The other side was wooded with a clear channel for water coming off the highway and the hillside above. They looked around for any obvious hiding places and saw none. A mound rose above the right side of the channel, and they climbed up to it. They each made their way into the surrounding woods and Molly called, "Look, here's an opening in a tree, but I can't reach it."

John hiked over to where she was pointing. The cavity was about eye level for him. He looked in. "It looks like a plastic bag, but I don't know what's in it."

"Don't touch it," Molly cautioned.

"We need to make sure it's not a bird's nest or something," John said as he pulled his work gloves out of his back pocket. He lifted the bag enough to see what looked like cash and papers and maybe a plastic pouch. He gently set it back into the tree hole as Molly again called Detective Bell.

This time he answered and told them he would be there in forty-five minutes. They were to stay in sight of the cache.

Molly started to explore the surrounding area, but then decided she shouldn't be tromping around. She and John sat on a rock while Bingo hunted for prey. The leaves were changing and a brilliant red maple tree stood beside a yellow poplar. She tried to relax and enjoy the beauty of the day, which she hadn't had time to do lately. Bingo chased a squirrel up a tree, and they laughed at his frantic barking.

Bell crashed through fallen leaves and approached the mound. He climbed up and John showed him the tree.

"Did you touch it?" he asked.

"Only enough to see that it held something. And I had my gloves on."

Bell nodded. "Trouble is, I have no way of knowing you folks didn't plant this."

John looked him in the eye and said, "I didn't. Molly couldn't reach it. But we got to thinking if Royal were being chased, he may have tried to hide whatever this is before they caught up with him. That might explain why he was down here with the golf cart. And we didn't know how thoroughly you had searched this side of the culvert."

Bell snapped several pictures before donning gloves and lifting the package out. He set it down in a cardboard box he had brought and aimed a flashlight into the opening to make sure there was nothing else.

"Aren't you going to open it?" Molly asked.

"Not until I have impartial witnesses," he said. He took a picture of the bag within the box and lifted it up to carry it back to his car.

They called Bingo to leave his prey and follow them back to the car. The culvert held no terror for Molly now.

"What does this tell us?" John asked as he guided the car back out to the highway.

Molly thought for a minute. "Royal knew he was in trouble. Don't know if he was feeling bad or being chased, but he wanted to hide whatever was in that bag. If he did crash the ATV, he might have been feeling a little wobbly, and someone was able to give him a shot of the drug that led to his death. He might have even been knocked out. No, that doesn't work, because they would have taken the cash and whatever else they wanted. So he couldn't have hidden it."

"Unless he hid it first and then fell or passed out and they found him?"

"That works. I wish we knew what drug they used and how quickly it acts," Molly said.

"It would also help if we knew what was in the bag besides cash. I don't think it was large enough to be much of a drug stash, but there might be a list of gambling debts or payments. Sometimes I'm too honest. I should have at least looked at everything before we called Bell."

Molly closed her eyes for a moment. "Especially since he thinks we might have planted it anyway."

They stopped at a diner on the way home, and Molly shared the information from the doctor's visit.

"You need to take care of yourself and not worry about what Ellen says."

"Yeah, but that means more work for everyone else. But maybe right after Christmas."

Molly called Juan and told him that Detective Bell needed to talk to him. Juan was concerned, but Molly explained, "He already knows who you are, and he doesn't care about your immigration status. He needs to talk to you about your brother, Royal, and the farm. I'll give you his cell number and you can call him."

Reluctantly, Juan promised to call the SBI detective.

Chapter Twenty-Nine

LIFE WENT ON AS USUAL at the barn. If there were any developments in either murder investigation, no one had shared them with Molly or John. Late November brought a polar vortex and temperatures fell below freezing. At the end of the day on a Tuesday, John took Bingo home with him. When Molly brought the last of the lesson horses out, she remembered she hadn't checked the water tank. The temperature had only risen to twenty-five and skies remained overcast all day. She went to the tool room to find an axe. A hammer was the best she could do, and she couldn't find a flashlight. Wrapping a scarf around her face, she hurried out to the largest tank. As she suspected, it was frozen solid across the top. Her hammer bounced off the thick ice. She felt around the ground beside the tank and found a broken piece of a metal fence post that had probably been inserted in the tank to keep it from freezing. She tried to pick it up, but it was frozen to the ground. Kneeling on the cold bare dirt, she tried to lever the post with the claw of her hammer. Horses walked by after sniffing the ice.

"Hey, can I talk to you a minute?" said a female voice from behind Molly.

Molly jumped, letting the claw slip out from the post, and the hammer swing back into her thigh.

"Ow! You scared the snot out of me," Molly said as she struggled to her feet, turning to see the speaker. "Who are you?"

A slender girl stood a few feet away in the dark. "Sorry, sorry. I'm Elsa. I was with the PETA group, you know? But I've watched you. I can see you care for these horses. I looked stuff up. Mr. Mills was right about those cribbing straps."

"Imagine that. A lifelong horseman knows something about horses. Help me pry up this post, and we can get water for these horses."

Molly went back to her knees and began to pry the post, and as it lifted a little, the newcomer grabbed the end and added to the pull. Finally, they wrenched it free. Molly had her hold it on the ice while she hammered at the top. After a few minutes, the meager light from the girl's phone showed spidery cracks in the ice. Molly began beating the ice with her hammer while Elsa hit it with the post. The horses crowded around, and Molly stepped away once the opening was almost a foot in diameter. Her gloves were sopping wet and her hands were freezing.

Molly pointed to her house. "Can't we go inside and talk? I'm frozen."

The woman looked nervously toward the road, then

nodded and started to walk toward the house. "I was here right before that man died."

Molly stopped in her tracks. "I'm Molly. Tell me more."

"I was going to take off those straps, but that man stopped me. Said I shouldn't mess with the horses. My boyfriend, Chase, was waiting for me out by the road. I ran back to the car and I was kinda shook up. He asked me what happened, and when I told him, he got really mad. He was drinking and he'd been doing meth. He told me to wait in the car. He was gone a long time and when he came back, he said, 'That guy messed with the wrong people. He'll wish he never saw you.'"

Molly could hear the fear in her voice. "You think he killed Freddy?"

"I don't know what to think. But when I found out about the murder, I was really upset. My boyfriend hit me and told me not to talk about it, and then he came home with a gun and told me he would make sure I didn't say anything."

Molly resumed walking, telling Elsa to go first. She believed her, but she kept a firm grip on the hammer in her hand. When they both walked into the kitchen, John raised his eyebrows and looked at Molly.

Molly said, "This is Elsa, and she needs to talk to me."

"Looks like you and Elsa are half frozen. Go sit by the gas logs, and I'll bring you hot chocolate."

Molly pulled off her boots and wet gloves before leading the way into the living room and using the remote to turn on the fire. Tears streaked Elsa's face, and she wiped at her nose. Molly pointed to the bathroom door. "There's the bathroom, if you want to wash your face."

Elsa nodded and walked that way. John brought two mugs

of steaming hot chocolate and handed one to Molly. They could hear water running in the bathroom. "She was one of the protestors. She thinks her boyfriend might have killed Freddy," Molly whispered.

"Looks like she'll talk to you better if I'm not around. I'll go upstairs. Are you okay with her?"

Molly nodded, and they heard Elsa walking toward them. John left and Molly handed a mug to Elsa, who was still trembling. "Get warm first, then we'll talk."

Molly could see the girl was young. Elsa blew her nose and took a small sip of cocoa. "Thanks. I don't know what to do. I packed up and stayed with a friend last night. Chase thought I was at work, but I called in sick because I was afraid he'd come there and hurt me or someone else."

"Do you have any family here?" Molly asked.

"No. My mom lives in Florida. I could go there, but I don't have a car and I don't have any money. He takes all my money for beer after I pay the rent. I'm so scared." She worried a nose piercing as she spoke, her fingers constantly in motion.

Molly looked her in the eyes. "You have to tell the police."

"I can't," she sobbed. "He'll find me. He'll kill me. And they might think I did it."

Molly watched her constant movement. "Are you high?"

"I took a little something so's I'd have the nerve to come. I've been a wreck all day thinking about what to do."

"How did you get here?"

"My girlfriend dropped me off at Circle K. I walked from there. If I could just get out of town…"

"Elsa, you think your boyfriend committed murder. And

he could hurt you. We have to call Detective Bell. He can keep you safe, and then you can go to Florida."

"How's he gonna keep me safe? Lock me up? I can't do that, I…"

"Elsa, don't you see? An innocent person could be charged. You have to tell what you know."

"Maybe he didn't kill the guy. Maybe they had a fight and he got killed later. Can you just get me a plane ticket?"

Molly hoped John was listening and had already called Detective Bell. Elsa's frantic tone and movements intensified by the moment. Molly was afraid she was going to bolt, so she changed the subject. "So, Elsa, how did you get involved with this animal rights group?"

"Well, I've always loved animals. We adopted cats and dogs when I was young. So, when I met Chase, he was all into caring about animals. We met at the restaurant where I work. He was cute, and, you know, he always talked about animals. His mom was into demonstrating and stuff. But I found out what he really liked was stirring up trouble. He liked getting high and threatening people and stealing pets if he thought they weren't being cared for properly."

Molly listened, biting her tongue before asking, "They told you to sneak in to take off the cribbing collars, and then you came out with them later, to turn the horses loose?"

"Yeah, but I knew the stuff they talked about was crazy. After your boss said that about the cribbing collars, I looked it up. I quit school, but I'm not stupid. I decided I should see for myself. I came out with a friend who brought her little girl for a lesson. I saw how you all groom the horses and give them treats and clean their stalls. That's when I realized you all really care about these animals and maybe what Chase and his mom said wasn't right."

She sank back against the chair, finally still, with deep circles under her dark brown eyes. Molly watched her for a moment, then got up and walked into the kitchen. "Elsa, are you hungry? There's chicken chili here I can heat."

Elsa looked up. "That would be super. I am hungry."

Molly put the pan on the stove and called up to John, "Have you eaten yet? I'm heating the chili."

"Be down in a minute. And no, I haven't eaten yet."

Molly wrapped leftover cornbread in foil and heated it in the toaster oven. She set three places at the table.

John came in and pulled a Coors Lite from the fridge. "Beer? Molly, Elsa?"

"Sure, thanks," Elsa said as she walked into the kitchen and sat down at the table. "I mean you all are being really nice to me, and I know I caused you a lot of problems."

Molly dished out the chili, set the bread and butter on the table, and sank into her chair before opening her beer and taking a big sip. "We want to help you get away from Chase," Molly said, "but we can't just buy you a plane ticket to Florida. You have to tell Detective Bell what you know or we can't help at all."

Elsa stared at the table while she ate. "Do you really think the police can keep me safe? I'm afraid of Chase, but I'm even more afraid of his mother."

John said, "I talked to Detective Bell a few minutes ago. He's coming over to talk to you about Chase. You can stay here tonight, and he will arrange a safe place for you to stay after that. Will you just tell him what you told us?"

Elsa took another sip of her beer and looked at Molly. "I think you all are being straight with me, and I haven't had too much of that in my life. I know I need to do what's right. Is he coming right away?"

John said, "He said it would be about forty-five minutes."

Molly offered, "Do you want to take a shower? I can lend you sweat pants and a top."

"That would be awesome."

Molly took clean towels and clothes and put them in the guest bath, then made up the bed in the guest room. Elsa walked out of the bathroom dressed in Molly's sweats with a towel wrapped around her wet hair. Molly brought her a hair dryer, toothbrush, and comb and offered to wash her damp clothes.

Bingo had been curled up on the couch, but he alerted everyone when Detective Bell pulled in the drive. A female officer in uniform accompanied him.

"Come in," Molly said. "Elsa just finished her shower. Coffee?"

"No thanks. This is Officer Bullions. She'll be working with Elsa to find her a safe place to stay tomorrow."

Elsa walked into the living room, and Molly introduced everyone. Molly and John started to go upstairs, but Elsa asked, "Can Molly stay with me?"

Bell nodded. "Sure, if that makes you feel better."

Molly decided to start the narrative. "Elsa was here the night Freddy died. She was going to take the cribbing collars off the horses, but Freddy tried to stop her."

Bell said, "I need Elsa to tell me her story."

He then asked for and received permission for Officer

Bullion to record Elsa's words. Elsa spoke haltingly, but repeated the story she had told Molly about the night of Freddy's death. Elsa gave them Chase's full name, address, and cell number and also told them where his mother, Janice Pruitt, lived. Bell asked several questions to clarify things. Elsa cried when she talked about that night and Chase's subsequent threats. Molly believed her and wondered if Bell did.

Almost an hour later, Bell stood and thanked Elsa. Before leaving, they arranged for Bullions to pick her up at eight the next morning.

"Good night, Elsa," Molly said. "Do you need anything else?"

"I'm fine. I actually will sleep tonight, because I haven't been sleeping much this week. Thanks."

Molly put the clothes in the dryer and wearily climbed the stairs to join John in bed.

Elsa was still asleep when Molly brewed coffee at seven. Seeing the outside covered with heavy frost, she put water on for oatmeal and pulled out brown sugar and cinnamon. At seven-thirty she knocked on Elsa's door and heard a croak. "I'm up."

Elsa stumbled out and accepted a cup of black coffee. "You're making oatmeal? I love oatmeal. My mom used to fix it on winter mornings."

"Your clothes are on the dryer," Molly said, nodding to the pile of neatly folded clothes sitting on the dryer in the corner of the kitchen.

"Thanks, again," Elsa said. "When this is all over, would there be any chance I could like work here? I mean, learn to take care of horses. I think that would be so cool."

Molly smiled at Elsa's resilience. "We'll see. Eat up and get dressed. Officer Bullions will be here shortly."

Molly ate her oatmeal and served a bowl for John, who was shaving. Then she went back upstairs and tried to decide how many layers of clothes she needed for the day. Sometimes a frigid North Carolina morning could evolve into a pleasant afternoon, but sometimes not. It was in the teens now, and the forecast was for thirties and freezing rain later. *Yuck.* Molly pulled on silk long johns followed by fleece-lined jods and heavy socks. She dug out a turtleneck and a moth-eaten but warm cashmere sweater. She was downstairs looking for her phone when Bingo announced Officer Bullion's arrival.

The policewoman wore a heavy coat and gloves. "It's frigid out there, for sure." She looked at Elsa. "Do you have any clothes or stuff?"

"I have things at my girlfriend's apartment. If you could take me by there? My purse and license and stuff are there. The rest is at Chase's place, but I don't want to go there."

Molly wished Elsa good luck, and she surprised Molly with a quick hug before leaving. Molly locked the front door and called Bingo before heading to the barn. She turned on the bathroom heaters and did minimum cleaning due to the weather. In the office, the space heater made slight inroads to the cold. She sat at the desk with her hat pulled down over her ears. John came in to warm himself by the heater.

"Did she go off with Bullions?"

"Yes. She even hugged me and asked if she could work here someday."

"Huh. At least she was willing to talk. I believed her. Did you?"

"I think so, although I'm not sure she's telling us everything. But hopefully the police will figure it out."

Molly spent the morning thinking about Elsa and how she had come to be with Chase. She wondered if Elsa's mom had kicked her out for bad behavior or simply abandoned her. Or maybe life at home was so bad that Elsa had to leave. She knew the best parents sometimes had troubled kids and vice versa. Never having raised a child, she was in no position to judge, although as many kids as she worked with, she often wondered about parents and the choices they made.

She couldn't imagine being dependent on an idiot lowlife for a place to live. Her parents had always encouraged her to get an education, to be independent. She and John had met as equals, and her parents liked and respected him. In some ways, it was probably good that they weren't around to analyze her current job situation. They had both died within a year, almost five years ago. But all the same, she missed them and wished she could mull this over with them. Feeling maudlin, she went out to help John and Ed work horses.

By noon it was sleeting, and Molly sympathized with the poor lesson horses who lived outside. She took them an early feeding of afternoon grain and made sure they had plenty of hay. Horses stood out happily in snow and cold, but freezing rain was tough. Their thick winter coats got wet and it was hard for them to keep warm. One pasture had a run-in shed, but the horses seldom used it. Because most of her students canceled for the coming evening, Molly called the few remaining to reschedule. Then, after they fed the show horses, she brought the oldest two lesson horses into the indoor round pen for the night. They stopped shivering after she gave them a generous four sections of hay.

Carter had left early and the rest of the crew went home at four-thirty. Lorenzo promised to do the night barn check since he only had to walk from his trailer to the barn. Molly confirmed that the bathroom doors were closed with minimum heat running.

The rain changed to snow, a much better option, but footing was treacherous. Molly and John slid home with Bingo leaping and sliding beside them. They charged in the back door and began peeling off boots and layers of clothing. Detective Bell called to tell them that Elsa was safely ensconced in a women's shelter. "But," he said, "I wanted to warn you about Chase's mom, Janice Pruitt. She served time in Arkansas for breaking into a pet store and turning cattle loose from a feedlot. She was charged with terroristic threatening in Charlotte, but nothing ever came of it. I'm texting you a picture. If you see her around there, call me immediately."

Molly gasped when she saw the picture. She said to John, "It's the woman I told you about at the funeral. The one who hassled Freddy's sister."

She called Bell back to tell him she had seen the woman at Freddy's funeral.

Molly turned on the gas logs and brewed cups of tea. They sat in front of the fireplace and watched the television news, which mainly dealt with weather-related closings. Carter called to be sure everything in the barn was secured for another cold night. John didn't mention Elsa or Chase or the detective's warning.

Chapter Thirty

CARTER FUSSED AT MOLLY FOR the manure in the round pen where she had put the lesson horses. She didn't try to argue but said she would personally clean their droppings, which she did while everyone else cleaned stalls.

The sun came out and the six inches of snow on the barn roof began to melt. Cold water dripped everywhere. Thankfully, there was very little hay in the lofts to be ruined by the water. Carter had a backyard handyman patch the roof last fall, but it should have been replaced. Instead, he'd spent money on enclosing the lofts so they couldn't be seen from the barn aisle. That increased the heat in the lofts, limited the ventilation, and accelerated molding in any damp hay.

The roads began to melt, and Molly taught her almost full schedule of lessons. A few students came early since school was out and parents wanted to be home before the slush refroze. Carter asked John and Ed to take his truck to pick up a load of hay about fifty miles away. They were not yet back when Molly put the last horse out and finished cleaning the holding area.

She was trying to think up a dinner solution as she and Bingo slipped and slushed home. Her key would not work in the backdoor lock. This was not an uncommon experience, and she had opened it with a credit card on a few occasions. But not having one with her, she slogged around to the front door where the key usually functioned. She pulled her boots off on the front stoop and, after she opened the door, carried them across the carpet to the kitchen. She shut Bingo out and went to the back so she could let him in on the vinyl floor where a towel waited for his wet, dirty paws.

As she scoured the refrigerator for BLT ingredients, she thought she heard a noise in her pantry cabinet. Probably a mouse. Bingo barked, and as she opened the door, growled specifically at the tin which held his dog food. He was probably starving. Molly unscrewed the lid and quickly reached in for the dipping cup.

She caught movement out of the corner of her eye before she felt a sharp sting to her hand. "Ow," she yelled as she jumped back. Bingo ran up and began to bark hysterically at the snake writhing in the container. Molly thought it was a copperhead and slammed the lid back on the bucket before grabbing a towel and to hold against the throbbing bite.

She sat on the floor with her hand low while she dug her phone out of her pocket. John answered.

"I've been snakebitten," she shouted into the phone. "I thinkitsacopperhead."

"What? Slow down. Snakes aren't out now."

"It wasn't out. It was in the pantry."

"Oh. We're about thirty minutes away. Think you should call an ambulance? Wait, I'll call someone to take you to the emergency room. Ellen or Lorenzo. You need to stay calm."

Molly took a deep breath and tried to calm herself. She knew increased activity and panic would make the venom spread faster. Lorenzo was at the back door in minutes. She struggled to her feet and let him in.

"Miss Molly?"

"The snake was in the dog food. It bit my hand. Go upstairs and get my purse. It's hanging on the side of the bed. My keys are on the table. Help me get my shoes on."

"I'll carry you."

"No. I can walk. Just help me pull on those boots."

"I bring the snake in case they need to see it," he said, grabbing the container and making sure the lid was secured.

They hurried out to the car, and she directed Lorenzo to the nearest emergency room. He pulled up outside the door and ran to get a wheelchair. Molly told the intake person she had a snakebite.

The woman was incredulous. "At this time of year? Is it a pet snake? Do you know what kind?"

"We have it contained in the car. I think it's a copperhead. It was in my house."

With difficulty, Molly used her left hand to pull out her wallet and then her insurance card. She tried to keep the bitten hand in her lap. She couldn't really sign the consent form but used her left hand to initial it. A nurse wheeled her back to an exam room. They helped her onto a table and told her to let her right hand dangle off the edge in order to keep the bite below her heart.

"You have antivenom, right?" she asked.

"We can get it, but it carries serious side effects. We need to see how badly you were bitten and how much toxin you received. Have you had a tetanus shot recently?"

Molly remembered having to pay a lot for a Tdap shot, the only choice for tetanus at her local pharmacy. Since she worked around horses, she and her doctor tried to keep her shots up to date. "Yes, I had one this year. We brought the snake. It's in the car."

"Good. I'll try to find someone who knows snakes to look at it. Meanwhile, I'm going to start an IV and give you a little calming medicine."

Molly tried to relax. A guy wearing a flannel shirt and jeans under his white coat came up to her.

"Ms. Lewis?"

"Yes?"

"I'm Tom Nelson, a physician's assistant here in the emergency room. You have the snake in your car? Loose? Is that where you were bitten?"

Molly grew very sleepy. She tried to focus on his words. "Yes, I mean no. We have the snake. It's locked in my dog food container—that's where it was when it bit me. Lorenzo—he works with me—he's Mexican—he should be in the lobby. He can show you."

"Okay, thanks. We'll take good care of you, not to worry."

Lorenzo had called John and told him where they were. John and Ed came straight to the hospital, hay wagon and all. John jumped out and spied Lorenzo and another guy beside Molly's car in the emergency parking lot. Protected by thick gloves and boots and armed with a tire iron and a flashlight, a bearded guy instructed Lorenzo to dump the contents of the container on the asphalt and step back.

John ran up to them. "Where's Molly?"

"Inside," the PA answered. "I want to make sure what kind of snake we have."

The cold night air had stilled the snake and it lay motionless amidst the dog food crumbles. John stared, fascinated, while the PA shone his light over the snake's skin. "It's a copperhead, sure enough, and a pretty big one. Wonder how it ended up in there?"

John thought back to Detective Bell's warning.

"Anyone care if I send this bad boy to snake heaven?" the PA asked. "I'm Tom Nelson, by the way, a PA in the emergency room."

"Please do. John Lewis, Molly's husband. How is she?"

"Being carefully observed. We don't give antivenom unless we need to. It can have bad side effects." With that he swung the tire iron hard, connecting with the snake's head. Then he hit it again several times. It moved once and lay still. He picked it up and dumped it into the empty container. "Let's leave that here, in case a doctor needs to see it," he said as he put it back in the car. "Come on, I'll take you to your wife."

John looked at Lorenzo. "Here, let me have the keys and you can ride back with Ed. He's over there with a load of hay." They looked over to the edge of the ER drive where Ed was being accosted by a security guard. They could hear the guard yelling and pointing toward the street. "Better go quick, and thanks for taking care of Molly."

"You let me know how she is. You call any time."

Chapter Thirty-One

ALTHOUGH SEDATED, MOLLY COULD HEAR background noises as well as the nurses coming in and out of her room to check the level of swelling in her arm and take her vitals. She had just closed her eyes and was beginning to doze off when John's voice broke into her thoughts.

"As soon as I let you out of my sight you get into trouble." She opened her eyes as he took her hand. "How are you feeling?"

"Kind of woozy and my arm hurts, but I don't seem to care." Molly was having trouble enunciating. They had given her the good stuff.

"I talked to your PA. He identified the snake and dispatched it to snake heaven."

"Where was it?"

"Lorenzo had it in the trunk of your car. I think they are still watching to see if they need to give you antivenom."

"A doctor told me. How long have I been here?"

John looked at his watch. "I guess about two hours. At least that's when Lorenzo called me. But you're not leaving anytime soon." He settled into the chair beside her bed.

"You can go home," Molly said.

"No way. But I might run downstairs and get food. Do you want anything or are you allowed to eat?"

"Not hungry, don't know." Her words sounded even more slurred to her own ears. She wasn't sure John could understand her at all.

He leaned over and kissed her on the cheek. "Don't go anywhere, I'll be right back."

~ * ~

Barring an allergic reaction, Molly should be okay. But how did a copperhead get into the dog food container? They kept the plastic tub sealed with a screw-on lid to prevent bugs or mice from getting in. Unless Molly had left the top off and a copperhead had come in from under the house.

Or someone had put it there. Cold chills ran up John's spine at the thought. Both he and Molly had been diligent about locking the house ever since Freddy's death. But the lock on the back door was hinky. One time they had used a credit card to open it because the key wouldn't work.

That animal rights woman had been accused of several pet store break-ins. Had she kept venomous snakes? The back of the house was visible from the arena and the pasture, but only if someone were looking. Could she have snuck up to the door?

John realized he had better call Carter and tell him what

was going on.

"A copperhead? In the winter?" Carter asked, clearly incredulous. "How would it get in the dog food?"

"Did you notice anyone strange around our house or anywhere today? It had to happen after breakfast."

"No. Wait. I saw a lady parked in your drive when I stopped to fix a board in the front fence. She said Ellen had called her about a possible gas leak. She wore a brown uniform. I went and got her a key. You didn't call Ellen or the gas company about a gas leak?"

"No, I didn't, and I don't think Molly did."

"Well, I'll be. Did she steal anything?"

"Don't know. But I'm pretty sure that's how the snake got in." John gave him a summary of what Elsa and Detective Bell had told them as he walked toward the hospital cafeteria.

"So, you think this girl's boyfriend killed Freddy? What about Royal?"

"Can't see the connection. But anyway, I'm staying with Molly. I'll call you in the morning."

"Okay. Tell her to feel better."

John selected a pre-made ham and cheese sandwich, along with chips and a cup of coffee. He paid for the food and headed back to where Molly was being observed. She had been hurt chasing down a murderer at their last farm. She was smart, and she couldn't help trying to figure things out. But she was his partner in all things. He didn't like the idea of her being in danger. Maybe when she was released from the hospital, they needed to get out of town for a while.

He remembered Detective Bell's warning. Speaking of which, John should call him and let him know the latest. He doubted that Janice Pruitt, if that's who had done this, would have left any evidence, especially since Carter had given her a key. What happened to the key? Did she still have it? He'd forgotten to ask Carter.

He stopped in the lobby so he could put his food down and called Carter back. "What about the key? Did she bring it back?"

"Let me think. Oh. She said she might need it for a technician to come out but that they would leave it on the table when they left since I told her you all had other keys."

John took a sip of hot coffee. "Can you call a locksmith tomorrow and have the locks changed?"

"Well, if they left the key…"

"Might have made a copy."

"Yeah. I see. I'll call someone in the morning. You gonna call the detective?"

"Right now."

John took time to wolf down his ham and cheese and open the chips before trying to call Bell. The phone went to voice mail and he left a message. When he got back to Molly, he noticed the swelling and redness on her arm had increased significantly. A nurse was measuring it, wearing a frown on her face. Molly appeared to have dozed off.

The nurse recorded her measurements and went to get an extra blanket. "She said she was cold. I think her temperature's coming up. To be expected, but still concerning." She took Molly's temperature in her ear and nodded. "103. Hope it doesn't go any higher."

John thought Molly looked paler and not peaceful, even though she lay still. She would occasionally moan softly.

The nurse handed him Molly's call button. "If anything changes, you ring me. I'll be back directly."

Molly's entire arm was red and swollen. She shivered and tugged at the blanket, mumbling, "Cold, so cold."

John wrapped the blanket around her shoulders, before smoothing her hair with his hand. "You have a fever. But they're watching it. Said it was to be expected."

She mumbled and shivered again. John took her hand and squeezed it. She squeezed back and grew still.

John sat back in the chair and let his gaze wander back and forth between the muted television and his wife. He let go of her hand as he dozed off.

~ * ~

The hospital was full of noise, and weak light shone in a window. John looked around, confused, and then remembered where he was. He stood up to stretch and went to use the bathroom. When he came back, Molly was tossing and turning, trying to throw off her covers. A sheen of sweat coated her forehead. He took a washcloth and wet it to wipe her face. She opened her eyes. "Now I'm hot."

He looked at her arm. It hadn't gotten any worse, and it might even have gone down. He pushed the call button. A new nurse greeted them. "I think her fever's broken," he said. "She seems better."

The nurse took her vitals before agreeing. "It might spike again, but this is a good sign. I'll tell the resident."

Molly looked at him. "You spend the night in that chair?"

"Yep. And I'm a little stiff and itchy from the hay we loaded."

"I'm better. Why don't you go home to take a shower and

get some real sleep? And Bingo will need to go out. And you'll need to buy him more food."

"Okay." He handed her the phone from her purse. "Call me if you need me. Maybe they'll let you out by this afternoon. Are you hungry? Here comes your breakfast."

"Actually, I am. Starving."

"Need me to stay and help you eat? You still can't use your right hand."

"No. I'll manage. I can eat toast and bacon with either hand."

Relieved that Molly was on the mend, John kissed her goodbye and left for home, calling Carter on the way and then trying Detective Bell again before he stopped at the store for dog food.

Bell answered and John brought him up to date.

Bell said, "We already have an APB out on that woman, Janice Pruitt, for her past robberies. Barricade your doors until the locksmith comes. I'll send a tech out to look for prints in about an hour. Try not to touch anything."

Bingo was franticly barking and jumping when John unlocked the door. He let the dog out and poured fresh kibble and water in his bowls.

John had a much-needed shower and pulled on sweat pants and a hoodie. The evidence techs arrived just as he finished, and they elicited a flurry of barking from Bingo. John grabbed the dog and went out to the car to let them work in peace. He drove around to the barn to find Carter.

"How's Miss Molly?" asked Lorenzo.

"Better, I think. Thanks to your quick action. She might even get to come home this afternoon. Where's Carter?"

"In the office."

Carter was on the phone with a locksmith. He scheduled an appointment for early afternoon. John told him the evidence techs were at the house and, as soon as they were finished, he was going to sleep for a few hours. He noted that Lorenzo and Ed had already unloaded the wagon full of hay and felt not one bit of guilt. "If Molly's still doing okay, I can teach her lessons tonight," he offered.

Carter looked at him. "Hadn't even thought about that. Yeah. Good."

John and Bingo walked home, and John remembered to check the mailbox. He sat on the couch to read through the mail and the next thing he knew, he had fallen asleep and woke to banging on the door. Bingo carried on and John yelled, "Coming," as he fumbled for his glasses and shoes.

The locksmith replaced both the front and back door locks and handed him the keys. John paid him and insisted on a receipt to present to Carter. He rummaged in the fridge for sandwich material and found cheese and salami. Finishing off with an apple, he debated calling Molly. Since she might be sleeping, he decided not to bother her. He thought about going back to sleep, but he might have to pick up Molly, and he had promised to teach her lessons. Better find out when they started.

He pulled on long underwear, jeans, a turtleneck, and a sweatshirt. His phone chirped with a text from Molly. They say I can go home. Doctor released me. It'll be about an hour.

John smiled and felt a weight lift away. Ellen called next. "I was so sorry to hear about Molly. How is she doing?"

"Better. The hospital is releasing her. I was coming to the

barn to check her lesson schedule. I told Carter I'd teach for her, but I need to go get her first."

"Don't you worry. I'll go pick her up. She's at the Medical Center, right? Her first lesson starts at four."

Molly wouldn't be happy, but that was the best way to take care of her and his bosses, so he agreed and realized he needed to get to the barn right away. "Thanks, Ellen, that will work. I'm going to the barn now. Molly should be ready in less than an hour. The locksmith was here. I'll bring you a key right now so you and Molly can get in."

~ * ~

Molly was cuddled on the couch in front of the gas logs watching TV when John finished for the night.

"Have you eaten?" John asked.

"Ellen brought pinto beans and cornbread from Carter's mother. Not my favorite, but I ate. The beans are on the stove."

John pulled a beer out of the fridge and got a bowl for his beans. "Do you want a drink?"

"No alcohol. I have antibiotics and painkillers, but I'd love a cup of hot tea."

"How do you feel? How's the arm?"

"Wiped out but better. I'm supposed to take it easy tomorrow, then if everything is okay, I can go back to work." The doctor had also told her she was seriously anemic, but she knew that was due to her monthly issues. She could take more iron to help that. She held up her arm for John to see. The bite was covered with a bandage and her arm looked slightly swollen, but nothing like the red angry flesh he had seen before.

He set his bowl and beer on the coffee table and snuggled against her, kissing her gently on the cheek. "You had me worried, you know."

Molly smiled at him. "It wasn't exactly fun, but I'm mending and we have new locks. If Chase's mother left the snake and Chase killed Freddy, how does that connect to Royal?"

John thought for a moment. "According to Elsa, Chase is a druggie, so maybe he bought from Royal or picked up from Pedro?"

The tea kettle whistled, and before John could get up, Molly said, "I'll get it. I need to move around." She came back, carrying her tea cup carefully with her left hand. "That's plausible, but why kill him? And would Chase know about drugs that would mimic a heart attack?"

"He could probably Google it or his mother could. Maybe she killed Royal because he was supplying her son with drugs? I can't see him being organized enough to plan a murder in advance. So, none of this is helping Jose."

Molly yawned. "I think we're too tired to make any logical conclusions. Let's go to bed."

Weak winter sun was beginning to creep across the horizon when Detective Bell called. John fumbled with the phone. "Hello?"

"Bell here. Have you heard from Elsa? She left the women's shelter. I hope she didn't go back to Chase. We haven't found him yet."

"Why would she leave? Was there a problem at the shelter?"

"I don't think so. Her roommate told the housemother she got a phone call. Said she had to leave or something really bad was going to happen. Is Molly home?"

"Yeah. She got home yesterday afternoon. We had the locks changed."

"I'm going to ask the county to send a deputy to stay at your house. These people are loose cannons. What time do you go to work?"

John squinted at his watch on the nightstand. "Eight o'clock. But I'm not leaving Molly alone. I'll stay until a deputy gets here."

Chapter Thirty-Two

MOLLY WOKE WHEN SHE HEARD John's voice. "What's going on?" she asked as she struggled to sit up without leaning on her injured arm.

"Elsa's missing. She apparently got a call and told her roommate she'd have to go or something terrible would happen."

"You think she went back to Chase? Maybe he threatened suicide or worse?"

John considered the thought. "From what you said, she's afraid of Chase and even more afraid of his mother. But if one of them threatened to hurt us or the horses or the people Elsa worked with…"

"Yeah. Does Bell know?"

"He called me. He's sending a deputy, and I'm not going to the barn until he gets here. Stay in bed. I'll get you breakfast."

"I'm okay." But when she stood, she realized she wasn't. She eased back on the bed.

John hurried to her side. "Easy there. I can help you to the bathroom."

Using the nightstand to brace herself and then leaning on John's arm, she slowly made it to the bathroom. After splashing water on her face, she felt more awake. Taking it very slowly, she crept back to bed. "Laying around will kill you for sure," she said with a rueful grin. "But I promise to be good and take it easy."

John went downstairs to make toast and brew coffee. He brought up a tray of buttered toast, a clementine, and a large cup of coffee for each of them.

"Thanks, dear. This will help. Then while you're waiting for the deputy, you can help me take a shower. They said that's fine but to put a new bandage on the bite afterward."

Molly said she felt stronger after eating and showering. She pulled on clean sweats and awkwardly combed her wet hair with her left hand. With John's help, she walked downstairs and parked herself on the couch in front of the TV for local news. They were just in time to hear the newscaster. "State Bureau of Investigation and the local sheriff's department have identified a person of interest in the July murder of Freddy Pedigo at a local horse barn. Another suspect is being held in connection with a murder on a Mock County horse farm, which happened around the same time. Police are not saying whether the two killings are connected. This man, Chase Pruitt, is considered armed and dangerous. Anyone having knowledge of his whereabouts should call 911 immediately." A driver's license photo and description of his truck followed. There was old footage of the Mills Stables barn, Molly's clash with protestors, and a shot of Royal's Mock County farm.

John chuckled. "There she is, the mad horsewoman of Mills Stables."

Molly used her good hand to throw a pillow at John. Bingo began to growl at the front door. John looked out the window and saw the deputy's car.

"Your security team is here. Guess I'd better get to work."

The deputy came to the door and introduced himself. He stated he would be out in his car, with occasional walks around. The severe cold had abated and ice now melted and dripped off the roof, making for a wet, slushy mess everywhere.

John walked to the barn, wondering where Elsa had gone and what Chase or his mother had threatened to do. He had no doubt that Elsa was in danger, but who else was in their crosshairs? His mind was not on his work, and Carter chided him for bringing out a driving horse without blinkers and another horse without bell boots. He tried to focus and also do lesson planning for Molly's students, who would be coming later.

~ * ~

Molly was soon bored with daytime television and decided she was well enough to do laundry. The recent excitement had left her further behind than usual, and she knew they were both running out of clean barn clothes. She couldn't help but wonder about Elsa's whereabouts and safety. When John came in for lunch, she had managed to wash and dry two loads worth, but her injured arm wasn't strong enough to carry the basket of clean clothes upstairs.

John opened a can of soup and put it in a pan to heat while

he carried the clothes upstairs.

Molly found cheese and crackers, and they sat down to eat. The food helped, but Molly's laundry efforts had worn her out, and she promised to take a nap after lunch. John gave her a hug and went back to work. The deputy was in his car and assured John he had his lunch with him.

Molly's phone chimed with a text from Juan. *Came out to feed the horses, but there's a strange truck here. Don't know what to do.*

Awkwardly using only her left hand, Molly texted, Get away. Could be dangerous. Go back later. Could this be Chase and Elsa and maybe his mom? Had they been involved in Royal's death? But even if so, why would they go back there? She tried to call Bell but got only voice mail.

She remembered the deputy sitting outside. She grabbed a jacket and slid on her boots. He saw her coming and stepped out of the car. "Deputy, I don't know how much you know about all of this, but I just heard from a friend out at Royal's farm— you know, the other murder site, and there's a strange truck there. It could be the guy and the woman you all are looking for. I tried to call Detective Bell but I got his voice mail."

The deputy looked at her and started to ask for a repeat, but said instead, "Ma'am, can I use your restroom? Then we'll talk about this."

She said, "Of course, come in. Come in anytime, as long as you knock. I'm keeping everything locked." She wondered how long the poor guy had sat out there needing a bathroom.

After pouring him a cup of coffee, she showed him the text and explained who and where it had come from. He made notes in a small notebook and started out to the car to call it in, but he stopped in the doorway. "Ma'am, if you wouldn't mind coming with me. In case they have any questions?"

"Sure." Molly pulled her jacket and boots back on and followed him to the cruiser.

She explained that the other farm was in Mock County and the deputy asked to be relayed to their office. Together, they described the situation and that no one was supposed to be on the property but Juan, and he was the one who had notified her. They finally agreed to send a car, but Molly didn't think they felt any urgency.

"Can you get a message to Detective Bell? I mean other than his voice mail?"

"I can try to relay it through our headquarters. I'm sorry but I'm not authorized to go to another county, and anyway, my orders are to stay with you until your husband gets home."

Molly listened while the deputy asked the dispatcher to try to send the message to Bell. She also texted him. Then she asked the deputy, "Can you drive me over to the barn to speak to my husband?"

"You mean right here?"

"Yes, just turn left and then drive in the barn driveway and let me out for a minute, or we can walk. Whichever."

"I guess."

The deputy followed Molly into the barn as she looked for John. Carter was working a horse and Ed was getting another horse ready. Carter had sent John to return the hay wagon. He wouldn't be back until time to start teaching Molly's lessons at four. She was getting a bad feeling about whatever was happening at Royal's farm. She texted Juan. *Are you away?*

No. Afraid to leave. Afraid horses will be hurt.

She got back in the deputy's car. The radio squawked about an incident in Mock County.

Molly asked the deputy to interpret. "That's a domestic situation. Just over the county line. Everyone's going to be focused there. The welfare check or whatever you requested will have to be on the back burner."

Molly thought for a moment. "Your orders are to stay with me, right? Wherever I may go?"

"Ah, ma'am, you're recovering from an injury. You're supposed to stay in your house."

"I know, I know. Take me home."

Molly unlocked the door and went upstairs. She traded her sweats for jeans, a warm sweater, and heavy coat. She grabbed her gloves and a scarf before leaving by the back door and going to her car, which sat behind the deputy's. She started the car and pulled around him.

Startled, he tried to block her but moved too late, and Molly squeezed by him and turned onto the road. He followed but without lights or siren. She figured he was asking for instructions. She sped up and headed for the interstate. She had no weapon, but the deputy did, and she was pretty sure he would keep following her. But he might try to pull her over. The traffic gods were with her, and the westbound interstate was sparsely populated. She sped up but tried to keep close to the speed limit so that he wouldn't have an excuse to stop her.

As she crossed the Farling county line, she exited and turned toward Royal's farm. She pulled over on a side road a few hundred feet before the farm drive. The deputy parked and stormed up to her car. "Ms. Lewis, you have put us both in a world of trouble. We shouldn't be here. I have no jurisdiction in this county."

"But you are here. Please radio in your location, and we can go take a look. If nothing's wrong we go home, or if needed, you call for back up. But I think there are lives at stake, and I can't ignore the situation." With that, she got out of the car and put on her gloves and scarf before starting down the road. Once at the farm, they walked over against the pine trees and cedars lining the long driveway. Molly was not back to normal and had to slow her pace. But her fear kept her going.

When they were in sight of the house and barn, she stepped behind a large pine tree and texted Juan. *I'm here with a deputy, out in the driveway. Can you meet us and tell us the situation?*

She spied a large rock and gratefully sat down. The deputy said, "A lone officer wouldn't go in without backup."

"For a welfare check? We're checking on Juan, and he's coming out to meet us."

They heard a noise in the brush and the deputy unholstered his weapon, keeping it by his side. "Miss Molly?" asked a tentative voice.

"Over here, behind the tree, Juan. This is Deputy Harris. Tell us what's going on."

"Look, someone's coming," said Juan.

They all peeked through the pine branches to see a cloud of dust rising on the long driveway behind a white SUV pulling a horse trailer. As the trailer drew closer, Molly whispered, "Holy shit, that's Ellen."

Juan and the deputy whispered in unison, "Who's Ellen?"

"My boss," Molly said. "What's she doing here?"

Chapter Thirty-Three

"**WHO ELSE IS HERE, AND** what are they doing?" Molly asked Juan.

Juan said, "A man drove in with a blue truck. He parked in front of the horse trailer, like he was going to hitch to it, you know? I thought maybe he was going to steal it, but he's been here a while, so maybe he's trying to steal something else."

Molly looked at the deputy. "What kind of vehicles do you have listed for Chase and his mother?"

"I'll have to go back to the cruiser and look it up for sure, but I don't think either one was blue."

Molly thought for a minute. "It doesn't look like Elsa or Chase are here, so my hunch was wrong, but it does look like this guy or Ellen are trying to steal a horse or trailer. We need to block the drive. Where's your car, Juan?"

"It's down there by the house. Can't the deputy block the drive?"

Deputy Harris said, "Remember, I have no authority in

Mock county. I only came because Ms. Lewis came and I am supposed to be guarding her."

"You can stay here. I'm going to find out what's going on. Come on, Juan. I don't think either of these folks are dangerous."

Deputy Morris's ruddy complexion grew redder. "Ma'am, I can't let you do this. I'm supposed to keep you safe. Can't we go back and let this young man take care of things?"

Molly didn't think he would restrain her physically, but he did have a point. She didn't really know about the man in the truck. "Okay, fine. I'll get my car and sit in the drive. Come on, Juan."

"But…" The deputy had no choice but to follow Molly and Juan as they walked back to her car.

Molly started the car and drove to the farm entrance, effectively blocking the drive. Deputy Morris pulled to the side of the road behind her. Molly's arm ached and throbbed. She dug in her purse for aspirin and swallowed two tablets dry. "Juan, tell me about the horses. Are the ones your brother was working still in the barn?"

"Only one. Two of them had keg shoes and short feet, so I turned them out in the front field. But Jojo had show shoes, and he was body clipped, so I couldn't turn him out. I clean his stall and turn him loose in the round pen once a day. He's a nice horse. My brother said a buyer was coming to look at him before all this happened."

They sat there for thirty minutes before they heard the SUV and trailer rattling down the driveway. A horse kicked and stomped in the trailer. Ellen accelerated until she saw Molly's car and then slid to a stop in the gravel, throwing the horse around and making a lot of noise.

She got out and recognized Molly. "Molly, what on earth are you doing here? I need you to move your car."

"Ellen, this is Jose's brother, Juan. He's been taking care of the horses since Jose was arrested. He told me someone was at the farm, so I came to see."

"Uh, well, Jose wanted us to pick up this horse so Carter can work him. He doesn't need to stay here."

Molly looked at Juan. "Do you know anything about this?"

"No. And I talked to my brother yesterday. He didn't say anything about it. He said keep turning the horse out in the round pen and to call the blacksmith to change his shoes."

Jojo was stomping, pawing and kicking, shaking the metal trailer. Ellen said, "You know the horse is better off with us, being worked every day, Carter wanted to do that for your brother." She ended with a big smile. "It's a surprise. And Molly, I thought you needed to be in bed after your ordeal. I can't imagine what you're doing out here."

Deputy Harris walked up. Ellen's smile disappeared. "Hello, officer, is there a problem?"

"I don't know, ma'am. Is this your horse?"

"In a way. I mean, my husband is going to train this horse. He's coming back to Mills Stables."

"Ms. Lewis?"

"I'll move my car. We'll know where the horse is."

The blue truck, hitched to Royal's horse trailer, was coming out the drive. Molly pulled her car out of the way, but stayed by the edge of the driveway. The blue truck came to a halt and an older man in dusty jeans and boots stepped out of the truck and walked over to Molly and Juan. "Hi there, I was hoping I would see somebody. I'm supposed to put a new floor in this trailer, but I got behind and haven't been able to pick it up until today."

Molly said, "You know Royal is dead, right? And Jose is in jail. I mean, I'm not sure who can pay you."

"No worries. Jose and Royal let me use this trailer all last summer to go trail riding. It needs a new floor and I told him I'd do it for free. I try to honor my word. Name's Jeb Clemments. I did take a little lumber he had, and I took the Reese hitch off Jose's truck. I always use it to pull this trailer. He'd told me I could use it. I live just down the road. And for what it's worth, I'm sure Jose didn't do anything wrong."

Juan said, "That sounds right. I've seen him borrow the trailer, but he had a different truck then."

Jeb smiled. "Yep. I traded about two months ago. That's part of the reason I hadn't got around to it yet. My old truck kept breaking down."

Deputy Harris stood at a distance, then walked up to Molly's car as the truck and trailer pulled out. "Ready to go home? I'll feel ever so much better when we get back to Farling county. Think your boss will report me for being out of the county?"

"I'm pretty sure she didn't know we were in Mock County. Anyway, she's the one stealing a horse. I don't think she'll say anything. Let me take Juan back to the barn so he can feed the horses. And I'll head home. Have you heard anything more on the search for Elsa and Chase and Janice Pruitt?"

"No. Ma'am. Can we please go?"

Chapter Thirty-Four

JOHN ARRIVED BACK AT THE barn barely in time for Molly's first lesson. He was relieved that she was safe at home with a deputy guarding the house. After he finished cleaning up and walked home, he noticed a new deputy was in place, a woman this time. He walked up to her car. "I'm home now, so I think we're good. And Molly plans to work tomorrow so she'll be with everyone else at the barn. We'll be sure to lock the door."

The deputy thanked him and radioed in before leaving.

John noticed the upstairs lights were out, so he tried to be quiet as he opened the door. Bingo came barking. "Shh, come on out." The dog did his business and followed John back into the house.

Molly was out cold. He was glad she'd been resting all day.

~ * ~

Molly woke up to hear John whistling in the bathroom. Was it already morning? She had slept hard. She sat up slowly and realized she was much better. Her arm hurt a bit, but nothing a few aspirin wouldn't cure.

"Hey, sleepyhead, looks like that day of rest did you good."

If he only knew. But she was not about to confess. "Yeah. I feel much stronger. I can work today."

"If you're sure. Just don't do too much. By the way, there's a new horse in the barn. Don't know where it came from."

Molly almost spoke, but reined in her tongue and said, "Yeah, what's it look like?"

"Chestnut gelding, flaxen mane and tail. Sort of looked familiar, but I can't place it."

Molly went downstairs to start the coffee. She poured a bowl of cereal and covered it with blueberries from the freezer.

Carter and Ellen were both gone, and Molly was glad of the peace. She swept out the lounge and bathrooms, emptied the trash and went to the office. She was making good progress on her to-do list when Jean Montrose called.

"Hi Molly," Jean said. "Are Carter or Ellen there?"

"No, but I can take a—"

"Good. I need to talk to you. Privately. Don't worry, what you say will go no further. How about I bring lunch at twelve?'

Molly was caught off guard. "Ah—sure." Ellen hadn't taken care of things and now Molly was on the hot seat.

"What do you like on your hot dog?"

"Just relish."

"Potato salad and a Diet Coke okay?'

"Sure, thanks."

This had to be about her mare. Molly was tired of getting caught in the middle of Ellen's lies. She would tell the truth as she knew it but not volunteer anything else.

John came by. "Ed and I are going out for lunch. Do you want to come?" She told him no, she had her lunch and would see him later.

Jean carried a large Baker plaid tote bag. Her thick, dark hair was piled casually on top of her head with a few tendrils falling softly along her cheeks. She wore designer jeans, boots and a down vest over a red fleece. She was a pretty woman, probably at least ten years older than she appeared. Money can do that, Molly thought. Jean set her bag on the desk and began unloading it. "Two grilled hot dogs with relish, a side of potato salad, Diet Coke, and M&M's for dessert."

"Thanks."

She got out her own hot dogs and sat down. "Molly, I'm in a quandary here. I love my new mare, but you and I both know she isn't a ten-year-old pleasure horse from Pennsylvania. I've talked to Judy's friend, and I know this mare is not Pendiana Poppy. Can you please tell me exactly what happened so I can decide what I need to do?" Jean spoke with a deep southern accent. Molly thought she had grown up on a plantation in Mississippi. She played at being a carefree southern belle, but Molly had misjudged her. She was shrewd and concerned.

Molly took a bite of hot dog and tried to recreate the sequence of events. "Carter called me and said a new horse was coming. The driver brought a mare and unloaded her. Her Coggins had been pulled in Pennsylvania, but her health certificate said she was shipped from CC College in

Kentucky. Said her name was Pendiana Poppy.

"A few days later, on a Sunday, Carter had me drive up the mountain to Wytheville to pick up a horse at Monty Blair's barn. Monty didn't know anything about it, but a guy from West Virginia brought me a horse. She looked like the first mare, except she was taller. He had forgotten the Coggins and told me he'd mail the paperwork."

"That was my mare, right?"

"Yes. A few days later, the Coggins came in the mail. And they were the same. The first mare fit the bill as a ten-year-old pleasure horse. Carter had me look up her show record. She was talented and well broke, but nowhere near as hot as your mare. I mentioned the duplication to Ellen, and she sloughed it off. Then Carter told me to take the first mare to Hickory to the auction barn, with no paperwork. A horse trader bought her."

Jean had been making notes while Molly talked. "I paid a fair price for the horse, maybe even low for as nice as she is, but not if she's not registered. I pulled a piece of mane hair for a DNA test, but I can't decide if I should send it to the registry. I'm not accustomed to cheating. She may have never been registered or she may be stolen. I might never get her real papers or I might lose my horse. Knowing what I know, I could never sell her and there will be a problem if I breed her."

Jean took a deep breath before she continued. "I carry on around the barn and like to have a good time. I also get involved in people's stories because I'm fascinated. But I'm not a fake person in any way. I asked Carter to find me a nice horse and gave him my budget. I'm sure he didn't pay anything near what I paid, but that's okay. He found the horse and took the risk. But now I'm taking a bigger risk. I know you and John had nothing to do with this, but I need to know the truth."

Molly took a sip of her drink and nodded. "I understand where you're coming from. I try to do my job and stay out of Carter and Ellen's deals, but it's getting uncomfortable."

"I have a good reputation in the horse world and I'd hate to lose it. Thanks for talking to me. I'll go home and talk it over with my husband. And I won't mention your name. I'll say I talked to the former owner." With that, she gathered their trash and walked to the door. "And, Molly, I'll warn you when and if I take action."

The manure was headed toward the fan. Molly tried to put the conversation out of her mind. A text from Elsa did the trick.

Chapter Thirty-Five

ELSA HERE. SORRY, HAD TO leave shelter. Chase wd hurt my girlfriend if I didn't come with. At rodeo.

Molly remembered there was a bull riding event at the local coliseum. Were they planning to turn the bulls loose? She called Bell.

He was not pleased. "I believed her story enough to put her in a safe place and then she leaves. Goes back to the abuser who threatened to shoot her. I'll call the city and warn them. You stay away. Got that?"

Molly hesitated and then replied. "I will be right here, working."

When John returned from lunch, she told him about Elsa's latest and her conversation with Jean. He said, "If Jean takes action, you'll get the blame. You know that, right?"

"Yeah. She said she would tell them she only talked to the former owner, but yes, Ellen will blame me, and I can't lie like she does. And I couldn't not tell Jean what I know. I didn't fill in any blanks for her, but I did tell her the sequence of events. She has a right to know."

"Bell didn't say I couldn't go, did he?"

"Your name was not mentioned. But neither of us knows what Chase looks like. Only Elsa."

"I can at least hang out around the horses and bulls and look for anything hinky."

"Be careful."

Molly helped Ed and Lorenzo finish working the horses and prepared for her lessons. She taught late that night because a group from the local college came at eight. But she never minded them coming that late; they were fun and they all could ride. She never knew for sure how many to expect, since the college kids' plans changed from minute to minute, but two of them, William and Courtney, were pretty consistent.

She made it through her earlier lessons but needed aspirin for her throbbing arm and more caffeine before the last group. Courtney was clearly smart and a good rider, but at times a bit of an airhead.

When they were mounted in the arena, she asked them to ease into a slow trot. After a few rounds, she told them they could begin calling on their horses. William lifted his horse's head and tapped him with the whip. "Up here," he said, and his big gelding responded.

Courtney's horse broke into a canter.

"Don't let her break," Molly yelled.

"I'm not," Courtney answered, as the mare continued to pick up speed.

"Whoa, everyone, walk," Molly said.

When Courtney had brought her racing mare almost to a walk, Molly went over to her. "I told you not to let her break, and you were galloping."

Courtney said, "I promise I wasn't letting her take a break, she was going fast."

Molly couldn't help but laugh. "No, Courtney. I meant don't let her break into a canter, don't break gait. Not take a break."

Courtney laughed, too. "Oh… well, I am blonde, after all. Sorry about that."

The class went back to work and finished strong. Molly let them put up their horses while she picked up the manure from the arena. She bid the students good night and went to do a stall check. The Hackney road pony was snorting and pawing. What on earth? Molly reached for the switch to his stall light and was flung backwards by the shock she received. She picked herself up and ran for the breaker box. The circuits weren't labeled so she switched off the main, giving a sigh of relief when the barn went totally dark.

She reached for her phone, but realized she must have left it on her desk. She felt her way toward the office slowly, bumping into a mounting block and a pitchfork along the way. Once in the office, with Bingo jumping at her, she pulled up the blind covering the window. The security light on the pole outside was still burning and gave her enough ambient light to find her phone on the desk. She tried to call Carter and Ellen, receiving only voice mails for each.

A text from John read, *No sign of Elsa.* She still needed to check the horses, but she decided to walk around the barn to go home and get a flashlight. She locked the office, and she and Bingo trotted around the outside of the barn. Lorenzo might have one, but his trailer was dark. She remembered him saying he was going to the bull riding event with friends.

Molly felt her way slowly alongside the arena, hoping no obstacles waited in the dark. As she rounded the corner, Bingo stopped and growled softly. She froze. Elsa's text was a ruse. Someone waited for her in the dark.

Where to go? She quietly retraced her steps, hoping Bingo would follow. She knew the premises better than the intruder, but if she hid, Bingo would give her away. She hurried to the back of the barn where she could see. Grabbing a halter and lead from a stall door, she ran behind the shavings shed which abutted the pasture. After punching in 911, she climbed the fence and tried to find a possible mount in the dark. The dispatcher had trouble hearing her whispered remarks. "Intruder, Mills Stable, 3636 Brandt Road, Farling County." Despite instructions to stay on the line, she shoved the phone in her pocket and found Patty, one of her favorite ponies, behind the round bale.

"Easy girl," she whispered as she slid the halter on the munching pony. She tied the lead to each side of the halter and climbed onto Patty's wooly, fat back. She turned the pony away from the hay and squeezed her. Patty obediently broke into a trot as Molly headed for the back of the pasture. At the edge of the woods, she slid off and removed the halter. Using her phone for light, she made her way through the brambles, thorns catching at her down vest and fleece headband. Reaching the back fence, she climbed through. Safe for the moment, she stopped to text John and Detective Bell. If she kept going in the same direction, she should come out on the street where her bosses lived. She used Google and found she was only slightly off course. If she didn't get shot by a homeowner, she should be safe enough. She was cold and shaky, not yet fully recovered from her snake-bite ordeal. Suddenly dizzy, she sank to the ground to rest and realized she hadn't eaten for a very long time. She bent to put her head down and surrendered to the dark.

Chapter Thirty-Six

SOMETHING WARM AND WET ABRADED Molly's cheek. What, where… was she bleeding? She opened her eyes to dark and the smell of dog breath. "Bingo, hey boy. Thanks for finding me." She hugged the squirming bundle of fur and tried to figure out where she was and what was happening. As her memory surfaced, she wondered how long she had been out and if law enforcement had made it to the barn. She hadn't heard sirens, but then they might approach quietly. Not knowing, she decided to continue walking to her bosses' home if she could. She touched her phone and found it totally dead. What time was it?

She sat up and slowly climbed to her feet. She felt a little woozy, but she took a deep breath and a small step and that worked. She was so thirsty. Probably dehydrated. A security light shone ahead. Slowly making her way into an unfenced yard, she spied a dog bowl with ice and water. Bingo ran up to it and lapped, wagging his stub tail. Molly looked for another source of water and, finding none, cupped her hands in the dog bowl and took a big sip. It tasted fresh, and she got another handful. Her hands were now really cold, but she tried to dry them on her fleece before continuing.

Molly worked her arms to warm up, then added a jumping jack but quickly decided she didn't have enough energy for more. She walked out to the street and toward her bosses' driveway. She was weak and shaking when she reached their front door and rang the bell. A light shone from Ellen's office, so maybe she was still awake.

Ellen looked out a sidelite to spot Molly and then threw open the door. "Molly, what on earth? You look a wreck. What's happened?"

As she walked into the warm house, Molly's last ounce of strength drained away. Bingo felt fine and ran in happily. She slid into a chair. "Intruder at the barn. Tried to call."

Ellen said, "Who? What were they doing? I guess I turned the phones off after Carter went to bed."

Molly tried to explain. "Got a text from Elsa that animal rights people were going to rodeo. John went. Let me back up. Girl who took off cribbing straps, Elsa, came around a few days ago. Thinks her boyfriend killed Freddy. Detective Bell found her a safe shelter, but she left.

"There was an electrical short in the barn. I shut off the main breaker and was going home when Bingo sensed someone hiding. I grabbed Patty and rode to the back of the pasture."

"Are you sure Bingo wasn't just chasing a rat? Molly, it sounds like you're overreacting again. Did you call the police?"

"Yes, and the detective and John. But I was afraid to go back." Molly realized she hadn't seen or heard the intruder, only Bingo's reaction. Could she have panicked over nothing? The dread she felt had been very real.

"I see. Do you need coffee or anything?"

"A glass of water would be great." Seeing the fruit bowl on Ellen's counter, she added, "Could I have a banana? I'm really hungry."

"Of course. You need to eat better. I'll wake up Carter and he'll go up there with you. Help yourself to whatever."

Molly went to the powder room and washed her hands. Her reflection showed deep circles under her eyes, a scratch and mud on her face, her light complexion now ghostly. Her fleece headband shoved her hair in all directions. She pulled it off and tried to pat down her wild hair. She washed her face and walked out to pour a large glass of water. She downed that and a banana while she waited for Carter. She added an apple and a protein bar from a bowl on the counter.

Carter came striding into the room and sat to pull on boots. "You think it's those damn fool animal rights people again? What are they trying to do now? Put another snake in your house?"

Molly said, "Remember Elsa, the girl who took off the cribbing collars? She was here the night Freddy died. Thinks her boyfriend killed him. I think John told you that. Anyway, police took her to a safe house, but she left and texted me that they were going to rodeo. I think it was a ruse. I think they're still after me."

"Get in the car, we'll go see."

Chapter Thirty-Seven

THE STROBE LIGHTS OF A deputy's car greeted them in the barn driveway. John's truck was parked behind it. Carter said, "Why don't they turn the barn lights on?"

Molly just then remembered. "There was a short. It was grounding out in the pony's stall. I turned off the breaker."

"Well, hell. I'll get Possum here tomorrow to check it out."

Molly had seen Possum, but she didn't know he was an electrician. Well, he probably wasn't a licensed one, anyway. Could be why there was a short to start with.

Bingo ran up to John, barking. "Molly?" he asked, "Where have you been, why didn't you answer your phone?"

"Long story and it was dead."

John opened his arms to enfold her. "Was Chase here, or his mom?"

"Don't know. Bingo growled and I ran."

Detective Bell pulled in behind John's truck. He spoke

briefly to the deputy before walking over to where John and Molly were standing near the security light. "We didn't find anyone, but we did locate Chase's truck parked down the road. We're towing it in. What's with the barn lights? Did he cut your power?"

"No, I shut off the breaker. There was a short, grounding out in one of the stalls. I was walking back to the house in the dark when Bingo growled and I ran." Molly's desperate fatigue was returning. She began to shake with cold and emotion. "Can I sit down?"

John led her to their truck. "Get in, I'll crank up the heat and see if we can go home."

She was about to pull herself into the truck when Carter walked over. "Show me where you think there's a problem. I'll cut the power back on."

John said, "Can't she show you in the morning? She's exhausted."

"Just show me where," he said as he walked back toward the office and the breaker box.

John muttered, "Arrogant S.O.B."

Molly said, "Come on, might as well show him now."

The lights blazed on as they walked into the barn. There was a ping, and the pony hit the back of his stall, snorting. Molly pointed to the light switch on the wall beside his stall. "I got a shock trying to turn that on," she said.

"Uh huh," Carter said, nodding. "Coulda just turned off the breaker for the stall lights."

"If I knew which one it was," Molly retorted. "They're not labeled. And I didn't know how widespread the problem was. But maybe you'd rather the barn burned down and…"

John squeezed his arm around her and whispered, "Easy, let's not get us both fired tonight."

Carter stared at her. "Okay. You show Possum in the morning. I'll call him first thing and I'll cut the main breaker back off."

Molly hoisted herself into the warm truck, Bingo jumped in next to her, and John drove back to the house. He insisted on checking the house before returning to the truck and telling her it was safe. She collapsed onto a kitchen chair and pulled off her boots.

"Food? Drink?" John asked.

Bingo barked. Molly and John both laughed, and John gave the hungry dog food and water.

"Too tired," Molly mumbled and dragged herself upstairs. She pulled off her filthy clothes and crawled into bed.

Molly woke up to bright daylight and rolled over to look at the clock. Nine o'clock. John had let her sleep, and she'd never heard him get up. She threw her dirty clothes in the hamper and took a very hot, very long shower. After trying to check the weather on her phone, she realized she hadn't charged it. She plugged it in, pulled on her plush bathrobe and went downstairs. She cooked scrambled eggs and added two pieces of toast to her plate. Turning on the TV, she found it was already in the forties and headed for sixty. She dressed accordingly and added make up to her pale face.

She wondered if Possum had come yet. John could show him where the problem was. Feeling almost human, she walked to the barn. John was riding Poppy. He pulled her up and grinned at Molly. "Morning sunshine, you look a lot better. Possum should be here around ten."

"Thanks for letting me sleep. Has Carter been here?"

"Nope. Your late arrival is our secret. Now get to work."

Possum determined the short was caused by rat-gnawed wires, and after leaving and returning several times, said he had the problem fixed. Molly was skeptical, but at least the switch no longer shocked her and the horses weren't acting strangely.

When she returned to the office, she found a message on her phone from Jean. "Molly, I'm afraid we have to pursue this, not just for us, but for the industry. We can't let people get away with fraudulent registrations. If I can't get the real papers on my mare, I'll just show her at the smaller shows. I want to keep her, and I won't ask for my money back, but she is going to a new stable."

Judy Franklin had left a message for Molly to call. Her stomach dropped. Was Sarah leaving as well? Molly had really hated leaving her students when she and John moved from Marsa Farm to Carter Mills Stable. Her only consolation had been that many of them would soon be off to college or too busy with other activities. Even if she wasn't fired, she no longer wanted to be associated with this stable. She had built a relationship with many of her students here and leaving them would be difficult. However, it seemed as though many of them might be going elsewhere. But where would she and John go?

Should she warn Carter and Ellen about Jean? She tried to be a loyal employee, but she knew she would get the blame. She and John needed to make decisions.

The next phone call, from Detective Bell, brought good news. Chase had been arrested when he tried to steal cigarettes at Circle K—a deputy pulled up to the gas pump just as Chase ran out. Joyce Pruitt was still at large, and who knew where Elsa was?

Molly was rolling all this information over in her mind when she realized Bell was still talking. "Molly, are you there? I have more."

"Sorry. What?"

"Royal didn't have fingerprints, but his DNA was on file. Royal was in the witness protection program. His family was into the numbers racket in Pennsylvania. A rival blew up a car, and Royal's cousin was killed. He went to the authorities and turned state's evidence. The feds set him up in Arizona. He had a family. But of course the mob came looking for him. He left Arizona and disappeared. We're trying to track his family."

"Did you say Arizona? Jose mentioned a woman who came last year. He said she had Arizona plates and seemed to know Royal. Maybe his daughter?"

Bell sighed. "Another detail no one cared to share with me."

Molly dropped into her desk chair and ran her hand through her hair. "Sorry, I had forgotten until you mentioned Arizona. Do you have a lead on her? Would whoever set up the trust know?"

"We're on it, thanks. Gotta go."

So, Royal had a daughter, and presumably at one time a wife. How sad to be so disconnected from all of your family, regardless of the reason. She wondered if the daughter would have any interest in the farm or the horses. Was she even the heir? Jose said it had been left in a trust. Was she the trustee?

Chapter Thirty-Eight

HAVING FREDDY'S KILLER ARRESTED brought closure of a sort. But with his mother still at large, Royal's death remaining unsolved, and Jose remaining in jail awaiting trial, Molly continued to worry. And now, there was the question of where she and John would end up after Jean confronted Carter and Ellen. Ed was considering leasing a barn, because he too was growing tired of the problems in their workplace.

Molly had been playing phone tag with Judy and the thought of losing Sara as a student concerned her. Sara had canceled lessons for the week due to exams.

Lessons, barn chores, and office work kept Molly occupied during the day, but her nights were often sleepless. John usually fell asleep when his head hit the pillow, but Molly noticed he tossed and turned more than he used to. Ellen hadn't been at the barn, and Molly had tried to call her to no avail. She told Carter that Jean had talked to Poppy's former owner and was concerned. He brushed it off.

"She's got a damn good horse for her money. No way she'll mess that up. Ellen will take care of it."

The next evening brought good news. Jose was free. He was still a person of interest, but the authorities had failed to find any further evidence connecting him with Royal's death. Detective Bell called the next evening.

"You should know, we finally found Royal's home. He rented a cabin in the woods, on a vacant property, not far from his farm. Paid cash month to month, no written lease."

Molly said, "That seems in character. But have you found another murder suspect?"

"Can't discuss that, but we did find out he wasn't actively dealing drugs. One of the gamblers who owed him paid up with a small stash of coke and a list of who was to pay and pick it up. Since Pedro owed him and couldn't pay, he asked Pedro to do the collections."

Molly said, "That makes me feel better about Royal. What about the daughter or whomever? Have you found her?"

"Not at liberty to discuss that, either. I'll probably come by tomorrow to talk to your boss. He around this week?"

"He was there yesterday, but I haven't heard from Ellen all week."

Molly shared the news with John and they talked as they finished washing the dinner dishes.

"Even if we aren't fired, do you still want to quit?" John asked.

"I think so, but how do you feel? I mean, you could stay and I could get a job doing something else. I hate to leave my students but I'm afraid Sara may be quitting anyway and who knows about the others?"

"We both want to work with horses and kids, and we still own a few horses ourselves. So, either we both quit and find jobs right away and buy property for our own horses or we find a training job and pack up and move. I've been looking around here—either the land doesn't really work for horses or there's no house or it's out of our price range."

Molly sighed. "Yeah, I've been looking, too. Maybe we should have taken that job in Pennsylvania."

John laughed. "Yeah, hindsight and all. But that would have had its own set of problems, and we hated to leave Carter and Ellen right after they had hired us. But let's keep our eyes open and hope we have another week or two before we have to make a decision."

They trudged upstairs to shower and bed. Molly's phone chimed as she climbed under the covers. She was tempted not to answer but saw that it was Judy. She took a deep breath and said, "Hi Judy, sorry we've been playing phone tag."

After listening a minute, Molly said, "Dinner, tomorrow night? It will have to be late but, yes, we ought to be able to make it by eight. Let me check with John." She looked over at John and whispered, "Judy and Kent want to have dinner with us tomorrow night."

John nodded and Molly continued, "Okay, see you there."

"What's that all about?" John asked.

"Maybe they want to let me down gently when they tell me Sarah has to quit riding with me. Or maybe Judy wants to tell us about the murder case. Now, I'll never get to sleep."

~ * ~

The next morning, a joyful Jose came to work. Carter kept calling him "Jailbird," but the groom was too happy to let that bother him.

"Miss Molly, thank you so much," Jose said.

"I didn't really do anything, but you didn't kill Royal and there was no evidence to say you did."

"You believe me and that was good. But I wish we know who kill him."

"We all do," she answered before going to her duties in the office.

Ellen walked in about ten with a load of paperwork and sat down opposite Molly. "Good morning, Molly. I have a list of things for you, better get your notebook."

Molly jotted down upcoming events to add to the calendar, lists of volunteers to recruit, and other errands.

"Do you have anything to tell me?" Ellen asked.

Here it comes, thought Molly. "I told Carter that Jean Montrose had talked to one of Poppy's former owners and was concerned about her papers."

"How did she even know who the former owner was? Or how to contact her?"

"It's on her papers. Even if she didn't have the official copy yet, she could look it up at the registry. The woman who raised Poppy was at Raleigh and excited to see the mare she used to own, but told everyone it wasn't the same mare. And she's a friend of Judy Franklin."

"Judy Franklin needs to mind her own business. What did you tell Jean?"

"I told her when the mare arrived and that I didn't know the person who brought her."

"You know, Molly, there are many confidential things that you can't be telling the customers. I'm meeting with Jean tonight, so we'll see what happens." With that, she walked out to her car and drove off.

Molly wanted to say that she had been avoiding Jean's questions for months and that Ellen hadn't handled the situation and furthermore, caused the situation, but there was no point.

Chapter Thirty-Nine

HUSTLING HER HELPERS TO CLEAN up and put the last lesson horses out, Molly took one last look around and waited impatiently for the last student to be picked up. Then she ran home to shower before their dinner with Judy and Kent.

John was already dressed in khakis and a sweater. "Hurry, Molly, we're supposed to meet them at eight, right?"

"Yeah. I'm going as fast as I can."

She threw on corduroy jeans and a sweater, then combed her wet hair and tied a scarf around her neck. "This is as good as it gets. Let's go."

The restaurant was nearby and one of her favorites. A fire was roaring in the fireplace and the smell of sizzling steak blended with wood smoke. Kent and Judy met them at the door, and they secured a table near the fire.

Judy and Molly ordered wine while John and Kent settled

for drafts. They had only met Kent at academy shows where Sarah was competing, but he seemed supportive.

"It seems strange to see you two without a horse in your hand," he said. "Glad we could get together."

"How are Sarah's exams going?" Molly asked.

"Okay, I think. All I hear about is how much she misses being at the barn," Judy said, "and frankly, I miss it too. But we'll talk more about that later. What looks good to you on the menu?"

Molly was, as usual at this time of day, starving. She started in on the bread basket while she sipped her wine. "I haven't had a steak for a while, or maybe the salmon. What are you having?"

"I'm going for the sirloin. What about you Kent, and John?"

They ordered steak all around, and they chatted about the weather, the latest sports news, and the colleges Sarah planned to visit. They declined dessert, and over coffee, Kent said, "This has been fun, but I know you're wondering why we wanted to get together."

Molly felt cold in spite of the nearby fireplace. She looked at Kent and Judy without speaking.

Judy said, "We have an opportunity we want to discuss with you."

"Okay, we're listening," John said

Judy continued, "Sarah doesn't know for sure yet, but we're moving to Virginia. I've been offered a teaching position at William and Mary Law School. Kent will be working remotely for his engineering firm, and they do a lot of work in Virginia. We've been looking at property up there."

Kent interjected, "As in, property with a horse barn." He looked to John and Molly for their reactions.

Molly asked, "Ah, how big a horse barn?"

Judy smiled. "Twenty-five stalls, with an arena and thirty acres of pasture."

John said, "Wow. So, what are you thinking?"

"We're thinking we'd like to lease the barn to someone who would start a Saddlebred lesson and training barn, maybe breeding, too," Judy said. "We know most of the barns in that area are hunter or western, but we know you built your own program before you came to Mills Stables, and we wondered if you'd be interested in doing it again. We'd have to work out the details, and we realize you might not want to leave North Carolina. We don't expect an answer tonight, of course."

A dream come true, thought Molly. She smiled at John and he smiled back before asking, "What kind of time line are we talking about?"

"If all goes as planned, we close on the property at the end of January," Kent said. "The house needs work, and we don't want to move before school's out for the summer. It will be rough on Sarah to change schools for her senior year, but with a barn in the deal, I think she'll be willing. If you all are interested, we'd like you to start working on the barn as soon as the first of March, or even sooner if you wanted to. And by the way, there's another house on the farm. You can tell us if it would work for you."

Molly's eyes filled with tears. "We will talk and get back to you. Thank you so much for this offer."

Judy patted her arm. "There's no one else we'd trust like you two. Sarah and I want to be right there beside you, mucking stalls and everything. It's late, and I have an early court time tomorrow. And I know you have an early morning."

Molly hugged them both as they walked out, and she reached for John's hand on the way to the car.

"We have a lot of details to work out, but I assume you want to do this?" John asked.

"Are you kidding? Of course—do you feel the same?"

"Yeah, boy. Good thing we saved all of our equipment." When they moved to Mills Stable, they had sold their driving cart, but all the tack and other equipment was in a storage shed, except for a few lesson saddles she had sold to Ellen and their personal saddles which lived in the tack room.

That night they celebrated, briefly, in each other's arms until sleep took them both.

~ * ~

Jose called to Molly as soon as she walked into the barn. "Miss Molly, Royal's daughter is here."

"Here? Where is she?"

"No, I mean she is in town. She wants to meet you since you help find her father. She says she needs to tell you something."

"Okay, how do I get in touch with her?"

"She will be at the farm tonight. I tell her you could be there by eight-thirty, maybe?"

Molly thought about her lesson schedule. "If John will help me clean up, that should work. We'll get there as soon as we can."

She told John when he led a horse in from the arena. He

said, "Yeah, I'll make us sandwiches to eat on the way. Has she talked to Detective Bell yet?"

"Don't know, I only know she's in the area."

Molly and John hoped to avoid talking with Ellen before they finalized details with Kent and Judy. So far, so good. Ellen had not appeared or called, and Carter had not mentioned anything about Molly being in trouble or Ellen's meeting with Jean Montrose.

Molly finished her lessons and saw that John had finished cleaning the holding area and swept the lounge. They climbed in the car where Bingo greeted them.

"There are sandwiches in that little cooler," John said.

Bingo barked. "None for you, Buckaroo. I already fed you."

Molly opened the cooler and pulled out sandwiches and drinks, handing one of each to John.

"Wonder if Royal and his daughter stayed in touch?" John asked.

"Jose said an Arizona car was there. I guess she had visited at least once."

Chapter Forty

THEY TURNED IN THE FARM driveway and parked behind a Lexus SUV with Arizona plates. It also sported a Saddlebred decal on the back. Molly said, "She must be a horse person, too."

Bingo hopped out when they opened the door and ran toward Jose's house. The lights were on and his front porch was full of torn cushions and other broken items from the ransacking. Bingo checked them out as Jose opened the door. "Hey, Bingo. Come in. Sorry, is still messy. Come meet Angela, Royal's daughter."

The woman got up from her seat at the kitchen table and walked over to them. She was tall and slender, probably early forties, wearing jeans and a fleece, her long blonde hair pulled into a braid. "Good to meet you. Jose has been telling me good things about you."

John and Molly shook hands with her and Molly said, "So

sorry about your dad. When did you find out?"

"Thank you. The lawyer for the trust tracked me down about a month ago. I'm a critical care nurse and it took a few weeks for me to clear my schedule to come East. And I'm in the middle of a messy divorce, but that's another story. I'm sure you have questions—let's sit down. Jose made coffee."

Molly didn't really want coffee, but she figured it might be less awkward to hold something in her hand. She walked with Jose to the coffee maker and accepted a cup.

When they were all seated at the round table, she began, "What I've been telling Jose is that I don't think my father was murdered."

Molly started to say, "But the police—"

Angela held up a hand. "Wait, please hear me out. My father was paranoid. In fact, he used to sit around and rub his fingers over bricks for hours at a time. He wore his fingertips out doing that. He had Parkinson's disease and because he was so paranoid, he wouldn't see a doctor. He would research on his phone and self-medicate. I'm sure he thought someone was after him, and I'm pretty sure he injected himself with the drug that killed him. He emailed me once or twice a month, but I became concerned. The emails made less sense and then they stopped. He told me he wouldn't talk to me if I came because I would want to put him in a hospital or nursing home, and it wasn't safe."

Molly asked softly, "Was his paranoia the result of his disease or his past life? We know he was in witness protection."

Angela wiped a tear from her eye and took a moment to answer. "Both, I suspect. When one of the mob guys from Pennsylvania found him, he took off that night. Didn't want us to be in danger. Didn't even contact us for a year. We thought he was dead."

John asked, "Have you talked to the local police and the state detective, Bell?"

"Not yet. But I plan to contact them tomorrow. I'm so sorry Jose ended up in jail and that you made the grisly discovery…" She looked away from the table and fought for emotional control before pulling a notebook out of her purse. "If you could give me the contact numbers and tell me who these people are?"

"Of course." Molly pulled out her phone. "Detective Bell from the State Bureau of Investigation has been spearheading this investigation as well as a murder at the stable where we work. I think you should call him first and then he will notify the Mock County folks."

Angela wrote down the number and made notes beside it. Then she looked up. "This farm and the horses are beautiful. I'm so glad he had this to enjoy. The trust takes care of the farm and Jose for a year, but I'm divorced and I was looking for a change. I think I might like living here very much. I could carry on my father's legacy." Then she chuckled and said, "Not the gambling, only the farming. I'd like to stay in touch, if you don't mind?"

They exchanged phone numbers. Molly asked, "How long will you be here?"

"I'm not sure. I have to work with the lawyer to wrap up the legal issues, but I don't know what all that involves. Jose said your boss was one of my dad's friends and gambling customers. I'd like to meet him."

"You'd enjoy seeing the show horses, too," Molly said. "I

take it you ride?"

"Yeah. I have a five-gaited pleasure horse I showed in Arizona, but with the divorce and all, he's turned out in dry lot right now."

"Maybe you can come to the barn this Saturday? The customers will be there to ride their horses, and Carter will probably let you ride one of his horses. We can have dinner together, after. If that works for you?"

"That would be lovely. I'll plan to see you then. Thank you so much."

Molly and John got up and Angela followed. She looked at her phone. "Oh, I didn't realize it was so late. You have to work tomorrow. I'm sorry."

John said, "Not to worry. It was great to meet you."

Molly and John were both yawning as they got into the car. Molly said, "Do you think that's really what happened?"

"Hard to tell," John said. "But I guess she knew him best, even if it was from a distance, and she would know the kind of drugs he had been trying. Makes as much sense as anything else we've been able to figure out."

Chapter Forty-One

MOLLY AND JOHN FOUGHT TO stay awake on the way home. John turned up the radio and Molly dug in the console for stale crackers.

Relieved to be home, they set the alarm in time for morning showers and crashed. Bingo's frantic yips brought Molly awake. He sounded far away. What now?

John slept on. Molly sat up and realized the dog was downstairs. She ran down the steps without turning on the light. Bingo was at the back door, growling and barking. The back light was out, but Molly was pretty sure they had left it on. She reached for the switch. Flicking it did nothing. She glanced at the microwave. The clock wasn't flashing as it changed from one-fifteen to one-sixteen. Should she let Bingo out? The light may have burned out, and he might sense a stray dog or cat. Or a fox or coyote. As she eased the door open to let him out, she could smell a strong odor of gasoline. She slammed the door and yelled for John. Her yell was swallowed by a whooshing sound from the front of the house. She turned to see flames licking the front door. The stairs were beside the door.

"John, wake up, fire, John, John," she yelled.

She remembered there was a fire extinguisher in the closet which housed her washer and dryer. She ran for it, continuing to yell for John. As she pulled it out and ran for the front door, the entire front of the house exploded into flames, blocking the stairway. She pulled the pin on the extinguisher and tried to douse the flames on the stairs, but although the foam was smothering the fire at the door, the flames were already running up the stairway.

John, coughing, appeared at the top.

Molly yelled, "Go out the back window, I can't stop this. Call 911."

The flames were jumping around the living room now. Molly moved to the kitchen, laying down foam as she went, pushing Bingo ahead of her, before running out the back door and looking up to the small dormer window from their bedroom. John had opened the window and was trying to climb out.

"Hurry, hurry."

The air from the open window was fanning the flames behind him. Molly looked around in desperation for a way to reach him. Finally, he shouldered through the window casing and slid down the shingles toward Molly. He grabbed the window frame and tried to find purchase on the steeply sloping roof, slippery with melting frost.

Molly saw him let go as the flames reached the window.

Molly tried to reach for him, but he was too high above her. She saw him slide and ran to catch him.

John yelled, "Get out of the way, I'll crush you." He slid off the roof and on top of Molly, and they crashed to the frozen ground, Bingo jumping on top.

They were too close to the burning house. Molly wiggled, trying to move them both away. John coughed and rolled. "Come on, this way." The smoky air distorted everything, but as John rolled off of her, she could feel cooler air behind her and scrabbled to turn around and crawl that way. John was crawling, too, and she didn't know if he was seriously hurt or trying to stay below the smoke level. It was taking forever to move out of the smoke.

They heard sirens and voices and firemen pulled them both away from the conflagration. An EMT offered hits of oxygen to help relieve their coughing. John reached for Molly's hand.

"Okay?" he asked between coughs.

"Think so, what about you?"

"I might have twisted my ankle when I landed on you, but we're lucky, I think."

"Where's Bingo?" she asked and despite the EMT wanting her to be still and breathe oxygen, she called for the dog. He appeared out of the gloom, sneezing and gagging. The EMT held an oxygen mask on him as well. One of the first responders brought water bottles, and Molly made a cup with her hands for the dog to drink.

"Thanks," John said. "He saved our lives."

The enormity of the situation hit Molly, and she began to shake as tears ran down her face. A fireman brought a blanket and helped them into the back of an ambulance, although they both protested that they were okay. "Just sit here a few minutes," the EMT said. "Someone will want to ask you about the fire."

John held her against him, pulling the blanket tighter around both of them. He wiped her face with the edge of the blanket and said, "Guess we're moving."

Chapter Forty-Two

THANKS TO THE FIREFIGHTERS' EFFORTS, the blaze died down and the shell of their house began to appear in front of them. Fortunately, their quick arrival had managed to save the truck and the car. The rear of the house was more or less intact. They might be able to salvage a few things.

Lorenzo came running from his trailer. "John, Miss Molly, are you okay? I call Carter, he's coming."

Molly said, "Yes, Bingo woke us up."

John said, "Speaking of calling, I threw my phone out the window right after I called 911. Lorenzo, can you look for it?"

The groom went off in search of the phone. A short, slender firefighter walked toward them and removed her helmet. "Glad you folks are all right. I'm Captain Austin. Do you have any idea how the fire started?"

Molly answered, "The dog woke us. I went to see what he

was barking at and when I opened the back door, I smelled gasoline, then the front of the house went up in flames."

The firefighter nodded. "Looks like arson to us. We'll know more after an investigator examines it. By the way, we found a purse by the back door, wet but not burned. I'll bring it to you."

Thank God for small mercies, Molly thought. Their lives were spared, their vehicles and now her purse. She remembered dropping it by the door when they came in. She saw Carter's truck pull partly in the farm driveway and stop. Carter and Ellen came running across the field carrying jackets and shoes.

"Oh my God," Ellen said. "Thank goodness you're okay. You come back to the house right away." She handed them jackets, a pair of men's clogs, and women's tennis shoes. "These might not fit, but at least you can walk to the truck in them."

Carter talked to several firefighters before being sent to the diminutive woman who had spoken to them.

The EMTs released Molly and John, but they stressed that the couple should see a doctor if there were any lingering effects. John was limping, but he could walk. Captain Austin and Carter walked toward them and the firefighter handed Molly her purse, which dripped water.

"Thank you so much. At least I have my license and credit cards. And thank you for coming so quickly."

"That's our job. Just glad we got here when we did. You can go now, but we're going to stick around to make sure no hot spots flare up."

Lorenzo yelled, "John, I find it."

John accepted the phone and gave Lorenzo a hug. "Thanks,

buddy." It came to life in his hands. He texted a message to Detective Bell and limped toward Carter's truck, his arm around Molly's shoulder. She shivered despite the blanket still wrapped around her. They climbed into the back seat of the truck and Carter turned around.

"They said it was arson. That Chase guy's in jail. Reckon it was his mother?"

"Don't know. Wish they could find her and lock her up," Molly said. "Being a target is getting really old."

John and Molly hobbled into Carter's house and down the stairs to the guest quarters. Pepper eagerly greeted Bingo. Ellen said, "I'll get sweat pants and supplies for you. Take a hot shower if you want, and I'll bring you food. There's beer and soft drinks in the little fridge."

After John and Molly had taken showers and dressed in the borrowed clothes, they found Ellen laying out plates of ham sandwiches and bowls of chips and cookies on a small round table.

She sat beside them and ate a cookie. "We have plenty of room, there's no reason you can't stay here indefinitely. There's a microwave and a fridge, and you can use my kitchen and laundry whenever you need it."

Molly tried to process all of this, but it was just too much, too absurd. She simply said, "Thanks." She finished a sandwich and excused herself to go to bed. John followed. Carter had never come downstairs.

John and Molly huddled together in the queen bed. She cried and finally fell into a fitful sleep. It was bright daylight when they woke to the sound of John's phone.

He groped to answer it and simply said, "Yeah, give us

fifteen minutes."

"What?" Molly asked.

"Bell. He's coming over to talk to us."

Molly realized she didn't even have a toothbrush or comb. She found her wet purse and pulled everything out to dry, finding a comb in the bottom. She combed her wild hair and looked in the mirror at the zombie looking back. She set her wet phone on a towel and wondered if it was salvageable.

John walked up behind her. "Still beautiful to me," he said, patting her on the butt.

She handed him the comb and asked, "I guess we can get in the house to salvage what we can?"

John said, "Maybe, but not until the arson investigator is finished."

When they walked upstairs, they found Carter and Ellen were both gone. Molly let Bingo out and then looked in the utility room for Pepper's dog food.

Ellen had left cereal boxes and bowls on the counter, and a Keurig stood at the ready for making coffee. Molly brewed them each a cup of coffee and poured cereal. Bingo barked as Bell pulled up outside the door.

Molly opened the door. "Come in and excuse our dress, but this is all we have at the moment."

He stopped mid stride to look at both of them. "You guys look rough. I'm sorry this happened."

"Do we assume it was Joyce?" Molly asked.

John said, "Come get coffee. We can sit at the table."

Molly handed Bell a cup of coffee, and they sat at a pine table.

"Thought she was long gone by now," Bell said, "but with

Chase in jail, she may have stayed close. But dammit, we ought to be able to find her."

Molly suddenly remembered Royal's daughter. Had that only been last night? It seemed like an eternity ago. "We met Royal's daughter last night at his farm. Seems like a really nice woman. She plans to call you, but I guess she hasn't had time yet." Molly looked at the clock on Ellen's stove. It was ten-thirty.

"Yeah. We finally learned she existed, from the lawyer's office, but I had no idea she was here. Where's she staying?"

Molly said, "Don't know. She gave me her phone number—but I guess my phone's out of commission for the moment, at least until it dries out. Jose might know. I assume he's at the barn, working.

"Anyway," Molly continued, "she told us she didn't think her dad was murdered. Said he had Parkinson's and self-medicated. Would try anything. She's actually a nurse, and she was very worried about what he was doing."

"Hmm," Bell said as he finished his coffee. "I'll have to run that by the medical examiner. And it would explain the paranoia, the reason he hid lists and cash in the tree."

"Do you know when we can get in the house?" John asked.

"The arson investigation may take a day or two. Maybe by tomorrow. From what I could see, it looked like you might be able to save some stuff."

He looked down at John's bare feet. "What size shoe do you wear? I've got boots that are too big. My dad gave them to me, but I wear a ten. I'll stop by at lunch and get them, try to bring them by this afternoon if you think they'll they fit you. I guess you guys have shopping to do. I'll talk to Jose and see you back here later. Thanks for the coffee."

"Wait, could you give us a ride to what's left of our house? Our vehicles are there."

"Do you have the keys?"

Molly smiled for the first time that morning. "Yep, they were in my bag."

John gave her a sheepish grin. "I will never again tease you about all the stuff in your purse."

They rinsed out their dishes and put them in the dishwasher. Molly locked Bingo in the utility room with a bowl of water. "You stay here, buddy."

The house looked in some ways better and others worse when they saw it in the daylight. The front of the house was only a burned-out shell, but the back corner appeared mostly intact. John reached over and squeezed Molly's hand before they climbed out of the detective's car. An SUV with the fire department logo was parked behind their truck. The investigator walked over to them. "No doubt it was arson. But I ought to be able to finish up this afternoon before dark so you folks can salvage what remains. But I can't let you in now, and I doubt you can get to the second level. It's not safe."

"Thanks," John said. "Can you call us when we can get in?"

"Sure, what's your number?"

John told him and he keyed it into his phone.

Molly and John started their car and headed for The Dollar General Store first for toiletries, then to Target for jeans, socks, underwear, and fleece. Ellen had texted John that she found boots in the lost and found that might fit Molly.

They stopped for lunch at Subway and tried to decide

their next steps. John answered when his phone rang.

"Oh my God," Judy said, "I just heard. Look, you guys can stay with us. Were you able to save anything?"

"Don't know yet. Here, I'll let you talk to Molly."

"Hey," Molly said. "Our lives are certainly never boring. Right now, we're in Ellen's basement. She's being super nice at the moment. So, let's see what happens. But we were going to call you anyway. We think we want to go ahead and work out the details on your offer. But we need to get ourselves situated and back to work first."

Judy said, "That's wonderful news. But I'm so sorry about the fire. Kent and I will talk and draw up possible scenarios. Do you know how the fire started?"

Molly answered, "We know it was arson and we assume it was Joyce, but that's all we know. They're supposed to let us in the house to see what we can recover by late this afternoon."

"But living in Ellen's basement, won't that be awkward?"

Molly laughed. "Yeah, especially when we give notice. But for the moment, they're being super hospitable. I'd better go, John's getting another call."

Chapter Forty-Three

CARTER WAS ON THE LINE, asking if John could be at work in the morning since several customers were coming. Ed would teach for Molly, but she was expected back to work the next day as well.

They drove back to the Mills home and changed into their new purchases. Then Molly thought about going through the house. "We don't want to ruin our new clothes—let's put these sweats back on and hope we can get in."

The fire inspector called at four and said they could go in, but no second floor and they had to be out by dark.

Molly suggested they stop by a grocery and get boxes, so they did, along with snack food and a carton of Diet Coke. The day was bright and sunny, so at least they wouldn't freeze in the unheated house.

Molly remembered she had stored their offseason clothes as well as their riding habits in the downstairs back bedroom closet, so that's where they went first. The clothes were smelly but otherwise undamaged. They boxed them up to go to the dry cleaners or Ellen's washer, whichever seemed appropriate. Molly found her work boots, soaking wet, by the back door. They might dry out okay.

Judy drove up about four-thirty, dressed in ripped jeans and an old sweatshirt, her hair covered with a bandana. "Help has arrived," she said. "How about I go through the kitchen stuff and pack out what might be saved. I can keep it in my garage if you want."

"Are you sure? That would be wonderful. But let's put those things in the back of the truck so they don't stink up your car."

A few pieces of furniture looked okay. The distressed china cabinet Molly loved would only look a bit more distressed. She decided to return in the morning to see what else could be rescued. It was growing too dark to see, and they were all exhausted. Judy invited them home for dinner, but John had a text from Bell asking them to meet him at a local Mexican grill at seven.

After dropping off a load at Judy's garage, Molly and John drove themselves and a few meager possessions to Carter and Ellen's. They showered and Molly started the first of many washer loads. Ellen had left a note that they were going out to dinner, but to help themselves. Molly let Bingo and Pepper out and fed both dogs. If this was Pepper's second dinner, so be it.

Bell was sitting in a booth with a beer when they arrived. "I'm off duty," he said, "just having a friendly conversation." He pulled a grocery tote bag out from under the table. "Here are the boots, John. They're yours if they fit."

Molly and John slid into the other side of the booth and ordered brews. They chomped on salsa and chips while they decided what to order.

"I must say, you look a little better than you did this morning."

"Make-up and a hairbrush can do wonders," Molly said.

"Speaking of wonders," Bell said. "Royal's daughter is in the wind."

"What? She didn't call you?" Molly asked.

"Jose said that right after you left last night, she supposedly got a text from her daughter in Florida. Daughter's husband had been in an accident, Angela needed to go help with the family."

Molly said, "Well, I guess that could happen."

Bell held up his hand. "But wait. She said she wanted to drive straight through the night. Borrowed two gas cans full of gas."

Molly's hand froze on the way to her drink. "Oh my God. You think she was our arsonist?"

"Arizona can't find her name, driver's license, or vehicle in the system, but we don't know the husband's name. If they were going through a divorce, everything might be in her married name. Don't guess you took a picture of her?"

Molly sputtered, "That can't be. She was so nice, so concerned, so…"

"Believable?" Bell asked. "Sociopaths often are. Don't guess you have her tag number either?"

"I noticed the Arizona plates, but I have no idea what the number was," John said. "It was a dark colored SUV, I think a Lexus, or maybe a BMW—upper end, I remember that."

Their server brought food, but Molly had lost her appetite. Could Angela have fooled them that badly? Her gut said no.

Bell continued. "On another note, we've heard from Elsa. She wants to go back to the shelter or turn herself in if needed, now that Chase is in jail. Officer Bullions is picking her up at her friend's house as we speak. She'll take her back to the shelter, and I'll talk to her tomorrow. Elsa says she has no idea where Janice is, but she has an ex-boyfriend in Charlotte whom she sometimes visits. She's not working, and there's no sign or her or her stolen exotic animals at the house she was renting."

John was still thinking about Angela. "Angela is the main heir, I guess?"

Bell nodded, his mouth full of enchilada.

"And if she really is a nurse, she would know her drugs and be able to get close to her father…"

Molly gasped. "You think she killed her own father and then tried to kill us? But why? What threat are we to her? We believed her story."

"You might have had doubts. We're trying to get more background from Phoenix, find out who she really is and if she's even Royal's daughter."

John said, "But the lawyer would have asked for proof, wouldn't he?"

Bell gave a tight smile. "When you've been in this business for as long as I have, you learn to be cynical. Good forgers are available everywhere."

Molly asked for a to-go box for her dinner. She was silent on the way back to their temporary abode.

John looked over at her. "I believed Angela, too. Maybe Bell is wrong."

Molly shook her head, cocooned with her own thoughts.

They spoke briefly with Carter and Ellen before excusing themselves for bed. Despite their turmoil, exhaustion ruled, and they slept, allowing Bingo to nestle beside them.

Carter was up before six, hollering downstairs that he had gone out to get sausage biscuits and gravy and to hurry up before they got cold.

Even though Molly had lived in the south for a long time, the thought of greasy sausage and gravy first thing in the morning was nauseating. Biscuits with butter and jelly, maybe. She knew John, on the other hand, would be thrilled. She could slip her sausage to him, or Bingo reminded her, he was always up for a sausage.

Ellen had still not said a word about her meeting with Jean Montrose. Molly was not about to ask. They went to work and tried, not very successfully, to concentrate on the duties at hand. Molly cleaned and answered the phone, tried to catch up on paperwork, and planned for the evening's lessons. John groomed and warmed up horses for customers, one right after another.

They all skipped lunch and at about four, John found her in the office. "I'm going to run by McDonald's and get us burgers. You've got to eat. You're as white as a sheet. Did you eat anything this morning?"

"A biscuit. But I start teaching at five." She stood up and the world started to go black. She slid back into her chair and put her head on the desk.

"Molly, what's wrong? Here, let me get you water."

Molly drank a bottle of water and ate the candy bar which John bought from the machine. Then he made her promise to sit right there until he was back with a burger. She agreed, unable to argue.

She finally got up and made her way to the bathroom. Her monthlies seemed to be every three weeklies now, and she knew she was becoming more anemic. She would have to take care of that soon.

John was back by five and insisted she eat before she went out to the arena. This was an intermediate group who could all walk and trot and beginning to canter. They were enthusiastic and improving each week. John stuck around to help and kept asking if he needed to take over.

"No," Molly said, "I'm okay now. I'm in my element."

At the end of the evening, he sent her to the office to finish while he supervised the clean-up.

"You know, I thought you were thinking of outpatient surgery right after Christmas."

"Mm, I was, but things got busy and all and I…"

"No more. Call your doctor in the morning to set it up. Okay? I need you to be healthy. I need you, period."

Molly couldn't help but laugh. "Pun intended?" she asked.

"What? Oh, not really. Come on, let's get back to our B and B." With that, he took her hand and helped hoist her out of the chair. John whistled for Bingo and they walked to the car hand in hand, with Bingo trotting behind.

The few customers who hadn't come on Friday planned to come on Saturday. But no birthday parties were scheduled. Molly and John could go back to work at the house after the customers left.

~ * ~

Molly was at the barn by seven-thirty, making sure the lounge and bathrooms were clean before the customers arrived. And they arrived bearing gifts. Leslie brought bagels and cream cheese, which Molly was enjoying when Jean sauntered in with donuts. She pulled Molly into the holding area.

"Don't you worry about Ellen. She was shocked that I wanted everyone to know the truth about my mare's papers, or lack thereof, I should say. I sent Poppy's DNA to the registry and we'll see what happens. I think Ellen's running scared."

Molly nodded, her mouth full of bagel. She chewed and swallowed before she said, "I wondered why she hadn't said anything to me. She and Carter have been great since our house burned."

"I hated to hear about that. Do they know who torched it yet?"

Molly still wanted to give Angela the benefit of the doubt. She said, "They have leads, but no definite proof yet."

"By the way, I brought gloves and hats that I never wear, my husband's flannel shirts he doesn't need, and boot socks. Remind me to give them to you before I leave."

At this rate, we may end up with more clothes than we had before, Molly thought. "Thanks so much, we appreciate it."

The customers were gone by noon, and Molly finished off the donuts for dessert, insisting to John that she didn't want any lunch. They drove both vehicles to the house and resumed their scavenging. It was a bittersweet task, joy at finding a few things they could save and sorrow at seeing the destruction of family pictures and treasured artwork. But it was all stuff, Molly kept telling herself, and stuff could be replaced. She tried to count their blessings.

~ * ~

On Monday morning, Molly's phone came back to life, and she called her doctor to ask for a referral. She could only talk to a receptionist, and she knew that the wheels of medicine turned slowly. But by Tuesday afternoon, she had a name and a phone number and soon everything was in the hands of the insurance gods.

Elsa came out to visit with her friend, Teri, and told Molly that she hadn't sent the text about the rodeo. "Chase called me at the shelter and told me he was going to hurt Teri if I didn't come back. I didn't want to, but I knew he had that gun, and I was afraid he might do something bad. I didn't tell him where I was, but I met him a few blocks from there. At first, he was really sweet and kept apologizing for scaring me. Then he stole my phone and sent that text."

"Which left me at the barn by myself while everyone rushed to the rodeo."

Elsa had tears in her eyes. "I'm so sorry. I didn't know what he said. And he wouldn't give me the phone back. Then he took me to a motel where his mother was staying and told her to keep an eye on me.

"He came back late and mad and we drove out of town. We met his mother at her friend's house, and she had all these snakes and stuff there. It was awful."

"How did you get back here?" Molly asked.

"Chase left. His mother locked me in a bedroom upstairs. There was no way to get out, the windows were painted shut. But they let me go to the bathroom, and I found some tranks. I saved them and put them in a pitcher of tea one day. They both fell asleep before they locked me up again. I ran out the door and kept running until I got to a main road. Then I hitched a ride with a guy. I told him I needed to call someone, and I called Teri at work."

"She was in rough shape when I picked her up," Teri said. "Chase had beaten her. I took her to my place and then we called 911 and asked for Detective Bell in the SBI."

Elsa looked down, embarrassed. "I know I shouldn't have left the shelter, but I was afraid for Teri and…"

"I understand, Elsa. It's okay." Molly hadn't been the only one to suffer.

"Are you going to testify against Chase and his mother when they catch her?"

Elsa looked up. "Of course. I told Detective Bell I'd tell everything I know."

"Good luck, Elsa. You did the right thing. Take care."

"I have a new phone. Can I put your number in it? Like, when this is over, maybe I could help you?"

Molly smiled at both girls. "Sure."

~ * ~

After lessons, John dove them to Subway for dinner. Molly recounted all that Elsa had told her.

John laughed when Molly told him that Elsa still wanted to come help her. "Did you tell her you didn't need any more help from her?"

"No. She's trying to do the right thing. I think there's hope for her if she doesn't hook up with any more bad apples."

"I have news, too. I walked in the office and overheard Ellen talking to the registry. I heard her ask, 'the signatory is Angela Lanin? Who's she?'"

Molly stopped chewing. "Lanin Enterprises. That's who owned the property. Wonder if Bell knows this?" She pulled out her phone and punched Bell's contact information. She eagerly spoke to his voice mail.

On Wednesday, Judy called to invite them for lunch on Sunday. She and Kent had worked out several possible deals and wanted to touch base. They thought the horse operation should belong to John and Molly, who would rent from them. They would hash out details Sunday afternoon after they ate. Molly was sure that Judy's keen legal mind would have done a thorough job in drafting plans.

John and Molly tried to spend as little time as possible with their bosses. Carter and Ellen went out for dinner often, and Ellen was busy visiting her relatives. Molly kept the clothes washer running whenever she was in the house. Most of the clothes she had managed to save were summer items, so she was glad to see hints of spring approaching.

Sunday dawned warm and sunny. Daffodils and forsythia bloomed. They left Bingo in the house while they went to church. The bell ringers and organ music brought great peace to Molly, and she thanked God for all the grace and protection they had received. The sermon dealt with being good stewards of the earth, and Molly felt in tune with the universe.

They picked Bingo up for the drive to Kent and Judy's. Sarah met them in the driveway. She ran up to Molly, her eyes sparkling. "Mom and Dad just told me we're moving to a horse farm and you might come too. That is so awesome."

Molly said, "I'm glad you're excited, Sarah, but won't it be hard to leave your friends?"

"Some of them, but my best friends are at the barn and I might see them at horse shows. And we'll keep up by texting."

Molly wondered how much time teens spent in physical presence with each other since they were always on their phones. It was a different world from when she was a teen.

Judy met them at the door with a smile. "Come in. Since it's so nice out, Kent's grilling chicken. Let me get you a drink."

Molly and John accepted Diet Cokes before joining Kent on the patio. Judy came out to the patio for a moment before retreating to the kitchen.

"Judy, can I help you?" Molly asked.

"You can bring the salad and plates to the table, otherwise we're about ready. Are you off tomorrow?"

"Yeah. I was planning to do a final check of the house, but what did you have in mind?"

"I thought we might drive up to the farm, let you have a look, assuming you like what we've worked out so far. It's about four hours each way, but I feel like you need to see it in person. I have pictures, of course."

Kent announced that the chicken was grilled to perfection, and they gathered in a pleasant, sunny dining room with a French country ambiance. Molly and John enjoyed the home cooked meal and lively conversation.

"Sarah's doing the dishes," Judy said, "so let's gather in the family room and I can show you what we thought."

Molly looked at pictures of a long barn surrounded by black fenced paddocks. Parts of the fence needed replacing, but the metal barn appeared to be a Morton barn in decent repair. Judy said, "There are twenty stalls with a wide aisle in between where you can ride. There's an office, a feed room, and a large tack room built on the front."

She pulled out another picture of an overgrown stone cottage surrounded by trees. "This is the farm manager's house. I think it could be charming with a little work."

Molly agreed. Then Judy gave them each copies of a possible legal agreement for them to lease the barn and house. They took time to read through the detailed document, asking a few questions as they went.

"We close on the property next Friday. Now that you are homeless, I realize your timetable may have changed," Kent said. "That's why Judy wants you to see the house tomorrow. I gather you haven't said anything to Carter and Ellen?"

"No," John answered. "And they haven't tried to fire us lately."

"Take this paperwork home with you and talk it over. Nothing here is set in stone."

"Would it be too early if we left at six tomorrow morning, so we have time to get up there and back?" Judy said. "I can drive if you meet me here. Kent will be at work."

Molly looked at John, who nodded and said, "That should work, we'll see you at six."

Sarah bounced into the room, her ponytail swinging. "Can I go, ple—eease?"

Her mother looked up at her with a grin. "That would be no. No missing school."

"But, Mom…"

"No buts either. Now I think you have an essay to write this afternoon, correct?"

"Yeah. I'll go start."

~ * ~

Judy was an efficient driver, paying attention to the highway with little conversation. She asked the pair if they'd ever been to the Williamsburg area.

"Once," Molly said. "We went on a long weekend. I remember it was very pretty country, lots of big farms along the James River."

Judy answered, "Yes, it is pretty country. Our farm isn't on the river, of course. We're not in that tax bracket, but it's close to some of the old plantations."

Molly fell asleep and didn't wake until she felt the car slowing to exit the highway. After a few turns, they drove down a tree-lined gravel drive. The drive ended at a tee, with a colonial house sitting off to the left and the barn to the right. A smaller drive from the barn led into a grove of trees.

"Barn or house first?" Judy asked.

John answered immediately, "Barn, of course."

Judy pulled out a key, and they entered through the office area. They walked into a large pine-paneled room with an adjacent tack room, saddle and bridle racks standing empty. A small bathroom, complete with shower, adjoined. An old stone floor complemented the décor.

They walked into the barn and Judy flicked on the lights. The stalls were airy with outside windows and a few having Dutch doors to the paddocks located behind them. Cobwebs and broken boards showed the need for work, but overall, the barn appeared very functional.

"This is great, Judy," Molly said. "Big enough to build a business."

"Yeah," John said. "Cool."

"I thought so too, but you needed to see it for yourselves," Judy said. "Now let's visit the house."

They walked a few hundred feet through the trees. An oak door flanked by tall, slender cypress centered the house. Crunching down the oyster shell path, Judy dug out the key.

They entered a stone-floored foyer which looked toward a large stone fireplace at the rear of the house. Large windows on either side looked out toward a creek. A corridor kitchen stood to the left with pine cabinets and ancient gold appliances. Hideous orange and gold daisy wallpaper adorned the walls between the cabinets, coordinating with gold Formica countertops. The sink faced a low wall which contained shelves and cabinets opening into a bright dining area. Molly had no trouble imagining the space sans the hideous décor.

To the right of the foyer a short hall led to a large bedroom looking out on the creek with a brick-walled bathroom complete with soaking tub and tiled shower. Another bedroom and bath lay on the front of the house. A carport on the kitchen side of the house led into a utility and mudroom, stairs to the basement and several closets adjacent to the kitchen.

The floors were hardwood, needing only some cleaning.

Molly was silent at first and Judy watched her carefully, trying to gauge a reaction. Finally, she said, "This could be lovely. The view, the tub, and the fireplace are wonderful. The kitchen needs work, but…"

Judy burst out laughing. "Ya think? We were planning on a new kitchen, for sure. Do you want to see our house?"

"Of course," Molly said, always interested in houses.

The colonial was not huge, but nicely proportioned. Original cypress woodwork framed generous rooms with views of the semi-formal gardens outside. Molly's favorite was the library, which would become Kent's office.

The kitchen in the main house was outdated, as well. Judy explained her plans. "But we have to sell our house before we can start work on this house or yours. Would that be a problem?"

"No," Molly said. "We can do a lot of it ourselves. Not the plumbing or countertops, but painting and things."

Judy added, "There's a full basement so you could put your salvaged stuff down there until you have a room ready for it. But think about everything. We don't want to rush you on anything."

Molly had brought a notebook, and she spent the drive back happily making notes about ideas for the house and the barn.

On Tuesday morning, Ed met them on their way into the barn. "I wanted to tell you guys first. I'm leaving. I rented a barn and some of the customers are going with me. I hate to do this, but the customers were leaving anyway after the deal with Jean Montrose's horse, and a lot of other things. I can't afford help right now, but maybe down the road…"

John said, "Have you told Carter and Ellen?"

"No, not yet. I told them I needed to talk to them. I'm going over to their house now."

"Good luck."

Chapter Forty-Four

A SOBERED MOLLY AND JOHN walked into the barn and began feeding the horses. Lorenzo and Jose started cleaning stalls, and John joined them.

Lorenzo asked, "Where's Ed? And Carter?"

"Having a meeting," was all John said, despite Lorenzo's pleas for more information.

John walked into the office. "I knew something would happen, but I didn't think it would be this quick."

Molly looked at him. "Now is not the right time to share our news, is it?"

John answered, "In spite of everything, I don't think we can leave them with no one—but let's see how many customers and riding students leave."

They didn't hear from Ed or their bosses for the rest of the day. Molly helped John and the grooms work horses and took care of bedding stalls. They decided not to go back to

Carter and Ellen's house until bedtime.

Piper barked when they attempted to sneak into the house. Ellen walked out in her robe and pajamas, her face showing signs of recent tears. She said, "Did you know this was happening?"

Molly looked at the floor and then up at Ellen. "We knew customers were unhappy, and I tried to share that with you, but you didn't really want to hear it."

"Has Ed been soliciting customers?"

John spoke, "No, I would say they've been soliciting him. You made out that he was by far the best trainer, the best instructor. I knew he was unhappy, but I didn't know this was coming now."

"I've never seen Carter this upset. He called every customer and told them to let him know tomorrow what they were going to do. Can you be there early tomorrow morning to help? By seven? And be sure every customer pays up before they leave? I'll give you a list of who owes what."

Molly and John agreed that they could and escaped downstairs as quickly as possible.

Molly said, "How can she be so surprised? Did she not hear the customers concerns?"

~ * ~

When Molly and John arrived the next morning, Carter was busy pulling out customers' belongings, blankets and saddles and show bridles, piling them in one place and then moving them. He instructed Molly to go through the dirty laundry and be sure that every customer had their horse's sheets and blankets, show halters and the like. Molly had no way of knowing what each customer had purchased, but she tried to organize the best she could.

A horse van was scheduled for ten o'clock. Customers came and went all morning, collecting their belongings. Others had not committed yet. The partings were sad. Some of these people had their horses with Carter for years. And some had owed money and been allowed to slide for months. Molly knew there were two or more sides to every story. Jean Montrose came out to see her mare, who was going with Ed. "I don't have any DNA news yet, but I'll call you when I do. I know you are curious—and so am I."

Finally, at two, she and John left for lunch. They agreed to rent a motel room, so as to give Carter and Ellen privacy. About half of the evening's students had canceled. All of Ed's and some of Molly's. While Molly taught, John collected their belongings.

Ten show horses remained, including the gelding Ellen had picked up from Royal's farm. Molly wondered what Jose thought about that. He hadn't said a word. But Carter didn't work the horse or tell John to do so. Jose worked him every day.

A week after Ed left, Detective Bell drove up to the barn. He found Molly in the office. "I have good news for you."

"You found Angela or Janice?"

"Charlotte police arrested Janice Pruitt last night. She broke into a pet store to steal supplies for her exotic animals. The manager was in his office, working late. He heard something and called police. She let all the animals loose in the store before they grabbed her. Our attempted murder charge trumps their breaking and entering, so she'll be coming up here to be arraigned."

"Have you heard from Angela?"

"What, you think she'd call to see if we burned up or not?"

Bell gave her a sheepish smile. "No, she might call to tell you she's on her way here from Florida. Her son-in-law is recovering at home and her story checks out. She changed her name a few times because of her father's past.

"And Janice Pruitt was spotted the night of your fire trying to shoplift a gas can. Apparently, she found one somewhere else."

Carter walked into the office. "Molly have you seen my gas cans? I thought they were in the shavings shed."

Molly started to laugh, and once she started, couldn't stop.

"What's so funny?" Carter asked.

Molly finally got herself under control. "I believe they burned up with our house."

The look on Carter's face was priceless. Bell had to hide his smile. "Mr. Mills, I think we've solved the arson. Janice Pruitt, the animal rights fanatic, torched your house, with your gas it seems. We've also solved Royal's death. His daughter explained it to us."

"His daughter? What's her name? I met her once when she was a little girl. He loved that girl, but he was afraid to spend any time with her, afraid his past would catch up with her."

Jose was the next person to walk into the office, which was becoming very crowded. He looked around at the group. "Carter, will you be here tomorrow? Ms. Angela, Royal's daughter, she coming to see her horse work, and she want to meet you."

"I sure will," Carter said. "Who'd have thought. Little Angela, all grown up. I told Ellen those horses would belong to her now, glad she's gonna come."

Chapter Forty-Five

ANGELA ARRIVED BRIGHT AND EARLY. She gave Carter a hug when she saw him. "My dad talked often about you. He was always emailing me 'Carter' stories."

Carter said, "Sorry about your dad. He was a character."

Jose rode the gelding while Carter popped a whip.

Angela watched for a minute before asking if she could hop up. A big smile lit up her face when the horse began to trot. "I've missed this so much," she said. "Keep him here now and I'll pay board, but come warm weather I plan to be back in North Carolina, and I want him on the farm for me to ride."

"Good enough," Carter said.

After dismounting, Angela followed Molly into the office. "I'm really sorry I didn't call you when I had to leave, but I was in such a rush. Detective Bell told me I was a suspect in your arson. And I'm so sorry that happened. Are you two all right? I hope you had renter's insurance."

Molly said, "We did. And we're going to be fine. What are your plans now?"

"I should finish what I have to do this week and drive back to Arizona. Finish our divorce, and then I think I will move to the farm. Or at least close by. Maybe build a house there. I need a fresh start, and there are good hospitals here where I can work. I look forward to seeing you this summer."

Molly leaned in and gave her a hug. "Good luck with all of that."

Angela's visit lifted Carter's spirits. Ellen hadn't been around. Molly did her job, but she was filled with impatience to be getting on with their new life. Sarah came to ride on Saturday. When no one was close she whispered to Molly, "My mother's sworn me to secrecy, but it's killing me. When are you going to tell them?"

The next Monday, Molly called Ellen and asked for a meeting late that afternoon.

Ellen agreed, curtly ending the conversation. Filled with dread, they drove up to Carter and Ellen's house. John said, "We're not doing anything wrong. We're accepting another opportunity and our jobs here were not quite as promised."

Molly said, "I know. I just feel a bit sorry to be leaving a sinking ship, even if they did sink it all on their own."

Their reception was cool as Ellen ushered them into the living room. "What's on your mind?" she asked. "Are you going to work with Ed?"

John answered, "No. We are here to give notice—two weeks or a month, your choice. But we're moving to Virginia. Judy and Kent Franklin are buying a farm with a horse barn.

She's going to teach at William and Mary."

Carter said, "There aren't many Saddle Horse people in that neck of the woods."

Ellen was quiet for a few minutes. "Well. At least you are acting honorably. And I know things have been rough on you, losing the house and all. I'd appreciate it if you could give us three weeks—time to get us up to speed on everything, such as it is now."

Molly said, "That should work. But we need our weekends to get ready, so no more birthday parties. But we'll be here during the week and Saturday mornings until then."

Carter turned away and clicked on the television. Molly and John walked out without looking back.

Molly gave a sigh of relief once they were in the car. "That went better than I thought it might."

"Yeah, it did. How about a pizza?"

"Sure. Then we call Judy and give her our moving date."

The rest of the week went by quickly, and both Molly and John worked with a new sense of purpose. Ellen had a possible intern flying in from CC College and wanted Molly to show her the ropes.

Saturday night, Molly sat cross legged on the motel bed making lists in her notebook. "You know we haven't heard when Chase or Janice will go to court. Won't they need us to testify?"

John looked up from the ballgame he was watching on TV. "Yeah, I'm sure they will. We need to tell Detective Bell what's going on. You'd better call him while you're thinking about it. Monday will be busy. He probably won't answer. But you can leave a voice mail."

Bell answered. "You find another body?" he asked.

Molly laughed. "No. We needed to tell you we're moving to Virginia. But we'll come back if we need to testify or anything."

"Good to know. What part of Virginia? I need to warn the appropriate officers."

"Very funny. The Williamsburg area, but our phone numbers will be the same."

"Good luck to you. I'm glad to hear you're leaving. That's kind of a toxic workplace."

Molly hung up, only to find out her outpatient surgery was scheduled for the following Friday. She'd be out of work Saturday and maybe Monday as well as Friday, and John would need to be with her on Friday. But she wasn't putting it off. Ellen wasn't likely to complain now. Actually, in the past few days Ellen had been really good to work with, appreciative that Molly was trying to leave things in good shape.

Chapter Forty-Six

MOLLY WOKE UP WITH A raging thirst. The nurse let her sip water and helped her to sit up. "Glad you finally decided to wake up," she said. "The doctor will be in shortly."

John walked over and sat on the edge of the bed. "How do you feel?"

"Woosey and so thirsty."

"Better not drink too much at once."

The doctor, a middle-aged kindly looking man with horn-rimmed glasses, walked in. "How are you feeling?"

"A little dizzy and very thirsty."

"That's from the anesthesia. But everything looks good, and hopefully we've solved your heavy periods. You can go home now. Be sure to call if you have any concerns. No lifting more than twenty pounds for a week. But you can go to work Monday, if you feel okay."

John brought the car around and they drove back to the

motel. Judy called to say she was bringing dinner. The front desk called to say they had a delivery of flowers.

"You weren't supposed to tell anyone," Molly said.

"I only told Judy. And the flowers are from Ellen. You had to tell her since you took off from work."

Molly sighed. "A bouquet is nice, however, I'd rather she spend it on de-wormer or vaccinations for the school horses. She said we couldn't afford either this winter. But it was kind of her."

~ * ~

The intern from CC college had a lot of horse experience, but she hadn't expected the long hours and physical demands of teaching beginner lessons. She'd learn, Molly thought, or she wouldn't stay in the horse business. Unless, of course, she had rich parents who would buy her way into her own barn and show horses. All Molly could do was model effective teaching and encourage a strong work ethic.

On John and Molly's last day of work, Elsa and Teri stopped at the barn. Elsa wore clean jeans, a sweater, and minimal make-up. She looked fresh and healthy. "I had to tell you the good news. I have a job working at a kennel. I can walk there from the shelter," she said, clearly proud of herself.

"Good for you, Elsa. How long will you be able to stay at the shelter?"

"Till the end of the month. I'm moving in with Teri because by then I can pay part of the rent. We're renting a house down the street from the kennel. And my mom said she would pay if I wanted to take night classes at the community college."

"That's wonderful."

"If you hadn't helped me, I'd probably be dead by now.

So, I wanted you to know your help paid off. And I'm not looking for a boyfriend any time soon. I need to make a life—like you have."

Molly, John and Bingo drove out of the Mills Farm driveway with a feeling of relief, but also the knowledge that they hadn't burned any bridges. Maybe Carter and Ellen learned from this experience, maybe they'd do better.

Jean Montrose called Molly as they crossed the Virginia line. "I'm so happy for you, Judy told me all about the farm. Maybe when you're all set up, I'll think about bringing my mare to you. Now that I know she can be registered."

"What did you find out?"

"She's a full sister to the other mare, born six years later. The people who raised her sold her cheap, as a yearling without papers, to a local trader. He sold her to a trainer who got in financial trouble. Carter got her from an Amish guy who bought her at auction but recognized she was worth money. He showed Ellen a video of the mare, and she had already seen a video of the CC College horse they wanted to sell, so she came up with the idea of substituting the papers. Thing is, if they had just told me the truth, I could have gone ahead and pursued registration—the people are still alive, and they are happy to sign the papers, thrilled that she is going to be a show horse."

"Are you going to take legal action?"

"No, it's water under the bridge, but it makes a great story. And I don't mind telling it."

The only cloud on their horizon was the text that Molly got from Detective Bell. *Janice Pruitt is out on bail raised by the animal rights group. Hope you're moving soon.*

ACKNOWLEDGMENTS

I am extremely lucky at this stage in my life to be able to indulge in two of my passions—writing and teaching riding lessons. I am grateful to everyone in my life who has allowed me to do either. There have been role models, employers, trainers, grooms, co-workers, students and editors—all of whom have helped me along the way. Special thanks to Jeanine Lovell, Sondra Warren, Margaret Poovey, Robert Weisner and Michael Eure for my recent teaching opportunities.

I could not pursue either passion without the support of my husband and soulmate, Wallace.

Narielle Living is a wonderful editor and encourager.

Jeanne Johansen is teaching me more about marketing.

I treasure everyone who has shown belief in me.

My critique groups are always helpful even when they say they don't understand all of the horse language. Thanks to Peter, Christian, Elizabeth, Cynthia, Barbara, Sharon, Patti, Dave, Robert, Mary, Caterina and Tim for your suggestions, even though I may have not always chosen to follow them.

My father was my first riding instructor and my brother taught me much about horses; I am so grateful to both of them.

This mystery is a work of fiction. I've never been involved in a murder, but I love to read mysteries and I hope you do as well.

About the Author

Susan Williamson grew up on a horse, cattle, hog and sheep farm in Western Pennsylvania. She completed a BS in Agriculture from the University of Kentucky and earned an MS from the University of California, Davis. After meeting at a horse show, she and her husband raised their family in rural Kentucky before moving to North Carolina to operate a horse training, breeding, lesson and boarding farm. She has been an extension agent, newspaper editor, educator, food coop manager, and professional horsewoman. She is the author of three novels: *Desert Tail, Tangled Tail* and *Dead on the Trail*. She currently resides in Williamsburg, Virginia with her husband and Labradoodle and is a contributor to *Next Door Neighbors* and *Tidewater Women* magazines. You can find her at susanwilliamsonauthor.com.

Printed in the USA
CPSIA information can be obtained
at www.ICGtesting.com
JSHW010958060824
67622JS00008B/76

9 781948 979429